The Convalescent

By Peter Gilmour

Vagabond Voices
Glasgow

First published in September 2013 by Vagabond Voices by
Vagabond Voices Publishing Ltd.,
Glasgow,
Scotland.

ISBN 978-1-908251-19-0

Printed and bound in Poland

Cover design by Mark Mechan

Typeset by Park Productions

For further information on Vagabond Voices, see the website,
www.vagabondvoices.co.uk

For Lil, Andrew and James,
and in memory of my beloved sister, Lorna

The Convalescent

CHAPTER ONE

At the beginning of May, 1986, the body of old Mrs Templeton, badly battered, was found in a shallow grave in the garden of her house. A local farmer had called. Finding that the lights were on, blazing indiscriminately at noon, and that the front and back doors were wide open, he had suspected robbery or sudden and insane flight.

It was a large house, set in a vast encircling garden and overlooking one of the most beautiful valleys in the county. The Templetons had planned to leave it after their two children had grown up, but firstly Mr Templeton's ill health, and then, after his death, his wife's weariness had got in the way of this. So Mary Templeton had lived on there alone, doing what she could with the garden, occasionally visiting, occasionally being visited. "What am I to do with the house!", at first a serious question, had become a joke, a piece of self-mockery. Latterly it had been followed by another question, asked in the lightest of voices: "What am I to do with myself?" It wasn't quite an admission that she had outlived her usefulness, but nor was it a question to which she seemed to want an answer. Her plans (she still made them – lists of them were found by the police) came to have the appearance of imitation plans, her visits of imitation visits. To those more truly involved with life she would have been an embarrassment but for her lightness, her self-deprecating tone, her tact (she never stayed too long, nor talked too much).

There was no evidence of burglary and none of struggle. The only odd signs were the blazing lights, the open doors and the central heating still on in May: it was as if the house was awaiting the return of a grand eccentric and her friends.

A light lunch, of tomato sandwiches and orange juice, had been prepared and set on a tray, and a daily paper, dated a few days earlier, lay beside it. The bread was hard, the tomatoes mouldy and the orange juice sour. Otherwise everything was where it had been when Mrs Templeton had lived. Only the wind which blew through the house from back door to front door, disturbing the curtains, blowing open magazines, suggested it had become a lost domain.

A search of the garden quickly revealed what had happened. Mrs Templeton had been murdered and then buried, quite carelessly – as if the murderer had been in two minds – behind some rhododendron bushes. They were in full bloom, beautiful pinks and yellows, but the smell of putrefaction, just beginning, was troubling their authority this spring. The old lady's head had been battered by a blunt instrument and her arms broken. She lay more on her side than on her back, her knees drawn up, as if the murderer, in some demented parody of sleep, had arranged her thus. Her false teeth had been dislodged, but not entirely: like a last laugh too bitter to be contained, they stuck out from her mouth at an angle. Mirth in outer darkness: it was unimaginable that here was a woman who had wept and laughed with grace and subtlety.

For days the garden and surrounding woods and fields were searched for the murder weapon; but it wasn't found. In perfect spring weather the police and their dogs – as in some new but degraded rite of May – moved up and down, up and down. On and on it went, until it was as if the search had become an end in itself, employment for the police in their shirtsleeves and for their robust dogs.

Then it stopped and the questioning began, some of the locals wondering why it hadn't begun earlier. Not that they had much to say: they had never heard Mrs Templeton speak fearfully or harshly of anyone; as far as they knew, no one had ever spoken of her in this way; and no one suspicious had been seen in the area at the time of the crime. All agreed that the apparent absence of a motive was almost as terrible as the murder itself. They couldn't quite understand it, but it seemed to them that had the house been ransacked and fouled by the murderer it would have been slightly less terrible. There would have been a context then, and, with a context, there would have been motives and with motives the possibility of linking the criminal to other criminals – and so to history. As it was, there was a feeling that some perfect trick of evil had been done in their quiet valley.

The police didn't find Mrs Templeton's address books immediately. They had been put away in a small wooden box, as if they belonged to a past even more unreal to her than the house in which she had lived on alone. Their concern was with the next of kin, the two children, about whom the neighbours knew little. The daughter was thought to have married and gone to America, the son to have been disowned by his father for drunkenness. It wasn't known if he still lived in Scotland, or if he too had gone abroad. If he had visited his mother, he had never been seen to do so, and she hadn't spoken of his visits. (It was possibly out of deference to her late husband that she had kept quiet; he had said that their son wasn't to visit them again.) What particularly struck people was the detachment of the children from the life of their mother – how close it seemed to the detachment, the invisibility of the murderer. Unbidden, Mrs Templeton rose before them, her life even stranger than they had thought at the time; but, their sense of coherence offended, they were keener to forget her than they would have been had she died surrounded by her family.

By calling at some of the most recent entries in Mrs Templeton's address book, the police were able to confirm that the daughter, Marion, was indeed in America, and that the son, William, was indeed a drunk. Ten years a drunk, they were told, now unemployed as well, unemployable, haggard, scarlet, once with a disgraceful retinue, now alone, from one rented room to another; possibly not even alive, but dead before his mother. No one had been curious enough to follow his decline beyond a certain point. No spectators, apparently, as the waters broke over him.

Eventually the police traced him though. It was another rented room, the landlady an alcoholic like himself. They were watching television, on a table before them their drinks and the day's racing news. White stuffing from the sofa clung to them as they rose. At first sight, William Templeton gave an impression of health: an easy manner, strong eyes, intentness. But it wasn't long before this was revealed as a trick of his charm, a fabrication. The ease was a kind of exhaustion, the strong eyes a kind of fixity, and not even his good manners could hide the fact that his intentness was really an inability to turn his head left or right without dizziness. Having said that, yes, he was William Templeton ('never been anyone else, I'm afraid'), he insisted that the policemen sit down before telling him why they had come. He himself remained standing, head agreeably cocked. Receiving the news, he staggered slightly, rolled his eyes, and made a clicking noise. That was all.

An hour later, he was being driven to his mother's house. How long since he had been there? He couldn't remember. He couldn't even make a guess in terms of years. It might have been last year, the year before, the year before that. Nor could he remember the season. The spring, as now? Until today, driving through the countryside, had he even been aware that spring had come again? Probably not. The road, which should have been entirely familiar, was only intermittently so. Certain stretches he imagined had been reshaped since he had last been here, changes made necessary by the greater volume of traffic. But then they too (a bend, a bank, a copse) would seem familiar – ancient, even, in their significance. The stone circles of childhood, inexplicably forgotten. He would nod and murmur and raise his hands, on either side of him a silent policeman. Such a silence. Now it made him feel that he was being scrutinised, now ignored. Now that he was being driven home, now into exile. Now. Onwards. Son and citizen.

He looked down at his clothes. How had he come by them? Blue jeans, a cardigan without buttons, a faded brown corduroy jacket. Malodorous too. He realised the policemen would be thinking it was he who smelled; but it wasn't, it was his clothes. The distinction was important to him; he was still fit to visit his parents. It wasn't quite what he was doing, though, was it? There had been an unexplained horror, and his father, of course, had been dead for years. (Sometimes he woke to a world in which the living and the dead conferred.) He couldn't recall if his father had been there on his last visit, talking about seven-year economic plans, their effect on the small businessman, the farmer, the big businessman. Such vagueness was disgraceful, he knew – almost as disgraceful as these clothes. He set himself to account for them, but he couldn't.

The greenness of the countryside astonished him. In the woods there were areas of blue and yellow, exceptionally sunlit: wild flowers, he assumed. The images came to him through a medium of flickering light, the police car, at about sixty, tilting now this way, now that. Having failed with his clothes, he tried with the trees and flowers, but he got no further than the names "oak" and "ash", and even these he couldn't use confidently. "Oaks," he said, and the policeman on his left nodded. "Ash" – this too he spoke like one visited by strange fragments of memory. "Ash." "Ah … celandine." The policeman nodded again.

He felt suddenly cold and, rocking a little, hugged himself. Then he felt sick and asked for a window to be opened. It was, though the policeman kept hold of the handle, as if he had instructions to close the window again after a few minutes. You could either smell nature or yourself, apparently. You were either uplifted or suffocated. Searching for some middle ground, where he and the countryside might meet, he began to fiddle with his trousers. He saw himself pull down his zip and stand, crouched, in the back of the car. Didn't he quite know what it meant? Had he been reduced to dropping hints, like the very old?

He was helped over to the side of the road by the policemen. They were just in time. His stream, amber and unhealthy, played on the hedge in the sunlight. The policemen stood back, evidently thinking he would be all right now. He wasn't: he pitched forwards, his stream arrested. One of the policemen caught him, saying "Steady"; the other laughed. Heads turned away, smiling, they held him under the armpits as, grunting, farting, he struggled to resume. Soon the tiny flowers in the hedgerow were receiving his stream again, though this time he didn't notice. He didn't notice how they trembled on their stems. Where had he relieved himself that morning? Into what colour of bowl and how supported? Bowls from his childhood came to him, from his schooldays too, from early adulthood. Then – so strong and simple it might have been coming from the hedge itself – there was a smell of soap. Lavender, surely. His mother's. One of her modest aids. She had been pretty, an unforced prettiness, an unhurried pleasantness. (How different his father: an angry contraction there, lips thin from unsuccessful disdain, a stoop.) It was brief, though, the scent of lavender. Then he could smell nothing.

Back in the car, the inspector, turning round for the first time, asked him if he was all right. They drove off, going slowly now, very slowly. William supposed they must be getting close. Surely they were, for wasn't this all familiar?

Hadn't there always been this track off the main road? Hadn't he and his sister carried milk along it? Hadn't it been impassable in the winter of '47? Too many returns for one day. The car swayed and bumped, shaking those in the back seat, causing William to clutch the seat in front of him. The hedges with their splendid blossoms were high above them. For some reason then he saw himself, older than he actually was, a sort of enfeebled herald, walking along the track in front of the police car with extreme care, now and then, as though baffled or simply exhausted, stopping altogether.

Then they were turning into the short drive with its one bend. The crunch of wheels on the gravel was familiar, but that was all. The rest appeared like extraordinarily jaded replicas – what had distinguished his childhood not to be discovered in them. The front door, he saw, was open – under the circumstances, a parody of welcome. Indoors, there was noise – laughing, banging, footsteps: carpenters might have been at work, dismantling the place. Two policemen were on the terrace, theorising apparently, another was on the lawn, adjusting a length of white tape. The garden looked as if it was being plotted for conversion. There were small red flags on the lawn, black crosses also, tape between bush and bush, tree and tree, arrows drawn in white, bollards. William's fancy was immediate and unnerving: a dress rehearsal for his mother's murder rather than an investigation of it.

There were moments when he thought his only feeling was curiosity. An object of curiosity himself – a suspect, in fact – he leant against the car door, watching. He knew that he was not only expected to move – out onto the lawn and towards the house – but to reveal in the first few steps whether he was guilty or not. Clues as he stumbled. He smiled, proceeding unsteadily across the gravel and onto the lawn, watched particularly by the two policemen on the terrace. All he could do, he found, was grin, grin, as he walked towards that space where, on summer evenings, his parents had sat, his mother knitting, his father reading the paper. A space for cocktails, now merely a space. He had no idea what sort of grin he was wearing – what degree of indeterminacy he was guilty of today. He walked on, round the edge of the lawn, past the rock garden (or what had once been the rock garden), occasionally staggering a little, his walk now hopeless, now affectedly upright (something of the air of a discredited architect briefly recalling that it hadn't always been so). For a little while – watched now by all the policemen – he feared that it was an absurd attempt to recover his childhood in which he was engaged. It would have been typical of him (his timing, always poor, had lately become almost crazily so). But then he realised that he was searching – not for his mother, exactly – but for where she had been found. Where? It would be there, behind the rhododendrons, where the bamboo poles and red twine looked like a child's construction (and, indeed, hadn't he and his sister made things there?).

Going up to the inspector, he asked if he could be shown the exact spot. The inspector nodded and went before him to the back of the lawn. None of the other policemen moved. Now William felt that he was shambling, and that there was nothing he could do about it. What else, behind the disciplined and oblivious tread of the inspector? He tried to draw level with him, but always four or five feet separated them – four or five feet which he imagined betrayed, if not guilt, then a terrible unfitness. To draw level – wouldn't that be to remake himself in the image of someone forgotten?

"Here, Mr Templeton," the inspector said, his tone casual, reminiscent almost. "Here. It's been covered, of course. You'd hardly know, would you?" "No," William agreed. "It's been covered, as you say ..." He stared at the spot. So trim was the earth, so evenly raked, that all he could think of was the combination of delicacy and toughness required for good gardening. He looked beyond, to what had always been an overgrown area. It was so still, high and rank with nettles and briars. The delicacy of hoeing and raking, the animation of hacking and felling: all at once and confused their sounds came to him, like echoes from an orchard.

"I've only your word for it," William said. "Not that you'd make such a thing up."

"I understand, Mr Templeton. I understand. Yes, you'll just have to take it from me. I'd appreciate it, though, if you'd come to the house now. Okay?"

Again the inspector went before him, while on the lawn and terrace the other policemen, as if released from a frieze, talked, joked, gestured, made measurements. Only with the end of the silence – babble of duties resumed – did William realise how deep it had been, how gathered.

"Where is my mother now?" he asked, the knowledge that the reply would specify a place concentrating him greatly. "Not buried, I hope?"

"Oh no. The funeral arrangements will be left to you and your sister. She's presently with us, in the mortuary."

"With you? But how long … I mean, isn't there supposed to be a limit to how long … Rot, you know …!"

He laughed abruptly, a wild sound, at once fierce and forlorn. To control himself, he placed his hand on his stomach, pressing it into his solar plexus (ground of such agonies, apparently). He felt how thin he was, his body as ill-used as his clothes. Why shouldn't he walk naked across the lawn? Long gone his sense of fitness. Didn't one undress a little before entering houses anyway – gloves, coat, hat, scarf? Why not entirely – a naked and abased entry?

The inspector was speaking: "Don't worry, there are ways of cheating time where bodies are concerned. On the day of the funeral it will be as if death occurred just three days before. Be assured."

11

"Thank you, inspector," William said, entering the house. "Thank you."

Entering – actually crossing the threshold – was more difficult than being inside. Fearing that he would be caught up immediately by the past, William found that the opposite was true. What was this place? As he walked down the hall what seemed to be about him was a whimsical reconstruction of his childhood, a folksy approximation organised by some tasteless but well-meaning aunt. The only thing that caught his eye with approval was a curtain moving gently before an open window. Didn't this mean a vanished spirit? And wouldn't this explain the pointlessness of these corridors? It was as if nothing would ever happen here again. The rooms, were he to inspect them, he was sure he would find in a state of characterless and apologetic waiting. So he wouldn't ask to see them, as he had thought he might, for it would be beyond him really to understand how a place could become a cheap imitation of itself. Could become exhausted.

He was taken to what had been his father's study, now the inspector's "enquiry room". A notice to this effect had been put up on the door. Inside, typing in a corner at his father's desk, was a secretary. His father had typed here too – articles on the countryside mainly – but never in a corner. His desk had faced the door in those days so that, entering, one was confounded, even humiliated by his aggressive industry. William had sometimes gone away without saying what he had come for, driven by the clatter of typing into the quiet hall with its soft carpets and consoling dimness. Once his father had flung the door open after him and shouted, "Yes!? Not nothing I hope!?"

The secretary leant back holding a pad and pencil, the inspector sat to her left, arms folded. William remained standing, his awe and apprehension running over decades, from five to forty-two.

"Please take a seat, Mr Templeton. I wouldn't have you standing in your own house. For it is your own house now. You and your sister will have to dispose of it as you think best."

"My sister's been told?" William asked, sitting down in a chair he didn't recognise, grasping its arms.

"Yes. We're expecting her any time. But, now, some questions."

"Certainly."

"Your age?"

"Forty-two."

"Profession?"

"None."

"Address?"

"Ah … c/o Mclehose, 10 Archiblald St, Glasgow."

"When did you last see your mother?" The inspector, who had not been looking at William, looked at him now.

"I'm afraid I can't remember."

"Really? You can't remember?" The inspector was grinning slightly.

"I'm afraid not. I'm sorry."

"Months or years?"

"I can't … Both, probably," William replied, smiling to admit his confusion.

"I beg your pardon?"

"I mean years and months. A manner of speaking. A long time."

"No recent visits?" This was asked quickly, as if the inspector had suddenly seen how he might proceed.

"None."

"How d'you know?"

"I don't understand..."

"Mightn't you, a drunk," the inspector said, looking away from William again, "have come and gone without knowing it?"

"I see what you mean," William answered, speaking carefully, "but I doubt it."

"You wouldn't deny though that you've done things and not been able to remember them the next day?"

"I wouldn't deny it," William said, nodding.

"Quite a few times?"

"Quite a few times."

"Why not this then – a visit out here?"

"I don't think so."

"But it's not inconceivable?"

"It would have been a big thing, a visit out here."

"And so not to be forgotten? A visit to one's mother too big to be forgotten?"

"That's my feeling. But your implication, inspector, is terrible," William went on, leaning forwards. "You're suggesting I might have come out here … have killed and buried my mother, but now have no memory of it!?"

The inspector was silent.

"I had no reason to want to kill my mother," William said, trembling. "None at all. Never."

"Thank you, Mr Templeton," the inspector said, as though suddenly tired or disgusted. "You are free to go, to resume your life, such as it is."

"Such as it is. Very good, inspector. Such as it is."

He rose weakly, nodding to the inspector and his secretary. His legs felt heavy and he had the impression that the light was strange: it seemed to be not of the day, not of the season, but to be left-over light – left-over light and left-over air. He went from the room in silence. Outside, a police car stood ready to take him back to Glasgow and Mrs Mclehose.

July 22nd, 1959

The occasion is my seventeenth birthday. I rise early (my impatience reminding me of my early childhood), not to greet my eighteenth year before the rest of the family, but because of the morning – a most beautiful one, as beautiful as I have seen.

Outside (the dew as remarkable as the birdsong), I look up at my father's bedroom window, the drawn curtains. He makes such a thing of sleeping alone (as he made such a thing of resolving to do so). His Saturdays start just before midday, but I am not around to witness his appearance, his descent in his dressing-gown to a breakfast laid hours before. Sometimes – though infrequently now – it has been laid by me. The grapefruit, the wide choice of cereals, the toaster placed so that he can work it without rising, the coffee percolator: it has the appearance of ritual, though I know (painful knowledge this) that there is more sloth than ritual.

I am impatient with my breakfast too, eating it as I stand, looking out at the lawn, its quiet glistening (a kind of radiance, if I am not mistaken). There has been no talk of my birthday so I can be forgiven for thinking it has been forgotten and that I can go out for the day. I do this often at weekends. I don't like companions on my hikes. The point is to be alone. Who can hear the countryside with a companion's tread always beside one? (Not to mention with a companion's talk?) The unsociable is an important part of personality, I think. My father would agree, but we don't mean the same thing. Not at all. God preserve me from such ill temper.

Going up to my bedroom for my camera, I meet my mother coming down. She has remembered, and her preparations have been as thoughtful as ever. She is descending with the present and the care that has gone into the wrapping makes me laugh. She has never known what to make of my amazement at her tact. Do I consider it irrelevant or beautiful? I hardly know. Actually, I hardly know what I think the virtues are. The vices I can list and understand, oh yes (who cannot?), but for some reason I don't know what I'm saying when I list the virtues. I experience no sort of palpitation or quickening, for example, when I say "mercy". What reality answers to this name? What but the hope that the word is not without meaning is touched? Arrange them how you like, I sometimes think, empty drums are empty drums.

I will remember this present. I wouldn't have thought I'd appreciate such a thing. A barometer. We have never had one, and apparently have never noticed the lack. But with my hikes and weekends away, what could be more helpful? I kiss my mother to banish her fear that she has chosen something absurd. My father often chooses something absurd, and can't be moved from the conviction that it is deeply appropriate. His presents are didactic, one might say, implying a future to which we are either indifferent or actually have an aversion. Vain forecasts. The occasion when he gave my sister Marion jodhpurs and a riding crop comes to mind. A month before, he said, he had seen her talking to a horse, stroking it. But my sister is indifferent to horses and too concerned with her appearance to wear jodhpurs as a joke (it was I who wore them as a joke).

We hang the barometer in the hall and tap it gently, expectantly, for it has to be admitted that it is wrong. It is not a stormy day but a perfect one and one cannot imagine that there are storms on the way, crossing the Channel or the Irish Sea. Then my mother reads in the instructions that barometers, if laid on their side, won't work, but will eventually recover themselves if placed upright. We laugh in relief, for a broken present is a terrible thing, more terrible than no present at all (I have the feeling that there will be no present from my father this year).

I walk then for most of the day. My sense is that I am walking away from my birthday – not from the unalterable fact of it (that is consoling), but from these undercharged or overcharged ceremonies. Or is it just that, when a walk is a good one, one is drawn in by it, nothing existing before or after? Today I am lucky. I study birds, I see foxes and deer (brief but beautiful in glades), I meet only one other person – an old lady studying fungi with the help of a magnifying glass, and I have lunch by a waterfall. The sound or sight of running or falling water: what excites the capacity for reverie more deeply? Listen long enough and one's aspirations are recalled, renewed, extended. I rise from the waterfall refreshed. Before and after, though, are heavy with claims and directions – the bedrock of normality – to which I know I will return, or be returned, one or the other.

And so it is. Always such returns. I descend towards the house from the hills behind it. Plenty of evidence of before and after. I see my father rise from his deckchair, move to the house, return, readjust his deckchair, clean his spectacles, put them on, pick up a newspaper. From this height, and returning as I am from an inspiring walk, it has all the appearance of an exercise in idleness. Footling variations, the theme more apparent than real.

I enter the house from the back. My mother and sister are out. The barometer still says stormy. I tap it again, suddenly moved. I contain myself though because my father is exceptionally alert to turns of sentiment. He can sniff them through walls, be home early from the office on account of them, to spy or remonstrate.

But there is no avoiding him. It is one of the days when he is badly troubled by flatulence. The visits to the lavatory, once disguised, are now blatant. It is hard to see how they help, however, because they follow each other so rapidly. Indeed it is tempting to think that they give rise to one another somehow. It explains the number of books in our two lavatories, by the way. Some of the titles interest me, but I never read them because they are my father's companions during his trials and they must surely smell of him.

It is perhaps hard to wish someone happy birthday with a cistern hissing behind you and other evidence of your distress in the air. Let me be fair. That is maybe why my father doesn't shake my hand when we meet (too proud, of course, to be seen suddenly realising he has forgotten). His present – so I think of it – is an invitation to me to come and discuss my plans. My career. The unfolding of my talents in inherited forms. He is always on about it. But the harder he presses the less I can imagine what I might ever do. Under the weight of his enquiries, in fact, I become disorientated. There is no before and after. Not as at the waterfall, however – not at all. It is a kind of vertigo, a moment squirming on its axis.

My anger is purer than it has ever been. An exceptional outburst. I shout that on a day out of time one doesn't bother with plans. He looks at me, looks past me. How he might have looked and what he might have said but for the need to go back into the lavatory (ours is a house of tired cisterns) I cannot say. He shuts the door gingerly, his eyes pained, remote.

Outside, on his deckchair, a sudden breeze flicks over the pages of his book. I start up the hill again.

CHAPTER TWO

Eleven days after her murder Mrs Templeton was buried. It was as she would have liked it, with her dread of cremations: a small country churchyard, a minister neither too casual nor too sympathetic, a small group of mourners. Even William, as he stood by the grave in this churchyard which seemed to be definitely tilted – tilted towards the sun and the delights of the valley below – recalled his mother's horror of fires. It was the one fact about her he could recall in his distress. Otherwise her life and character were mysterious, the violence and strangeness of her end seeming to have thrown a long shadow backwards, obscuring the details by which she might otherwise have been remembered. (As if – William thought – it was a usurper's corpse before them.) He swayed, liverish and fearful, noting the exceptional self-possession of his sister opposite him.

Marion had arrived two days before, but he hadn't seen her until today, for she had been staying with friends. He hadn't even been sure, arriving at the church, if she would be there. And, seeing her, the aloofness with which she held herself, he wondered why she was. Questions occurred to him, the sort for which drunks – with their tactless insistence, desperate muddled perseverance (the drunk's prerogative, if there is one) – are noted. Is it perhaps the violence of our mother's end that has called you from New England? The murder or her death – which has summoned you? Would you have come had she died in bed? (It is not everyone whose mother is murdered, Marion.) Would either of us have come had she died in bed? Would you from the higher and I from the lower regions have budged at all? And what difference now, here, by the graveside, between you from on high and I from below? Sensational children. A sensational mother. His dear mother, her unforced prettiness: briefly recalled, it made his sister behind her half-veil seem merely glamorous. He faced her across the grave, careless of his tears, his unsteadiness, the impression he knew he was giving of mounting abandon. He wasn't drunk – only weak from the habit of being so – but he could see that it was assumed that he was.

Some of the mourners, old friends of his mother, had barely acknowledged him. He had dressed as well as he could, but it was not well – certainly not well enough to make them think they might have wronged him. A certain sense of style, though, had survived his ruin, but it didn't show in his clothes – only in a capacity to make light of that ruin, to make a riddle of it. He had been quite theatrical, greeting the mourners, quite cavalier, coming up with appreciative phrases when he couldn't remember the names. And mainly he couldn't remember the names. Some, it appeared, barely recognised him, and some he could have sworn he had never met. Others clasped his hand with a kind of awed forbearance, as if the son's disgrace and the mother's murder were somehow connected.

And one, whose name he immediately remembered, looked at him with more than simple disgust. It weakened him considerably, this look. Indeed, it may have been the main reason why he forgot most of the other names. Alice Fox. Alice Mary Fox. He remembered her role in his mother's life well: the pert and inflexible confidante. In this woman, for some reason, his mother had confided, by her she had been advised, mocked, admired. It had been one of the mysteries of their family life.

It was as his mother's grave was being filled that William realised the meaning of the look. In Alice Mary Fox's eyes, he, William, was the murderer. Cleared by the police ("too broken to want to kill anyone but himself"), he had not been cleared by Alice and would probably never be. Several times during the service she looked at him from her position behind Marion. Marion's detachment, Alice's accusation: their two heads came together, appearing to share the one pair of shoulders. He was used to these illusions of grotesque reassembly. In his time, he had seen men with the heads of giant crows, women with no heads at all, crowds with heads horribly swollen, as from a plague of hydrocephalus, dwarfs with wild grins and enormous bellies. There had been spells when these illusions had threatened to become more frequent than his times of normal vision. So it was with a grin almost of recognition that he saw Marion and Alice sprung from the one pair of shoulders. A legendary alliance. A kind of immemorial dovetailing in malicious agreement.

By the end of the service, however, his eyes were closed against the possibility of further distortion. On the surface of his vivid inner darkness lights flickered, born from nothing, returning to it. He feared he was swaying disgracefully, but he didn't care. It was the sun on his face, wasn't it, rather than Mrs Mclehose's gas fire? He should have known the difference, he had spent so much of his time by that fire, on the floor. With Mrs Mclehose on the floor, with her sour breath and sour underwear, her words alternately romantic and vicious.

Marion and he, hardly having spoken, took up their positions by the churchyard gate. The path between the gravestones was narrow and uneven and the mourners mainly over seventy, so the line moved very slowly – a sort of stricken shuffle. Now couples passed them, marriages of forty years or so (dressed, it almost seemed, not just to show respect, but to try and appease death itself), now individuals, the unmarried, the once married. William became aware that Marion was as uneasy as he was himself. Her words were few and made slightly ridiculous by what struck him as a false American accent. His own voice, he knew, was thick, made so by lips still cracked and swollen from the winter. But he was able to vary his expressions of appreciation; he was nimbler than his sister, and after seven or eight people had passed he realised she was using some of his phrases. "It may have been a long time but it's nonetheless a pleasure." "How good to see you, under such terrible circumstances." "Thank you, I'm sure we're equally appalled." "An unusual awe unites us today." "It is shocking – doubly shocking." "Of course I know you – why should I have forgotten?"

Then they were alone with the minister on the quiet hillside. The sound of the cars going down into the valley in low gear grew distant, was gone. William stood smiling, glad of the silence, the sound of larks, the sun. Marion was smiling too, but uneasily, and she was holding on to her hat; though there was a wind, there wasn't even a breeze. William saw that it was her way of managing herself. She didn't seem aloof now at all. Merely ordinary. Ordinary grief; ordinary mortality. It was the same with himself. An ordinary embarrassment. He didn't know this minister and it was so long since he had seen Marion that it was as if he had never met her. Alone with two strangers, his drunk's impudence asserted itself.

"Who were all these people? Are you sure they had the right funeral?"

"They can be difficult occasions, William," the minister said. "One is confused."

"One is indeed," William went on. "You'd think some of them had climbed from their graves to help mother into hers!"

"William!" Marion said, but it was clear that she was relieved.

"Alice Fox, for instance. I could have sworn she'd died before mother."

"I'd forgotten you were a joker, William," Marion said gravely. "Alice Fox. Yes. I couldn't remember that name at all."

Sometimes a house seems like Noah's Ark, everything of worth stored inside, to be enjoyed under a new dispensation. Old objects become charged with significance and there is a feeling that those who live there have been entrusted with the elements of exceptional change. It is particularly so if the sky is torn and livid, the trees and bushes bent against a gale, and if the residents themselves have recently been afflicted. Then the windows suggest that such storms are the last rages of the old creation. The intimacy of those indoors is as perfect as their confidence and they part with no suspicion that either will be undone. Little in the poses they strike is justified by experience, but the poses are deeply suggestive nonetheless and, like signs or oracles, are never forgotten.

William and Marion had arranged to meet in order to sort out their parents' possessions. William joked immediately that he was beyond possessions: he had come to nothing and so he needed nothing; he had no place for anything. All he wanted were knick-knacks, a few souvenirs; and maybe he would find that he didn't even want these. But he wasn't unhappy; it meant that they wouldn't have the problem of how to divide their inheritance. It also made him feel generous, and since he hadn't had the means to be generous for some time this was a great pleasure. What failed to happen when he had entered the house with the inspector happened now. He moved about the rooms with simple curiosity, often touching things, occasionally being enthralled – rediscoveries so intense they recalled the discoveries of children. (There were moments indeed when, dizzy, staggering slightly, he might have been leaving the darkness of infancy for the first time.) Some rooms he barely recognised at first: he had to take up several positions before he remembered. Had their mother rearranged the house after their father's death? Sold some of the furniture? His gaze and questions were innocent, interrupting Marion's attempts to work out what she wanted. She didn't mind. Her brother appealed to her strongly today, and if there was a selfish reason for this – he had not been favoured in the will and he wanted nothing anyway – there was also an unselfish one. His very absence of status or position was arresting. It was a touchingly bare disinterestedness. It was not an achievement, she knew, but a few times, hearing him say – "D'you remember this?" or "There it is!" or "I'd take that, if I were you" – she was close to feeling that it was. Her smile was of wonder, and wonder at her wonder: her brother was ruined and the house was hers, but as he accompanied her from room to room, opening doors for her, sometimes taking her arm, he didn't seem ruined and the house didn't seem important.

"What about Margo and the children?" Marion asked.

"Haven't seen them for years. They may have joined you in the New World for all I know."

"I mean, wouldn't they like some of the furniture?"

"No need. Margo is well provided for. With my demise her father stepped in. Huge cash injections. He threw a castle round her."

"Would it help if I saw her?"

"It wouldn't help me," William said quietly, realising that Marion hadn't quite grasped how far he had fallen. When had he last seen her? Had he seen her off to America or had he just heard that she had gone, imagining so many farewell scenes that he had come to believe that one of them must have happened?

"When did we last meet, Marion?" He asked it very directly, almost as if he believed that unless he were told he wouldn't know how to go on.

"Oh, William, you don't recall?"

"No. Most of the lines between my past and I are down."

"Margo rang me because you'd passed out at breakfast."

"So you saw me but I didn't see you? No wonder I don't remember! There would have been too much toast. Always was. Yes. But which year?"

"Let me see," Marion said, looking carefully at her brother. "It would have been nine years ago. You still had a few years to go with Margo."

"So nine years ago I was asleep on a bed of toast," William said, standing up from the window seat on which they had been talking. "I see."

He was rueful, not from some affectionate feeling for the details of that time, but from the realisation that he had no such feeling. Except for the children, there were no images, and even his images of them, he suspected, were sentimental. They were always grave and always together: in the bath, for example, or waiting to be read to at night, or coming into their parents' bed in the morning. Saving images, images which allowed him to pretend that his children hadn't grown. But they wouldn't always be summoned, and then the children, tall and thin now, would seem to be in a wood of some kind, crows' heads on the ground, the air thick with hawks. Thick too with sanctimonious babble. On their way to a lake of pitch, spellbound by their mother's plans. Margo in a lake of pitch, pointing, commanding. It was unfair, he knew, and it was uninteresting, but they were the images which assailed him when the other ones – the cameos of innocence and vulnerability – failed.

"William?"

"Sorry. Unnecessary reflections. Easily banished. There!" he said, clicking his fingers as for the amusement of a child. "There!"

"I've brought some dinner. I thought we'd be hungry."

"A carry-out?"

"Oh no. I'll cook it."

"That's kind of you," William said, going with her to the kitchen. "But I should say – please don't be offended – that my appetite is poor. It happens, you know."

She paid no attention to him, as if she was confident that when he saw the meal he would eat it! She might have been back in New England, it seemed to him, preparing dinner for a dozen guests. His admiration turned her into a performer. She moved stylishly, like one giving a cookery demonstration – cooker to table, table to cooker – now and then smiling at him as he sat. She was wearing their mother's apron, but her kitchen manner was very different from Mrs Templeton's. Even for the simplest snack, William recalled, their mother's preparations had been halting. Marion's were soft, silent.

But his admiration wasn't confined to her kitchen manner. He noted that she had become heavier but also more graceful, with a way of throwing her head back and smoothing her hips. If she hadn't been his sister: but that was the trouble – it didn't feel that she was (ostracism so barbarous apparently it destroyed even the sense of blood ties). Changed by America, by marriage there – her face, at least, was fuller, kinder – she struck him as the sort of woman (suggestive of many types without herself being one) one might talk to on a train and find it difficult to forget. Wasn't that exactly it? This was a heightened interval, and Marion, more appreciative than he, was marking it with a meal. He stood up abruptly, but there was nothing for him to do, and so he sat down again, smiling at the preparations, approving them, not wanting them to end.

They ate in the old dining room. The evening sky was livid and stormy. Rain drove against the window in gusts, the background in wavering sunlight, or scoured the hills, the young forests there, the foreground or middle ground in uncertain light. Then there were intervals when there was neither rain nor sun, only gloom and a wind unsure of its strength and direction.

Marion hadn't allowed William to do anything. Now he sat above his prawn cocktail, a perfectly folded napkin on his left, a glass of white wine on his right, his hands clasped in his lap and his eyes fixed on the salt-cellar. Marion spread her napkin and then, as if it was her custom, her brother's deftly for him. They clinked glasses, the sound pure and high, but fading quickly, and Marion led the way with the prawn cocktail, eating with a slow relish she clearly hoped would be encouraging. William followed as best he could, but he could taste neither the prawns nor the wine. Still like one hoping to encourage by example (the optimism of her chewing and swallowing was exemplary), Marion went through the three courses – prawn cocktail, steak, fruit salad – finishing the third as William, apologising for his extraordinary slowness, was beginning the second. Was she, William wondered, simple enough to believe that she could persuade him of the importance of diet and the necessity of health by eating in this way? With this slow theatrical relish? He saw that she wasn't. It was all she could do, under the circumstances. Another mightn't have been as generous – mightn't have cooked at all, or might have swept the bravely prepared meal onto the floor in a paroxysm of confusion and grief.

"You'd never think," William said, as if to test the rituals of cooking and eating to the utmost, "that mother was murdered out there. And buried."

Marion looked as if she thought he might have got his information wrong.

"You'd never think it," he said again.

Marion was blinking, her tongue half out.

"To picture someone doing that: is it possible?"

"For me," William said, starting to push his plate away with his fingertips, "it's not who but why. Why."

"Oh really?" Marion said. "For me the need is... a face. To supply a face."

"She had no enemies," William offered.

"Only friends," Marion murmured.

But then, as if dismayed that the conversation was necessary at all, she banged her fist on the table.

William attempted to rise, to comfort her, but he couldn't. Then he tried to say something appreciative about the meal; but he couldn't do this either.

The meal remained with him however. In the squalor of Mrs Mclehose's lounge – the air hot and stale and smelling of whisky – he thought of it. In her bedroom, which had somehow also become his, he thought of it. His sister's nice and encouraging sense of ceremony. She had returned to America, promising to write, promising (he was to go over for a visit when he was ready) to send him his airfare. But when he was ready, he knew, it wouldn't be for that sort of journey. Not that he could picture his path (if there was one), only the first steps (into the wind and the dark if necessary). He started to look at the "situations vacant" page in the evening paper, the last part of the column for those without professions: the meretricious, the migrant, the half-hearted, the discredited, the damned, the dull. And one day he saw an advertisement for a caretaker on a disused farm. Trembling (unclear whether it was fear of rejection, fear of commitment or fear of abandoned farms), he applied, keeping his intentions from Mrs Mclehose, for thoughts of desertion drove her wild. Suffering himself to be embraced nightly, on the couch or in the narrow bed, he dreamt of the farm, its limitless acres, its silences, the room he would have there were he hired.

September 10th, 1966

I am doing well at this job. I seem to be well liked, and, what is more, I like everyone here. I'm not aware of the grudges, the misunderstandings I sometimes hear about in the pub, at the end of the day. Indeed, young though I am (twenty-six next month), I've been asked to intervene on a number of occasions. I've not thought of myself as a peacemaker, not at all, but it's a change from the uneasy opinions my seniors usually have of me. Between Mr Fraser and his secretary I arranged a reconciliation, and between Mr Fraser and Mr Arthur a handshake and a drink. The latter two came to see me in the pub, where I was sitting in my usual corner. It was clear that something was wrong, but it was also clear that they were hoping to be rescued from their disagreement. I seem to have that knack – particularly after a drink or two. Laughter: create the conditions for that and you create the conditions for ease and forbearance. If I believe anything, I believe that; I make no apologies. (For how many faiths have we seen crumble, burdened by their own complexity, thousands perishing as a consequence?)

It's taken me some time however to find a job that suits me. What a relief to find it! This is partly the explanation perhaps for my popularity. My relief is mistaken for the happiness of a mature man, for informed good nature. It's thought that I have wisdom, higher advice to dispense. I wish I had. I feel peculiarly ignorant, and if I have any virtues they are these: I make no claims to knowledge of an improving kind, and I live from day to day. This second, I sometimes suspect, borders on a vice, for the moment can seem to me all that there is. I try to arrest it by means of impromptu ceremonies, but I always end up (sometimes inside a circle of broken glass) by chasing my tail.

Jobs. It is as if they are embedded in the very substance of our world. One can break oneself against them. Just as there are more rock formations than people realise, there are more jobs. There are the professions, of course – we all know about these – but it is the world below them and around them that

I am speaking of. I am at ease where I am, but there are many who are not – who are bent double or actually twisted in ill-lit caves. I was frequently so myself. The little firm of Robertson's which sold diaries and calendars, for instance: I didn't prosper there. From the start (after a characteristically impressive interview – at once attentive and cavalier) I was considered to lack a concern for detail. Fatal, this, in the world of diaries and calendars. My Housewives' Calendar for 1984 featured a March with only thirty days. Now I know that March has thirty-one days, so what went wrong? Mr Robertson himself took charge of the matter. He was deeply aggrieved, and sat, as he interrogated me, with his hands on his two most popular calendars: the Dog Lover's Calendar and the Calendar of Favourite Cats. It is no wonder my facetiousness surpassed itself. Arguing from the stars, quoting Newton and Einstein, I said that every one hundred and sixty-two years there was what some of us in the trade knew as a double leap year – twenty-nine days in February, thirty in March. I told Mr Robertson that if he were to check the records he would find that 1802 had been just such a year. (A year of memorable frosts, I added, three assassinations and twenty-six wars.) He was shaken and obviously wondering how to reward me if I was right. He did check and I was sacked instead.

From here, my disregard for the clock intensified by my experience of diaries and calendars, I went into the flour industry. There have been no appreciable gaps between my jobs, firstly because I am good at interviews and secondly because I have always been able to convert my despair over a job into the conviction that the next one will be almost ideal. In the flour industry, however, I couldn't even bring myself to despair. A mild exasperation was mainly what I felt. The only thing I enjoyed was the sensation of the flour itself, running through my fingers. On my last day, I recall, it was what anchored me while I was being berated for my poor sales figures. I ran it through my fingers and onto my desk – ran it almost continuously. It was like exploring the substance of the time-glass. In the exquisitely fine grains which for centuries measured time I imagined I was taking up my position. Paradoxically, though, the effect was to destroy my sense of time's great categories. Century, Decade, Year, Month, Week, Day – all dissolved as the flour ran. On and on, just the flour and my idle graceful fingers. Beyond, the terms of my resignation (or, failing that, of my sacking) were monotonously spelled out to me by what seemed like the entire board of directors. First one voice, then another, then another, each with its own part of the official script, but each losing conviction, I thought, as I sat silent, the flour running, the typewriters going next door, in the secretarial pool. The only words I remember are Charlie Hutton's, himself a casualty of the next reshuffle. "You should be a fortune-teller, William, you have the hands of one."

After Robertson's diaries and calendars and Clapperton's flour I had a spell with a distillery. It wasn't the whisky which got me, but the drunkenness of so many of my colleagues. It disgusted me; at times it enraged me. The firm seemed to run itself, unless there were, hidden even from my exasperated gaze, sober, intelligent people who ran it while the official employees, my colleagues, played at being businessmen. No job has so deeply distressed me. There was no equivalent to running flour through my fingers (unless you want to count drinking from ten in the morning until six at night as an equivalent), and so I bought some of the very 1lb and 2lb packets I had been unsuccessful at selling. I got a reputation, running the flour through my fingers, for modelling in clay. (I was even asked to model a four-foot bottle of whisky – someone' retirement present.) All that I got out of my stay was the chance to speak in public. I did it well, though it wouldn't have taken much to impress these people (anyone who didn't get lost in his sentences impressed them). I pitched my speeches higher and higher, at an imaginary audience (who might they have been?), one quite other than that actually before me, in all its florid messiness. They were lonely speeches to make. And, after six months, loneliness and disgust made me resign.

From my corner in the pub I review my day. We are an Educational Publishers. It is a small firm, but expanding. I am one of two salesmen. I travel alternate weeks, which makes my weeks in and about the office special. My popularity is intensified, I think, by these arrivals and departures. People store up anecdotes for me, as well as problems. I am missed. Who would have thought that I would be considered a peacemaker, and that, day by day, life should appear easy to me, running by as surely as the lovely flour?

At ease, therefore, I wait for Janet Macpherson. She is pregnant, I fear, but by whom I don't know. What can I say?

CHAPTER THREE

William held back on his drinks the night before he left Mrs Mclehose for the farm, for it was important that he should get up at six, undetected, and follow his plan faithfully. He had been holding back on his drinks for two weeks, in fact, planning. The edginess and reserve in his manner he accounted for by pointing to his grief, his mourning for his mother. Funeral matters also. It was convenient, for there was much to explain: the interview, the letters, the greater concern with his appearance, with tidiness generally. His determination was to repossess his will. And his grief, far from hindering him in this, strengthened him: the more he mourned, the more he uncovered energies (they were energies, he was sure, rather than just whims or impulses because they did not desert him) which allowed him to aim at the farm. The farm which was his future. The farm whose boundaries were as far as he could see for himself.

His plan for the evening before his departure worked well. He got Mrs Mclehose so drunk that she passed out on the couch in the lounge. He covered her carefully with a rug, gave her what he realised was a farewell kiss (on the forehead, for her mouth was open) and spent the night in her bedroom. Under the pillow he placed his farewell letter, written some days before. He had had trouble with it, not being able to write it until he had overcome the feeling that he should apologise. In its final form it was a simple state-ment of his intentions. It had a certain elegance, though, and this he knew would defeat her, for in eight months he hadn't once been elegant with her. He had been as respon-sible for the grossness in their relationship as she. Indeed it had been her coarseness, her utter disregard for niceties of any kind, that had attracted him. He had been undone in her shadow; and she in his. At pains to reduce himself to vanishing point, his wit only apparent the instant before he had a drink – and then mainly used to curse his past – he had become Mrs Mclehose's idea of a man of culture. His past. She was the audience for his dramatisation of such of it as he could remember. He lied, he vilified, he stumbled across the truth without knowing it and cast it aside, he approached the same event from different angles without reaching it, lurching into extraordinary irrelevancies, and he wept.

But now he had written her a letter.

Dear Sandra,

I am lighting out for pastures new. There comes a tide in the affairs of men when it is called for. Do not be angry! I leave you, if not my best, at least my best under the circumstances. Do not grieve; it is not worth it. It will come to seem an insignificant departure.

Ever yours,
William

At twenty past six, wearing his anorak and carrying a small case, he laid the letter by the door of the lounge and went quietly downstairs. He had practised opening the front door silently and so his departure was as silent as a departure can be. His only pair of shoes were soft ones, which meant that by the time he reached the corner of the street he had made virtually no sound at all, but this very soundlessness of his flight had the effect of making him doubt its reality. Another joke for his own diversion? Another extended threat? There had been too many: his defiant quips to himself in the lavatory, his broken answering laughter. His move from one chair to another, one room to another (in no house had he slammed so many doors), each time with the illusion that he was putting Mrs Mclehose beyond him forever. He walked on, coughing slightly, until he came to the bus stop for the six thirty-five. There he reached out and grasped the pole, not for support, but to reassure himself of the reality of his venture. It worked; he felt suddenly jaunty.

The bus, its doors open to the June morning, was empty. William sat near the driver, for he had to be sure to change at the right place. The bus for the farmlands to the south of Glasgow left at eight and arrived at nine-thirty. A Mr Weir was to meet him off it and drive him to the farm. He would recognise Mr Weir, he had been told in a letter, by his height. He hoped that he had been described in turn, for his fear was that he would get no further than the village, and that, after waiting there for some time, he would discover that his plan didn't match reality at the critical point. He had heard of people who had been promised jobs that didn't exist, or which had ceased to exist the moment they were promised. In an age of such carelessness could he really expect someone to take him to a deserted farm, where he would be paid to keep an eye on someone else's property but where he would mainly be keeping an eye on himself?

No longer jaunty after three hours of travel, William got off the second bus in the village square. The clock above the fountain said nine-thirty. The bus waited for a few moments, then drove off the way it had come. The square was empty then, and the streets leading into it, some from below, some from above, were empty too. The buildings were very white in the morning light, and very still. Beyond, there was a wooded hill, as green as the village was white, and appearing, as William looked at it, to move closer. He listened: from the profound silence sounds slowly emerged: a tractor, dogs, cows. His thoughts were simple: he was in the country and it was very different from the city. A pleasant difference, with the power of making Mr Weir's absence less troubling than it might have been. For he was absent: in no shadowed doorway was he standing, watching the new caretaker.

Then he heard a vehicle approaching the village rapidly from the direction of the hill. There was a lull before, recovering itself after a series of bends, the vehicle, a Land Rover, burst into the village. It came straight into the square and straight towards William, still at the same furious speed, the impression given being not so much of purpose as of purpose imitated, William recognised it as almost his own state: purpose imitated. He watched as the Land Rover turned in the square and reversed towards him, the engine high and impatient, the driver manoeuvring by memory apparently, for he was looking straight ahead, as at the next point in his day. He reversed until he was beside William, and then, smiling, reached across and opened the passenger door.

"Come in if you're William Templeton."

"That's me."

"George Weir – at your service."

George Weir was indeed a large man. He stooped as he drove, a reckless smile (as in response to secret challenges) coming and going on his ruddy face. He was well dressed, however, almost a dandy, and the Land Rover was as neat as he was.

"Last ditch?" he said, his voice loud and definite.

"I beg your pardon?"

"Last ditch job?"

"Not at all." William smiled, without turning his head. "A fresh start. As fresh as the day. One gets sick of cities."

"Glad to have you whatever your reasons. Your hours will be your own. Fill them as you like. There are vandals, so watch for them. And there are those, not vandals, whose line is old farm machinery. Watch those too. If it gets difficult, ring me, ring the police. Don't try to be heroic; you're not paid to be."

"You're nearby?"

"Five miles. Ashby House. I'm a farm manager. My time's not my own. My wife is, though, and my children. But what will you do? I mean what will you do?" He was suddenly earnest, asking this.

"I don't know," William said, thinking that it was enough that he was arriving. "I'll have to find out."

"All the best anyway. I'll drop in now and then. My wife too."

"Thanks very much," William said.

They were driving through farmland, but it wasn't rich farmland. The dykes had crumbled in places, the fences looked unsteady and the cattle were poorly nourished. There was a greyness in the green of the fields, as if there had been too many droughts in the area, or as if the land had never recovered from a rain of ashes. As they drove – quite slowly now, quite calmly – George Weir appeared to be settled by their conversation and William's impression was that the land had never been meant for farming. Ingenuity and doggedness alone had made it farmland, kept it so. To get it all going, he imagined, there must have been a time when labourers crawled on the face of every field. The exceptional flatness allowed him to imagine it: after the storm of ashes, the generations of labourers.

At last they turned off the main road onto a rutted track, driving between trees to the farmhouse, a yellow building of two stories. Outside it, but facing across the fields to the horizon, the Land Rover stopped. The silence was overwhelming.

"I'll show you round, then leave you to settle in," George Weir said. "Don't worry about the silence or the flatness.

They seem to breed each other, I know, but you'll get used to it. I did."

But it wasn't this that was worrying William. It was his bowels. The lavatory was under the stairs, cramped, damp and windowless. But the water came generously from old fashioned taps and there was a small hard crescent of green soap.

In the old days (the days of soft carpets and dubious favours, he had recently heard himself say), he couldn't have stayed in a place like the farmhouse for a night. There was hardly anything in it. In the bedroom a chair and a bed; in the living room an old leather armchair; in the kitchen a cooker, a small table and two chairs. That was all. But now, with no possessions, no means of furnishing the place, nothing really, the farmhouse suited him. He saw why he had been given the job. What married couple, however down on their luck, would have taken it? The house suggested his state with a vividness that startled him. Walking about it, up and down the stairs, flushing the toilet to create a little sensation in the stillness, checking the cooker, he thought that for most conditions there is probably a job. If he didn't quite understand his condition, he might do so after a month of this arresting bareness, this bullying flatness. He had the sensation, walking through the farmhouse, of preceding himself into himself, of coming on a piece of script in a deserted place and only by reading it beginning to grasp why he was there (how far do you have to go to discover why you set out?).

It only took him a minute or two to unpack, but he did so carefully, laying his things out on the bed. He had one change of clothes, a toothbrush, a facecloth, a razor, a small cracked mirror and a small transistor radio. He lifted the radio to his ear, trying the area for reception. The flatness ensured that it was very clear. But what else could be said for the flatness? The bedroom was upstairs and as he tuned in to a talk on vegetarian cookery he fancied that the expanse was mocking him. Many acres of it were now his responsibility, but how could he impose himself on so much second-rate farmland – he a third or even fourth-rate personality? He was being paid to make the attempt, though, and it was a long time since he had been paid to make any kind of attempt. This knowledge that money would be coming in regularly again pleased him, not so much because he would be able to pay his way as because it meant that he was recognised, marked, registered. He was on someone's books; he would figure in someone's accounts. William Templeton, Caretaker, Fulford Farm, £260 per month (gross).

He took longer to arrange his things than he had done to unpack them. Should he keep them by him in the bedroom, or trust the other rooms? He held the mirror before him, moving it about rather as he had done the transistor, but it was harder, because of the crack in it, to get his face into focus than it had been the talk on vegetarian cookery. The crack had been there for a long time and it always dramatised his sense that he had lost himself. He had to be content with getting about two thirds of his face into the area of mirror to the right of the crack. This he did now. His hair, he saw, was dry and matted, his eyes a bloodshot dirty yellow, and his skin had a tight look, as if another month or two with Sandra Mclehose and it would have begun to crack open all over, to peel off, abandon the flesh within. He smiled at himself, but the effect was ghastly: what was recorded was his aversion to his own face, and his horror at that aversion. He seemed to see, he thought, a face that was ceasing to be a face. He put the mirror on the mantelpiece and, sitting down on the bed, switched off the talk on vegetarian cookery ("the versatility of the cauliflower cannot be ..."). A great silence again.

He thought that he might have to start talking to himself. To take yourself into your own confidence, however – how did you begin? The phone by the bed was an old one – upright, angular, black – and when he lifted the receiver the dialling tone suggested a mass of cancelled opportunities. Then it was cut off and there was a remote whine, which, after a few moments, was like another version of silence. William said, "How do you do, I'm glad to meet you, let's grow some cauliflowers together" three times, replacing the receiver with exaggerated aplomb, hands poised shaking just above it. It exasperated him that he couldn't hold anything without his hands shaking. That might be one of his first projects therefore: to stop them shaking, to be able to hold the mirror up to his face first thing in the morning without his hands in their wretchedness contributing to the ambiguity of what he saw.

It was nearly lunchtime. When had he last made a point of having lunch? He would observe lunchtime again – breakfast-time and dinner-time too. There was a general store two miles away: he would walk there after he had made his first tour of inspection. George Weir had given him an advance of twenty-five pounds. He had suggested fifty – he had even had fifty in his hand – but William, associating the sudden appearance of money with recklessness, drinking, perversity, had refused. To start as he intended to continue was all he could think of saying to himself.

He said it to himself again as he set out on his tour of inspection. It was June, and the air, warm and fresh on his face, made him raise his hands – a kind of apprehensive delight. Even in the winter though he would make these tours of inspection: three a day. He would work out various routes, each tour of inspection taking a different one. He would get to know the land as well as any farmer knew his – better perhaps – appreciating each feature, however broken or useless. Bold intentions, they made him walk more briskly than he had done for years, away from the yellow farmhouse – less yellow now, at noon, than it had been earlier – towards the first of the fields.

It wasn't clear where the garden – if there had been one – ended and the field began; the grass was as thick in both. A cherry tree, its blossoms almost faded, suggested there had been a garden. Near to it, William came across an old sink, its taps, like forsaken mouths, pointing up at him from the grass, and a line of empty paint tins. Someone's idea of a boundary? some lazy predecessor? Someone who, struck one day by the importance of boundaries, had then lost heart, become cynical? Gasping and stumbling, William carried the sink over to a hedge, and after it, two at a time, the paint tins. But then, his heart racing, he too felt the need of boundaries – felt it as one might the need for abrasive self-scrutiny – and drew a line with his heel where he thought the garden should end. He would make a lawn between the hedge and here – reclaim the lawn there had once been – first scything, then mowing.

He took a few steps into the field and stopped. It was bright and hot and still. He listened – straining above the racing of his heart – for birdsong; but he couldn't hear any. It seemed to him possible that it was there – indeed that it was all about him, remarkable sequences of it – but that he was as incapable of hearing it as he was of holding his mirror or transistor without trembling. He took the first path he saw, assuming that it would lead to the first group of outhouses. There were four groups of outhouses on the domain, he had been told, one of them, the most remote, with a small farmhouse. They were his main responsibility: he was to watch them closely. "Although," George Weir had added soberly, "you've not exactly got troops to help you. Not exactly."

But after about two hundred yards the path ended. At his feet there was a scattering of marigolds. He squatted beside them, breathless. He would need to be fitter than this to make these tours of inspection. At this rate he would reach the first group of outhouses in a state of collapse. He rose, dark spots before his eyes, and pressed on, through grass which was often up to his knees.

A walking stick would help – it could also be used as a weapon. When he was stronger, when his hands were steadier, when he did not have these spots before his eyes, he would fashion one.

Quite recently he'd had a watch – he felt sure of that – but he didn't have one any longer. He couldn't tell how long it had taken him to reach the first of the outhouses. They formed a long rectangle round a steading which he entered through an archway of red brick. In the middle of the steading was a pump, its handle up, a pail on its side before it, bales of straw on either side. The materials of pantomime: that was what struck William as he squatted by the pump, exhausted ("The Treacherous Pump", "The Secret Pump"). But the smells were of a real farm – hay, cows, milk, manure, loam and William had the fancy that he would only have to look up to find that life on the farm had resumed. He had simply strayed into a pause: in a moment or two a plump woman would be operating the pump, a child would be calling, a dog would be asleep in the sun. But he looked up and there was nothing. He tried the pump but its handle was broken and it made a clanking noise which, as in mockery of his images of continuity, gave the deadest of dead echoes in a corner of the yard.

There was more farm machinery in the outhouses than he had thought there would be, much of it strange to him. Modern equipment for milking, ploughing, harvesting? The only thing he recognised with certainty was a small fork-lift truck, its cabin bright yellow, the fork-lift up, ready. Going from outhouse to outhouse – assuming that in the other groups of outhouses there would be more such machinery, elaborately waiting – William was shocked by the extent of his responsibilities. Did they know who they had hired when they had hired him? Was it so thankless a job that there was no other option but to pick someone like him? Who else had done the job? (He had been told that he was the first, but was he?) If they could afford all this machinery, why not several caretakers?

Had there once been several? Had they quarrelled perhaps, so that the enemy were able to come and go virtually unnoticed? Drunk together too often and too much? Colluded with the enemy – finally gone over to them? Would he meet them one day therefore, face to face in a steading, and be offered a bribe? Might they know enough about him to try and bribe him with drink? How would he account for himself on that day?

His theories about his predecessors getting darker and darker, weakening him, causing a ringing in his ears, he returned to the idea that he had none, that the line started with him. It was enough to get him going again, in the direction of the farmhouse.

He imagined the great expanse of farmland then as a setting for the neglected machines. Soon, released from stasis, from the weeks or months of arrest, they would cross and recross the land, reclaiming it, redeeming it. And then, having done all that they had been built to do, having done it perfectly, they would stop, rusting until they disappeared. An idyll of redundant machines, the long silence of their rusting as perfect as their final performance.

As though to check that these were merely visions, halfway back to the farmhouse William sat down and looked behind him. The outhouses wobbled in the heat. The distortions of June: he recalled them from childhood. Beyond the outhouses, however, he did think he saw something. Small black shapes, like eels dancing on their tails in clouds of dust. Towards or away from him? He walked back slowly, hoping that steady motion would help him to dominate his world. Then he looked behind him again. One minute the shapes appeared to be moving towards him, the next to be going away, the next to be gone entirely, the next to be returning. Endlessly flickering away from him, towards him, in the pure heat of June, they were like variations on the idea of periphery.

He lay on his bed, utterly exhausted. Had he left it too late? Was he too weak for a job? He couldn't afford such suspicions. When he woke he would try and reach the store. He could return in the cool of the evening. Food might make the difference. Without adequate food, he knew, he had hardly been living. He had been like the figures, flickering on some periphery, some line between presence and absence, substance and abstraction. Between the creature and its shadow, foundering.

August 4th, 1968

I can't understand why I am so reluctant to meet Margo's parents. It is time I presented myself. We have known each other for seven months. Marriage is even in the air, though it hasn't actually been spoken of. Why do I feel it is in the air? Why do I feel – for the first time in my relationships with women – that I have moved from the definitely temporary to the possibly permanent? A grey line, mark you, divides the temporary from the permanent. It is not one I have sought to cross. Indeed some days I feel I have let myself down, straying across it. I don't relish the new territory, but I can't deny that it is where I am. Margo is there too, of course. She arrived before me, awaiting me, if not with open arms, at least with little gestures of encouragement. It is a territory in which she moves with confidence, though since (or so she tells me) she hasn't been seriously involved before, I cannot understand where she gets her confidence. Either she knows me better than I know myself (likes me better than I like myself) or she doesn't know me at all.

She is quite highly born, and this may account for some of

her confidence. She has been used to the settled society of the highly born. There have been excursions from it, flights even, but she has always returned, and she has always known that she can return. It is one of the things that slightly irritates me about her: her belief that she doesn't need what enables her to appear so stylishly independent. She doesn't see it this way, of course. She explains that her returns are the result of affection for those she has left, not of fear. The world has few fears for her, she says.

It is not so with me. Not at all. Doing well in my job, I am yet aware of being orbited by alternative lives. Sometimes they pass close enough for me to be able to make out features. If they are not quite my features, they are not unfamiliar, either. I have a sense of peril, for it seems to me that it wouldn't take much to change tracks. Who throws the points? How familiar – if he has any – are his features? I have tried to explain this to Margo, but she just smiles. I suspect that she believes that I will be all right once we are married, and this troubles me. Maybe I will, maybe I won't. One can't count on it. Should it be a requirement, anyway?

From this new territory I glimpse a permanence greater than that which can be enjoyed – if that is the word – in particular relationships. And that is in the province of the highly born. I think that it must be my dislike of this province that is holding me back from Margo's parents. God help me, I am perhaps being unfair, but I seem to be able to trace so much of what I find irresistible in Margo – her capacity for delight, her confidence, her resourcefulness, her irony, her inspired rudeness – to an environment of which I am deeply suspicious. One of the paradoxes that makes one gasp. That defeats deliberation. The flower emerging from the dung.

What a flower! The frequency with which I think of her (turning in a doorway to cap what I have just said, turning in a doorway very suddenly, as if to catch me beneath myself, turning in a doorway to undress, turning, dancing) is a sign. She is different each time I think of her, as if her will (it wouldn't surprise me) extends to how she appears in my thoughts.

We are in bed. She is lying on top of me, playing, I regret to say, with her hair. She does this quite often after lovemaking, and it always disturbs me. What is wrong with my hair? It is probably my best feature, brown and thick and wavy. I suspect it is because I don't satisfy her. Certainly I am not as good with her as I have been with others. I am too quick, and my attempts to overcome this make me quicker still. I was quicker today than ever before. It is partly because of the passion with which she launches herself into lovemaking. She acts as if an immediate climax is her objective. Why so impatient? Whether it is greed or generosity, or partly the one and partly the other, I don't know, but it is terribly exciting. I can't deny that, even as I am overcome, I'm glad of it. Not afterwards, however: I'm not glad then. We have just come to bed and she is lying on her back, sighing or silent, or, like today, on top of me, playing with her hair, eyes averted.

It is a sultry afternoon in early August and eventually we doze. I dream that I am making love to Margo in the grounds of a castle. I am doing it as I wish I could – slowly, passionately. The longer I go on the more she moans and the more concealed figures on the ramparts moan too. When we come, wildly and together, there is an ecstatic chorus of moans and the castle walls tremble before, in the following silence, showing themselves to be stronger than before. Is it polite applause that I hear then, with muffled laughter, or just castle life returning to normal after the little diversion it has enjoyed?

I wake up to find Margo leaning over me, laughing. It has been a wet dream. In her hand is a clutch of Kleenex and in her eyes light-hearted censure. I tell her about the dream and she is pensive.

"That is a socio-sexual dream," she says, and I know that we are about to have one of our pretentious sounding but painful exchanges.

"I know. What sexual dream isn't? There are many presences here. Not just my mother."

"Who then?"

"Your father, his politics. Your mother too. The dream would say that I sleep with your whole family when I sleep with you."

"You'd be better with a partner shorn of her background."

"There are no such people. You know that."

"Some women," Margo says wistfully, "can persuade their partners that they have no pasts. That they have made themselves anew. The contemporary Venus."

"Some men are foolish."

It is the end of the conversation. The dream has sobered her. She stops playing with her hair and lies quietly beside me. She is perceptive and cannot pretend otherwise. Even in her occasional imitations of sluts there is some flair and intelligence. She cannot help it. I suggest to her the August Bank Holiday weekend would be an appropriate time for me to meet her parents. She says all right, but in a low, almost reluctant voice. But then embraces me, half crying.

CHAPTER FOUR

The heat wave continued, week after week, June into July. William found it exhausting, but he feared any change, for regularity had come to obsess him. Regular weather, regular meals, regular exercises (press-ups and knee bends), regular tours of inspection, regular hours in bed, regular times in the lavatory (even if only straining). Regularity: it alone would make health possible, himself coherent, the world a presence again. There should be as many emblems or reminders of it as possible, therefore – the convalescent's icons – such as the sundial he had found in the garden (how he missed a good watch, though, regularity itself), the old cracked barometer he had found in an outhouse, the chart of milking times he had come across in a steading.

But there were days when he was sure he had left it too late. He would not reclaim himself now. There would be moments of terrible weakness then, William lying on his jacket in a field, still unable to hear birdsong, able only occasionally to smell grass. But he didn't allow himself to remain stricken for long (nothing more absurd than the self-consciously prostrate figure). He would stand up and continue on his tour of inspection, spots before his eyes (silent flies? he once wondered), a ringing in his ears, his nostrils as good as useless, walking still with a trace of the drunkard's teetering. Walking on eggs (his wife's description); peripheral neuritis (the doctor's): a condition, he knew, which could be fought with vitamin B. And so, tokens of his will to reclaim himself, to be a steady guardian of these fields and their machinery, bottles of pills he had taken from a cabinet in Mrs Mclehose's bathroom stood on a small table he had carried to the kitchen from one of the outhouses. They were ranged according to his sense of their importance: vitamin B, vitamin C, iron, calcium. It encouraged him, not just to take the pills with his meals, but to touch the bottles gently between meals, whenever he passed them.

He became sunburned, and the sight of his sunburned face in the cracked mirror pleased him. All signs of agreeable change held him. He watched admiringly as flowers in the garden bloomed and were gone, as the grass which he was still too weak to scythe and mow grew longer. Sometimes he looked so intently, like a man actually entranced, that it was as if he was trying to catch nature in the very act of renewing herself – discern the hand of God, even, in the splendour of the light.

Aware that his walk betrayed his past, he set out to change it. He tried out several walks, determined that if he found one that suited him (because it spoke, somehow, of what he hoped to became) he would keep it. His experiments took place mainly in the garden and were like rehearsals for a play that consisted simply of a prologue – a very confused one at that. He tried a pensive stroll, pensive down to the arm movements, but it wasn't right for an outdoor life like his and it embarrassed him deeply. He tried a forceful, rangy walk, but because it suggested a state more fiercely ambitious than any he could imagine himself ever reaching; it embarrassed him also. He tried a bright but modest walk, but, probably because it betrayed a sort of indiscriminate willingness, a sort of sweet servility, it caused his energy to go after about forty yards, and it sickened him anyway. The one he finally hit upon surprised him: brisk, semi-military, neat, the walk of one used to discipline and responsibility. Measured but alert, self-possessed but responsive. He practised it in the garden and around the house (up and down the stairs like some trainee adjutant) until it satisfied him almost entirely. He decided to try it out on a tour of inspection, one which would take in all four groups of outhouses and which would involve a check of all the machinery (over a period of three weeks he had made an inventory of the contents of each outhouse, right down to pails and stray spanners).

He thought of the groups of outhouses as hamlets, each with its own character. The first unsettled him, with its broken pump, its dead echoes and its unseasonal chill. The second he found welcoming – probably because of the cat which hung about there, the bright red and green woodwork and the generous spaces between the machines. The third troubled him – the harvesters so close together, the ploughs pointing outwards like weapons: it was like a stockade, and, in it, William kept turning round, coughing into the back of his hand when he saw that there was nothing there. The fourth he found welcoming also: its steady silence, the way it seemed to be visited by gentle breezes, its impression of having been abandoned with some dignity years before the others. His tours of inspection were painstaking, but there were days when he couldn't bring himself to visit the first hamlet at all and when he could only bear the third for a moment or two. He was sure that if he were to hear the sound of engines in the middle of the night, the clank and clatter of machinery, it would be from one or the other of these.

Trying out his new walk (believing that it was already giving him the measure of the alien hamlets), William approached the first hamlet, wisps of grass floating upwards on the thermal currents. He paused as he always did before entering the steading. And heard voices. To begin with he couldn't locate them; they might have been distant but sounding close or close but not really sounding so. He couldn't make out any words, but he had an impression of casualness. Then there was a clang of metal on metal and he knew that there were men in the yard. Stooping, he moved to a position from which he thought he could see without being seen.

They looked like farm labourers returned out of curiosity or nostalgia to their old place of work, but he knew that they were not. There were four of them, one standing, leaning against the pump, the others sitting. They had pulled a plough to the centre of the steading and were dismantling it. The one on his feet was smoking, and gave occasional advice. None of it was taken, but no one seemed to mind, neither the one standing nor those sitting. They made a practised foursome, their intent steady, their movements quiet and informed. So much so that William wondered if they might not have been sent out to service the machinery – a visit of which someone had failed to inform him. The placidity, the intentness: it wasn't easy to hold to his initial sense that they were doing wrong.

Exaggerating his walk, he entered the steading, smiling. He hadn't intended to smile and feared that it was the smile of one unused to command. He had also not intended to walk straight up to the young men but to address then – sharply, perhaps scathingly – from about fifteen yards. But, as though his new walk with its military overtones had given him the idea that they were soldiers lounging on duty, he found himself face to face with them. They didn't appear threatened however, and, for some reason, he didn't feel threatened either. He had expected defiance, abuse, but they were as practised at seeming innocent as they had been at dismantling the plough. He hadn't spoken; he had forgotten what he had planned to say. Too bad. With movements which might have suggested capitulation but for their astonishing insouciance, the young men turned away, two shrugging their shoulders, one smiling, the fourth, the one who had been smoking, stubbing out his cigarette on the concrete yard with his foot. William followed, confounded. Who were they? They left the steading and started running. Twenty yards, fifty yards, a hundred yards, two hundred yards: black shapes in the heat, angular, mercurial, in and out of dance, vanishing, reappearing, finally vanishing. William was still shaking when he got back to the farmhouse, but he was pleased, for it was the healthy shaking of fear, not the ignominious trembling of debility. He made himself some tea, and then, briskly, like one who has been awaiting the opportunity for years, he rang George Weir to make his report.

George Weir took a dramatic view of the matter, arriving in the afternoon with his wife, Sheila, who was pregnant, and launching into an immediate search of the house and garden. Sheila, fanning herself with a paperback, looked on silently. William stood beside her, looking on also. After a few minutes, however, he realised that it wasn't her husband she was regarding, but the landscape, the summer day (as if too used to these overreactions to pay any attention). So when George, unseen round a corner of the house, called out in his deep voice "Nothing!" or "Nothing here!" or "Not a trace!" it was impossible for William to respond. All he did was look to his left, at Sheila, as though for a cue. But – a musing and imperturbable profile – she gave him none.

"D'you mind if I sit down?" she asked.

"I'm sorry. Come inside. It must be particularly hot for you. How long to go?"

"Three weeks," she replied, entering the house, still fanning herself. "Not that I'm impatient. I like being pregnant; I always feel very well."

Sheila was small and dark, and moved easily in spite of her condition, wearing a white maternity dress and sandals, the sandals flapping on the bare floor of the kitchen. The kitchen seemed to amuse her; she stood in the middle of it, fanning herself, smiling. Respectfully almost, as for an opinion on which his sense of himself might depend, William waited behind her. She was wearing her hair up, but some strands of it, he noticed, had escaped from a comb at the back of her neck. As she fanned herself, regularly, rhythmically with the paperback – beads of sweat on her forehead, her nose and under her eyes – these strands or wisps moved lightly above the brown skin of her neck. A perfect brown. Admiring, William became aware of her scent, the first he had caught in months. It was a dry one, derived from musk, he supposed, and as he tried to convince himself that he was really smelling it, it filled the kitchen. Either you didn't smell it at all or you were overwhelmed. Either you sensed nothing or too much. What did it mean – that he was damaged or erratically recovering? Set to sensationalise the world or receive it fairly? Sheila turned to him.

"But you've nothing here," she laughed.

"To be frank," he said quietly, "I've nothing much anywhere."

"If you say so," she said, with a studied absence of sympathy which yet struck him as a kind of sympathy. "What is George doing? Do you suppose he thinks they've planted bombs?"

"I'm afraid I've no idea what he's doing."

"Nor have I. Is there somewhere we can sit down?"

He had found two deckchairs in the garage and these he set up for George and Sheila opposite the broken leather armchair he sat in each evening. Legs apart, appearing (now that she was sitting) as though stranded by her huge belly, islanded, Sheila lay back, watching William. It was clear that she regarded him as a curiosity; she couldn't conceal it. Not even by fanning herself. She lifted the paperback to do this, but, as if suddenly irritated by the artificiality of the movement, she dropped it again, her hand and the book trailing on the floor.

It was a book on breastfeeding, William saw, on the cover a breast and a feeding infant submerged together in a sea of pink. He couldn't make out whether the breast was dominating the infant or the infant the breast, and cocked his head to see more clearly. Sheila lifted the book and flourished it.

"What do you do here? Read?"

"Not yet," William said, aware that he wanted to be as scrupulous in his account of himself as he was in his tours of inspection. "I find concentration difficult still. But it'll come back, I hope. I did read once though – quite a lot. So you can ask me about that, if you want, but whether I'll remember much is a different matter."

"So you have a condition too?" Sheila asked, laying a hand on her stomach.

"Yes; but as far from yours as I can imagine. Would you like some water?"

"It's all right. I look more uncomfortable than I feel. "

George's footsteps were heard outside – quick footsteps for so large a man.

He passed the lounge window, head bowed, and, calling out to them, came in by the side door. Not speaking, flustered and perspiring, he lowered himself into the deckchair beside his wife, who, not speaking either, turned to him casually, and regarded him as from some remote but peaceable plain of pregnancy. He too a curiosity to her, with an unnamed condition? He made an impatient gesture, fretful almost, as in defence of himself (evidently, not for the first time) against his wife's calmness, the dead-ends and irrelevancies it apparently enabled her to see. She was smiling, fanning herself again, using the artificiality of the movement not just to expose her husband's distraction but to try and subdue it.

"Well," Sheila asked at last, "what have you got to report?"

"One can never be too sure," George said heatedly. "When they're around, they're everywhere. They're more cunning now than ever. You think they're gone and they're behind you. William says they didn't say a word. Not a word! Gone are the days when they shouted, came at you with spanners. You'd hardly know it was them."

"That's right," William agreed. "They could have been trainee mechanics, or unemployed mechanics."

"It wouldn't surprise me," Sheila said. "It might be the latest youth opportunity scheme. Summer therapy for our lost young."

"Good God!" George said.

There was a silence. Slowly, George's urgent manner subsided; but he didn't relax. Bleached browns and yellows as far as the eye could see; the dykes diminished by the haze, mere lines now; the hedges ragged and skeletal; no birds in the sky: for a moment he appeared weary before all this. But then, a different kind of excitement to that with which he had searched the garden, he became heated again. This time, he was like someone searching for a point of reference but failing to find it. Finding nothing instead; nothing at all.

"It's not warfare, George," Sheila said, taking his hand. "Their appearances are still very intermittent. Take it easy. Come on."

"You're right, of course," George answered. "It's the heat: it always gets me."

"It's cool in here," Sheila said.

William was struck by how easily she was able to calm George. She had calmed him, too. The scene in the steading of the first hamlet, at the time so ambiguous and unsettling, seemed merely odd now. Another curiosity.

"Have you any family, William?" Sheila asked.

Again he was aware of wanting to be as scrupulous in his reply as possible.

"I have two children, a son and a daughter. But my wife and I are divorced. I don't see any of the family. Haven't done for years. I've not been in a state to see them, really, so it's not as bitter as you might think. "

"Parents still alive?" George asked.

"No. Both dead, father for years."

He spoke then like one making a belated confession; challenging himself to see what his words really meant (wondering if he was succeeding); feeling his way into an abyss he had previously just skirted; taking more advantage of the forbearance of his audience than he thought he should (surprised that he had an audience at all); discovering himself to be on a kind of pilgrimage.

"My mother ... murdered earlier this year. The spring. Yes, I'm afraid so. They didn't find who did it. Or why. No clues at all. There are more of these cases than one thinks. Utterly ... The files are closed. Rarely reopened. Naturally we don't hear about it – bad for police reputation! But why look for the invisible? Coming and going like that. Astonishing! Took nothing. Did nothing – except that. I was suspected, of course. Why not? She wasn't a victim kind of person, though. Wouldn't have set herself up for the chop. I'm sure of it. Sure too she didn't know him. Or her. Are most killers male? I suppose so. Good God! Sorry! Enough said. Anyway, she's dead. Mother and father dead."

He looked out of the window. No birds, no wind: one species of fact. His mother murdered: another. Had he grasped it? Taken it seriously enough? Instructed himself adequately in the meaning of such an end? On all counts he doubted himself. The line gave out where it should not have done – at the point of the knife. There he had denied her. Awed, he turned to the Weirs, whose kindly presence had enabled him to speak. They were staring at him.

"How terrible, William," Sheila said. "You mustn't know what to think."

"Exactly so," he replied with pain, sucking in his cheeks. "Exactly so. I'm sorry, in your condition ..."

"Not at all," Sheila said. "Don't think of it."

Still telling himself that he was holding back from drink, that when he got the half-bottle of whisky he would be as scrupulous with it as he was in his tours of inspection, he went that evening to the general store. It was a stifling evening and he walked slowly. He didn't have a drink on the way back, holding the bottle as if it was for another, waiting until he was inside the farmhouse. In the kitchen, then, he poured himself a generous measure and drank it quickly. He poured himself another and went outside. Dogs barked in the distance (may even have been playing in the distance, for he was sure he could see quick dark shapes, coming and going, coming and going.) Purple clouds were banked in the west. He raised his glass to the flat land. But he could go no further. There had been too many savage mock toasts. Altogether too many. (Sandra Mclehose had drunk to the Pope, the Queen, Lord Byron, Henry VIII, those with too much money and those with no money at all.) He spilled the whisky on the ground and, coughing, embarrassed, went indoors. The rest of the half-bottle – as if it was a sick animal that had to be helped to relieve itself – he allowed to tip over in the sink.

April 9th, 1973

A man must have his hobbies. Without hobbies you shrink yearly. At least that is my opinion. Those who are claimed by their jobs or professions believe that they are rising when actually they are falling. Only their positions conceal the fact that, humanly, they are nonentities. For look at them in retirement: various kinds of nullity, of distemper. They are as powerless then as they were powerful when they worked. The captain of industry, left to himself at last, invariably falls to pieces. God save me from this. Walter Fairley, chairman of our firm, was dead after a year of retirement. Visiting him in hospital, I couldn't believe he'd ever done anything. Such a spiritless death – not to mention such a premature one – it made me reconsider the life. Between the interstices of his achievements in educational publishing (several of them major, it has to be admitted) what did I glimpse – or believe I'd suspected at the time but not credited? (You don't attend to the pupils contracting when the cigar is buoyant, the hands applauding.) A poorly fuelled soul hoping it wouldn't be found out.

My main hobby is birdwatching. Here I extend myself to the utmost. When the light is perfect, allowing me to do justice to the character of the bird, its movements, plumage (how the wind on this can disclose colours not seen otherwise!), I am inspired. The natural world can seen to me contained in this one small part of it. (Sentimental to believe so? Perhaps. Perhaps.) To appreciate one bird is to appreciate them all. To appreciate birds is, ironically, to appreciate their prey. And so on. I won't say that I ever feel (this would be truly sentimental) that I end up by appreciating mankind – we are a special case – but at times I think I have glimpsed the possibility. On the shores of our afflicted world the waves of my sensibility have, perhaps, lapped tentatively.

I sit down on a hilltop to a lunch of beer and ham sandwiches. (I have discovered that if you wrap cans of beer in newspapers they stay cold.) Usually I make my own lunch, but today Margo did it. During our courtship she sometimes accompanied me on these trips, but it was clear that she was bored. It was like listening to music with someone who is indifferent to it. She would get me to make love to her in the wildest spots. All right in romantic theory, I suppose, but these spots are good for birds. Once I missed an eagle because of her. I'm sure I did. I'm sure it was an eagle. I seemed to glimpse it over my left shoulder, soaring from a crag, angrily majestic, disturbed, who knows, by Margo's cries. It cast an enormous shadow on us and I can't think what else could have done that.

So now I go birdwatching alone, no more required to explain to Margo what I hope to see, to give her the binoculars, to train them for her on the place where a kestrel or a dove or a raven briefly has its being, to hear her – oh God! – say that all she can see is a rock or a post or a piece of old clothing. The number of things she was able to see instead of birds was remarkable. In glades, for instance, she spotted refuse, on moorland the twisted remains of vehicles, in fields dead rabbits and dead sheep. And dead birds: these she was especially quick to see. She would not have the natural world pure for a moment. Her wish, it seemed, was to unsettle my reverence, to persuade me that the world soiled itself indiscriminately.

There are larks above me. I eat my lunch. The peace I long for is assured for today. It is harder to find however than it used to be, I cannot understand why. The possibility that one day it will fail me, and then fail me again, and then clearly be gone forever, horrifies me. Wordsworth it was who lost the art of knowing it and became sterile. What will I do if that happens to me?

A falcon hovers over the valley. I watch it through my binoculars, forgetting my lunch, forgetting everything, held entirely by this tawny idling in the mid air. Now it appears to be beginning its drop, now its rise, as if its plan is to persuade those below that it has no intentions, that its movements are all to do with wind currents. A capacity to deceive a part of its nature? I rather think so, having studied these birds for years. I read their minds well now. And so I can follow them with my binoculars, anticipating most of their feints and delays, switching suddenly to another part of the sky, there invariably to find the falcon arrived before me. There was a time when, mesmerised by their command of the air, by their monumental solitariness, I would lose them altogether. They would have dropped and I would be scanning an empty sky. Now I can sometimes follow them all the way down (we plunge together), exclaiming aloud in wonder, "Look at that!" or "There he goes!" To whom am I calling? Myself? Some ideal other? Is it not strange to cry out in the open spaces like this?

Now and then, of course, I am disturbed, It is often at about this time, three-thirty, and often by a couple such as this that I see approaching: merry, garrulous, about fifty, holding hands. They are not bird lovers and nor, from the awkwardness of their movements, do they appear to be walkers. I can never make out whether they are exceptional in having been as intimate as this all their lives or whether it is the intimacy of those recently married for the second or even the third time. I know what they are going to say; they never surprise me. (I know what hawks are going to do, more or less, but they always surprise me.) They address me with what I can only describe as a kind of ostentatious peacefulness. This doesn't seem to have been inspired by the countryside, but to have arisen elsewhere: it is as though they have brought it to the countryside for the finishing touches. It is the other way round with me. Comparatively speaking, I am a mess at home and in the city. Why? Because I have built my life too much on my wit, my capacity to be the life and soul of even the most soulless parties. The clown dependable because of his thirst for clowning. But what I really want is to lose my wit, or, if not to lose it (for what else might go also?), to address it to other ends. What ends? It alarms me that I cannot say. I still – when listing the virtues – have no impression of what I am naming. It is like an anachronistic role call: the past may shift a little, saints and martyrs stepping forward to take their bow, but the present is stuck fast, redeemers tripped before they can go anywhere.

I stand with my binoculars half raised, but it doesn't deter them: they chatter on about the heather and the fresh air. Eventually I excuse myself and move on. I find I am walking back to the car, tired suddenly, though not concerned to go home. I drive to an inn and sit at a table outside, drinking beer. I like the whiteness of this courtyard. It is strong, dominating even a party of cyclists. I will have a few beers and then go home. Margo has asked me not to be late because we are dining at the Macraes.

CHAPTER FIVE

William always enjoyed breakfast-time; it was the simplest time of day. The day before might have been confusing, the day in front of him uncertain, but drinking his tea, approaching the moment when he swallowed his pills, he was at ease. It was when he planned his day. Since his meeting with the enemy (as, following George Weir, he now described them to himself), he had revised his idea of what he should be doing. He believed that he should be making it possible for himself to catch them, should they come again. The details of how he might do this escaped him, but the resolve was there. He worked at it daily – worked at it as if the only alternative was a boredom which would destroy him. He drew a map of the farmland (labouring until he got it right, convinced it would give him a decisive advantage) which showed the paths, the dykes, the fences, the hollows, the bushes, the trees and the outhouses. One copy he pinned up in the kitchen, studying it over the top of his teacup, one eye cocked, the other he took with him on his tours of inspection. He would stop quite often and consult it, as if he was inexplicably lost in his own domain, quite astray. It combined with his semi-military walk, which now came to him almost automatically (and from which he lapsed only when tired), to reassure him.

One day he remembered that he had once been a bird-watcher. He had had binoculars. When had he given up bird-watching? What had become of the binoculars? He couldn't remember. He would approach the edge of his former life and seem to see – before a well-kept house – a large pile of refuse, gravely smouldering. A vaulted pyre. However he approached it – this point where his life had ceased to make sense – he would be faced by the fire, slowly burning, absurdly slowly. He imagined that all his possessions were in it – his binoculars and his clothes and his watch and his books and his photographs – and that, though it might take a long time, they would eventually be consumed. But the pyre: that he saw smouldering without end.

His sense of responsibility made him irritable. Why hadn't he been given binoculars? Didn't they want the job done properly? Didn't they really care if the machinery was stolen or not? To protect machinery you needed machinery. Binoculars should have gone with the job: it was obvious. With binoculars, he would always have had the advantage. Lying on his stomach somewhere, he could have surveyed the horizon where the farmland dissolved in the haze, and, when he saw shapes emerging from it, danger approaching in one form or another, the chimerical becoming flesh, he could have taken immediate action.

Then he feared that he was overreaching himself. He got the impression, looking round the bare farmhouse, with its crumbling plaster and its ugly oranges and yellows, that this was a job for a simpleton, a semi-invalid or an old man on the point of death. He had been warned not to be heroic; but what was the alternative? The alternative was how he had been when he had arrived: that was how the job was viewed apparently. His feebleness, his debility, which he had feared would count against him when he tried for the job, had actually been in his favour.

His humiliation affected his walk. His stride got longer, his shoulders were hunched, his hands often in his pockets. He recognised that, unable to do the job as he wanted to – with binoculars, a walkie-talkie even (so he thought one morning) one of those small vehicles used by the obese or the elderly on golf courses – he was in danger of doing it badly. His tours of inspection became casual, occasional, as though he was mocking the job as he did it, or doing it in order to mock it. He knew that this would encourage those he had been hired to keep out; and he knew that this might be considered a form of collusion. (Was this how his predecessors, if there were any, had changed colours?)

One day, returning to the farmhouse in this mood, he found that Sheila Weir had called with some vegetables.

"Can I use your loo?" she asked. "At this stage of pregnancy …"

He let her into the farmhouse, half watching as, with little gasps of alarm and anticipation, she hurried to the lavatory. Standing in the hall, he heard her urinate (she hadn't closed the door), moaning slightly as she did so. Then he heard her stand up and adjust her clothes. He stood very still (as still as he had stood for years), telling himself that this was the innocent arousal of the convalescent.

"How are you?" she enquired, returning. "I thought you looked bored crossing the field."

"Bored?" he said, remembering how it was possible to be direct with her, scrupulous. "No, not bored. Frustrated. Angry even. I've been thinking that my job would be much easier with binoculars. I've a lot of ground to cover, you know."

"Of course," she said. "Of course! I know that George has two pairs. I'll get him to come over with one … later."

He wondered if she was making fun of him ("later" – she had emphasised the word, given it a flourish). He didn't think so. She was lying back in the deckchair, a hand on her belly, breathing heavily.

"I'm fed up myself, actually. I'm three days overdue and I can't sleep. I've run out of books, but even if I hadn't, I'd be too tired. Are you up to reading yet?"

"Nearer. I might try. What do you suggest?"

"Oh, I don't know, William," she said, as if it wasn't in her nature to make such suggestions. "I'll send some over with the binoculars." She lost interest, then. Remote eyes, her hand still on her belly. Flies on the windowpane, loud in the heat. Once she waved one away, and once, compressing her lips, she blew upwards.

"Can I get you a fan?" William asked.

"Don't worry, I can't be bothered."

"I'll do it for you," he said awkwardly, imitating the movements he might make.

She stood up slowly, smiling, and laid a hand on his arm.

"Thanks, but I must go; I've the children to collect. Come and see us."

"Thanks for the vegetables."

"A pleasure."

"And I hope you won't have much longer to wait."

But she was already reversing the car and didn't hear. His pleasantry, unheard, sounded suddenly peculiar to him, like part of a parable or incantation ... "hope you won't ... much longer to wait ..."

After she had gone, he found that the binoculars, promised so readily, seemed less necessary.

Early that evening, William was startled by the sound of rifle fire. At first it was scattered and occasional (in the pauses he imagined figures running about frantically or standing perfectly still), then regular, concentrated. It came from the east, where the land he was responsible for was divided from the land beyond by a dyke and a fence running parallel.

He walked up and down in front of the house with what after a few moments struck him as a purposeless briskness. What did it mean? He rang George Weir for advice – there was an especially loud burst of firing as he held the receiver – but there was no reply. He went outside again. The firing appeared to have spread out now, as if those responsible were moving in opposite directions. William found that without a hypothesis he couldn't make a move. He remained in front of the house, either walking up and down with that purpose-less briskness (as if, crazily, his walk had become an end in itself), or standing still, his chin cupped in his right hand, listening to the rifle fire as if he had never heard anything like it before.

He came to the conclusion that they must be vandals or poachers. If the vandals were capable of silent arrogance, they would be capable of this. And poaching, he had heard, was widespread, and, like vandalism, was taking new and strange forms. (Much, according to George Weir, was taking new and strange forms.) He knew that there were many rab-bits, most of them in the tussocky fields beyond the hamlets and most of them healthy. Only a few were ill, struggling with enormous eyes to regain their burrows. (One day, before he knew what he was doing, William had killed one, chopping it on the neck not once but three times, in death its enormous eyes more enormous still.)

At last, having repossessed his adjutant's walk and holding his map, he set off in the direction of the rifle fire, moving from tree to tree, or, where there were no trees, from bush to bush, once, when he thought that the rifle fire was getting closer, throwing himself on his stomach in the open. Leaning against the trees, he consulted his map, having pencilled in crosses where he thought the riflemen were. After each consultation (glad to notice that his hands hardly trembled as he held the map), he would run, bent double, to the next tree and the next consultation, arriving breathless but clearheaded.

Danger had concentrated him: he sprinted without effort and when he had to do so, he believed that he would be able to deal with the enemy without effort. His theory was that he would find them near the perimeter fence. There was a long gully just beyond it and the muffled quality of the rifle fire made him think that the riflemen had entered it. It was a favourite spot for rabbits and hares. William had often seen them there, basking or frisking between the tussocks and the gorse bushes. So, almost certain that the riflemen were poachers (he thought of a fraternity or guild of poachers, for some reason), he leant against a tree and wrote "poachers" beside the pencilled crosses.

There was a long silence. He could hear absolutely nothing. Crouched behind a bush (in the middle of which he saw torn stained underwear and beer cans), he waited. Without binoculars all he could do was try to interpret the silence. A hard task. Had they killed as many rabbits as they wanted? What were they doing – laying them in a pile before dividing them, or having a smoke? How many poachers were there? What age? Would they walk to the end of the gully before climbing out or climb out here, so that he could see them?

He remained behind the bush, looking at his map, drawing a circle round "poachers". The delay began to upset him. He knew that he should find out what was happening, and, if necessary, report it to the police. But he would have to cross about two hundred yards to the top of the gully, and he would have to cross it in silence and without cover. His initiative, certainly his most important since coming to the farm, would be taken under the eye of heaven.

He came out from behind the bush and walked towards the gully, the heat and the silence matching each other. He felt that if he could get his walk right – if he could maintain it impeccably across these two hundred yards – he would know what to do when he surprised those in the gully. But if, affected by his apprehension and the uneven ground, his walk went wrong; then he would run the risk of speechlessness at the top of the gully. He would have the air of a doomed trespasser or a half-hearted walker. Of an amnesiac, even. He might even appear only to disappear.

But his walk didn't fail him. Head thrown back, arms swinging regularly, heels coming down promptly, he approached the gully. A shout made him pause; two shouts made him crouch; a sudden chorus of shouts made him fling himself on his stomach. But in the long silence that followed he was able to get to his feet (saw himself do it, indeed, as from an admiring distance) and proceed without any loss of composure. He went on until he knew that his next few strides would make him visible to those below. He was now certain that they were poachers, and poachers, he believed, were less of a problem than vandals (rogues rather than criminals).

He moved to the top of the gully and saw, disposed below him in a semicircle, three jeeps and about twenty soldiers. They seemed – it was William's first thought – to be having high tea. They were eating in groups, their rifles beside them. The mood was convivial, almost hearty, young men in their prime together. Only one of the soldiers was standing. He was wearing a green cap and had a stick or cane tucked under his arm. He was eating a roll, his hand and arm – as though he was demonstrating how to eat rolls in the open – held well out from him. It was he who spotted William. He said something to one of the soldiers beside him, and, smiling, tapping his stick on his thigh, started up the side of the gully. His walk was complacently neat: out of uniform, away from the gravity of command, it might have been effeminate. All the soldiers had noticed William now, standing as still as he could on a dry and dusty patch between rabbit holes, his hands behind his back, waiting for the officer to reach the top of the bank.

Still smiling, the officer stopped in front of him. He appeared to want to be exceptionally agreeable. There was a silence behind them, as if the meal couldn't be resumed until William had been checked over.

"Shooting rabbits?" William said.

"One or two," the officer replied. "I hope you don't mind. But that's not our main business. We're T.A."

"T.A.?"

"Territorial Army. Captain Jenkins. Pleased to meet you."

"William Templeton."

"Farmer?"

"No, I'm caretaker to these acres," William answered, remembering how, faced by the professions, he had often been facetious. "A gentleman caretaker."

"That I see, sir," the captain said.

William noticed that there were potatoes hanging from the captain's belt. "I didn't know it was the potato season," he remarked.

"These are not potatoes, Mr Templeton," the captain replied, suddenly unsmiling. "They are grenades."

"I beg your pardon, captain. I'm fairly ignorant. I didn't know, for instance, that you had permission to use this land."

There was loud laughter from the waiting soldiers. The captain merely smiled; but when the soldiers continued laughing, he raised his hand, indicating that they should resume their meal.

"Oh yes: you might say that it's one of our favourite stamping grounds. We come here every five or six weeks. You must be new."

"Comparatively," William said. "I'm certainly new to potato wars."

"You wouldn't thank us for using the real thing. No indeed! Don't worry though; we're spoken for. We're licensed."

"If you say so."

"Perhaps you'll allow Lieutenant Jackson and I to visit you later? We can show you the authorisation. I don't suppose you have many visitors."

"If you like," William said, exasperated. "It's the yellow farmhouse. You can't miss it."

"Thank you, Mr Templeton," the captain said, half saluting. "I know the yellow farmhouse."

William walked away. By the time he had got back to the farmhouse the war in the gully had started again. He didn't know if it was some trick of the atmosphere or the result of his meeting with the captain and the soldiers, but the rifle fire sounded different now: remote, random, the echoes of shots rather than shots. He spread his map on the kitchen table and, rubbing out "poachers", wrote: "Territorial Army – Evening Antics."

It was quite late when the captain and lieutenant arrived. They came by jeep, taking off their caps and putting down their sticks and then lying back in the deckchairs William had got ready for them. Out of the gully and with their caps off, they looked very young. What did they do when they weren't in the Territorial Army? William didn't ask; it was enough that they did this.

"Operation over?" he asked.

"Yes. Most successfully, too," Captain Jenkins said. "Wouldn't you say so, David?"

"Certainly," Lieutenant Jackson agreed, lying back with his hands clasped behind his head. "Soon we'll be ready for the big one."

"The big one?" William asked.

"Yes," Captain Jenkins said. "But I'm afraid it's confidential."

"Of course. It wouldn't be the big one if it wasn't," William observed.

"Only the small ones are fed to the public." He was sitting forwards in his armchair, hands clasped about his left knee, holding it as if it was slightly injured.

"So long as you leave the farmhouse standing. And respect my land."

"Oh, it'll not be here," Lieutenant Jackson said, suddenly standing up and crossing to the window, as if thoughts of the big one made him restless. "The big one's happening up north. Destination unknown."

"I hope it goes well anyway," William said.

"Thanks," the lieutenant answered, returning to his deck-chair but not sitting down. Hovering, making a show of his restlessness, he looked down at Captain Jenkins who smiled at him, acquiescent, curious. A young officer in repose, his vulnerability betrayed by the way in which he was obliged to lie back in the deckchair, right back, his quiet easy relaxation under the army clothes making it seem for a moment that he had been miscast, he suddenly stood up and slowly and deliberately straightened his shoulders.

"Can we offer you some plonk?" he asked.

"You're welcome to have a drink yourselves. Indeed I can even give you some cups. But, as for myself, I'm on the wagon. I'll not join you, thanks."

Having said this, William stood up, squaring his own shoulders. There was a silence. It was clear that his guests didn't know how to take him. His accent was wrong for the job; his manner was variable, now almost friendly, now sarcastic; the farmhouse was extremely bare; and he didn't drink. Faced by their youth, their preoccupation with their roles, their matiness, he rediscovered his capacity for fantasy. It pleased him, for it was some time since he had been able to speak freely, without care and deliberation.

"I use my job as a cover," he said. "You must have guessed that. Of course you must! But please go and get your drink."

They began by drinking lager, for, as they explained to William, these summer manoeuvres were hot work. They gulped it straight from the can, belching between gulps, smacking their lips. Later, their thirst quenched, they would be going on to whisky. They had two bottles of this, one a malt, one a blended. (Would they be drinking it from the bottles too, William wondered, or using his cups?) Apparently Lieutenant Jackson was the regimental drinks buyer and, proud of his reputation, he tried (holding the bottle in his lap like an anaesthetised pet) to talk to William about malt whisky.

"Really, lieutenant," William protested. "My place on the wagon isn't that assured! How about women? Or cricket? Or stocks and shares? Or racehorses?"

"We upset you by our presence?" the lieutenant asked, making to rise. "You'd rather we left?"

"No. That's not what I mean."

"All right," Captain Jenkins said, scanning the ceiling and the landscape outside as if in search of other topics. "Tell us then … tell us what your job's a cover for? Unless it's confidential, of course."

The lieutenant laughed loudly.

"I could tell you that I'm a spy," William began, "appointed by the Home Office to study vandals. There are vandals here, you know. Thieves too. One day they may make my life hell. They come quietly and go for the machinery that's stored out there. I'm supposed to deal with them on my own. But I haven't even got binoculars – unlike you fellows – though a pair is promised. I too have superiors, you see, superiors who are rather too remote from the field to appreciate what's needed. It's tough."

He was leaning back now, relaxed so long as he was able to talk. The officers had started on the whisky.

"But if I were to tell you that I was a Home Office spy," William went on, "it would be a lie, and one can't have lies. One can't have lies anywhere. An accumulation of lies is like an accumulation of dead flies on a white windowsill. Eventually the light is affected. No! What I am is a writer. I've had a generous advance from a publisher – quite a well known one too – to write a book. A sort of autobiography. My life has been a curious one, quite off the straight and narrow. In a thicket, in fact, without lights and with the strangest noises. So what could be better than being a caretaker? Here, every morning, I write pages which show me what I am and how I became it."

"A man of education," Lieutenant Jackson said. His long face and close-set eyes gave him the appearance of one for whom shrewd conclusions were the only currency. "But tell me more about the vandals."

"Yes," Captain Jenkins said, "One can't take that sort of thing lightly."

"There's not much more to tell," William said, realising that it had been a mistake to mention the vandals. He chose his words carefully, but he could see that the officers took this as a measure of the seriousness of the matter. He could see that they pitied him: a writer, not in good shape, up against vandals. He had experienced it so often with drinkers: the sudden conviction that they knew where their duty lay, the imperviousness to all else. There was no way of dissuading them, so his words were lonely ones, barely attended to even by himself, escaping him almost against his will, leaving his lips dry, distressed. "I must make it clear that there aren't many vandals, and that the damage they do is minimal. I can't really say it's a problem. And the signs are that it'll disappear."

"Oh, but it may not, William!" Lieutenant Jackson exclaimed, "It may not! It may get worse. What we'd like to know is simply this: can we help?"

"Exactly," Captain Jenkins said.

"What do you mean?" William asked, though he knew what was coming.

"I mean," Lieutenant Jackson said, drinking from the bottle of malt whisky, "that we could drive them off once and for all. A few wounded vandals and they'd never come back. That's how it would be if our police were armed. As they are in America."

"You're not trying to suggest that there's less violence in America? That's not my impression. My sister ..."

"It'd work here. A different climate. I tell you."

"I'm sorry for you if you're serious. Anyway, I don't need that sort of help. I don't want it."

"You could say it's our job," Captain Jenkins said quietly.

"You could indeed," nodded the lieutenant.

"You couldn't," William objected, looking at then in turn. "It's a police matter. The police and the army have different roles. Don't tell me you don't know that."

"Our role is broad, William," the lieutenant said slowly, holding his hands about a yard apart. "Broad! Understand?"

William had stood up.

"No, I don't think I do understand. Not at all! I think perhaps you had better go. Take your plonk and go. Just keep it a game. All right? Throw your potatoes and fire your rifles in the air ..."

"But you've not been drinking, William," the lieutenant said, "you've not been drinking! You can't hold it."

"Will you go please?" William had stood up and was pointing at the door. "This is as pointless as it is unpleasant."

"We'll go," the lieutenant said, rising. "Your lavatory first though ..."

Captain Jenkins had risen too. He was swaying slightly, his look vaguely pitying (as though William was just one of many manifestations of the deviant he would have to meet with in his lifetime), his stick back under his arm. He didn't speak, adjusting his cap, looking at William – who looked at him in turn – his expression slowly changing, from drunken pity through indifference to contempt. Knowing that he had excited the contempt by standing firm, his silence more concentrated than the captain's, William stood firmer still, though with the contempt deepening and the lieutenant blundering about in the hall, cursing, it wasn't easy.

"All right, David," Captain Jenkins said when the lieutenant came back, "let's go. We can catch the boys at the Black Bull."

They left without saying a word, carrying their boxes of drink. The headlights of the jeep swept the farmhouse and William standing before it, the jeep passing very close to him as it made for the farm track and the main road. On the rutted track it bounced and lurched, its headlights picking out the birch trees which lined the track, now their trunks, now their branches, until, with a wild turn into the main road, it was gone into the night.

It was then as silent as William had ever known it. He remembered that with some drinkers certain subjects had to be avoided. Then he remembered that with many of them they could never be avoided, the subjects possessing then even in sobriety, even while their lives appeared moderate, well ordered. He remembered it well: it was the one thing which, in his tiredness, he could remember about them.

Later, going to the lavatory, he found on the cistern the remains of the bottle of malt whisky. Under it was a note.

"Dear Mr Author,

Here you are. Go on! Drink and be damned.

Jackson."

Very calmly, as though as sorry for the man who had tried to tempt him as he was for himself, who might have been tempted, he poured the whisky down the lavatory and went to bed.

May 10th, 1975

I have nothing against my wife – nothing serious anyway. I enjoy most of the occasions she arranges and I like most of the people she introduces me to. It's just that so many of the occasions are her occasions. Her stamp is on all of them; she is the sole architect. Have I any ideas of my own about how our social life should go? Sometimes I think so, but then I trace them – to Margo. It's not made any better by the realisation that it's to her that I owe some of my highest resolves. To listen to more music; to read more; to set aside time for reflection (though I've never been entirely sure what I should be thinking about. The virtues perhaps?)

The feeling that I'm not quite in charge of my own life disturbs me. Sometimes I have thoughts of running wild, of establishing my own terms with a vengeance. For some reason (this disturbs me too) I have few if any thoughts of establishing them quietly, by degrees.

Today I find myself at my daughter's birthday party. It is being held, not as one might expect in our own house, but in the house of one of Margo's friends. This is because it is a shared birthday party; the friend's daughter is exactly the same age as Kathleen. We are outside on the lawn, watching the children, about thirty of them, play about in a pink parachute. It lifts and flops on the lawn like a giant pantomime sea anemone, now showing its insides, now concealing them, threatening to imprison the children. There are screams; one can see the outlines of desperate or mock desperate limbs.

The fascination which we feel isn't one which will fade, to be replaced by boredom, for we began by being indifferent and then, almost against our will, became fascinated. Conversation died as the parachute, seeming to get larger and larger, more and more capacious, possessed the lawn. Only Margo and her friend, laying out cakes and sandwiches on a long trestle table in the background, aren't looking at it. But it wouldn't surprise me to see them and their piles of food enveloped also, for I have seen few things as unpredictable as this parachute. It is capriciousness itself.

Suddenly I notice that Kathleen is trying to get out from under the parachute. But each time she tries she is either dragged back by a child or claimed by a pink fold. I hear her screams, and they seem to me different in quality from the other screams. Pure terror. I walk over to see what I can do and my eye catches a label: Rentaparty Equipment Ltd. I position myself, kneeling, so that Kathleen will see me when the parachute next lifts. Her screams get louder; she has sensed my presence. "Daddy! Daddy!" At last she breaks free, crying distractedly, and falls into my arms. I lead her away. I don't think that anyone else has noticed. The clumsy will of the huge mobile fungus is still being done and the parents are still standing on the terrace, fascinated.

Soon however other children come out from under the parachute. Eventually it is abandoned. But it still moves. Indeed, in a sudden gust of wind it is blown against the legs of the trestle table, wrapping itself around them. Now Margo takes charge, dropping onto it half playfully, beating it into shape and docility, preparing it – calmly, confidently, as though she did it every day – for its return to Rentaparty Equipment Ltd. She is wearing a summer frock and at one point as she kneels this is blown over her buttocks. She doesn't care. Have I ever seen her discomfited? No. There are no pauses between her thoughts and the actions expressing them. Her hours and days are seamless apparently. The children sense it too, for no one dares to eat until, the parachute folded and put to one side, Margo returns to the table. She walks up and down its twenty yards – that fluent, slightly abstracted walk – offering cakes, sandwiches, crisps, biscuits, juice. She does three times as much as Elizabeth, her friend. She is also three times as tanned as Elizabeth, although as far as I know the summer has favoured them equally. Poor Elizabeth: no wonder she opts for unobtrusiveness.

Kathleen is reluctant to go up to the table. I try to lead her, pointing to her mother, to the children I believe to be her friends. She is not encouraged. I take her for a walk round the garden, hoping to calm her. She has perhaps noticed that there is no chocolate ice-cream in a golden wrapper on the trestle table, for it is this that she asks for. I sense the approach of one of her tantrums. These are terrible, terribly embarrassing. I couldn't bear to have all these parents, now themselves up at the table, choosing their cakes and sandwiches with such deadly niceness, witness one of Kathleen's tantrums. Margo can ignore them, as the books recommend, but I can't. I become foolish in my attempts to defuse them: jokes, flattery, presents, entreaty, anger. Why do I bother with them? (Is it my secret hope to be provoked into one myself?) Maybe it's because at their heart I sense the rawest kind of interrogation of reality imaginable. Who am I? Why am I here? Who will tell me?

Unseen, I lead Kathleen from the garden. We tiptoe along the grass verge of the drive, avoiding the gravel. Then we are in the road and our stride lengthens. Suddenly Kathleen is tearless, delighted, skipping ahead of me. I am taking her from her own party! She has promised, however, that if I buy her a chocolate ice-cream in a golden wrapper she'll return to it and eat cakes and sandwiches and play all the games. (Am I aware that it might be thought that I am handling the problem absurdly? That I am dancing to a perverse tune? Yes, I am aware.) We walk on and soon reach a cafe where an obese but deeply patient Italian woman gives Kathleen an ice-cream and asks about the paper hat on her head. I explain – laughing indulgently, for I too am wearing a paper hat – that we are brief exiles from a birthday party.

Now that she has her ice-cream, I regret to say, Kathleen pays no attention to her surroundings at all. Her shoulders hunch as she eats it, her eyes become hooded. For a moment it seems to me a waste that she has such lovely fair hair. The tantrum and this sullen satisfaction: how upsetting that they are the two poles of her being.

Again we tip-toe along the grass verge of the drive. It is surprisingly silent. I am embarrassed to see why: the children are sitting on the lawn in a circle, eating chocolate ice-creams. Margo is observing me from behind them, standing very still, her dress whipped by the wind, clearly in tension between exasperation and outrage, her eyes dark and her mouth enquiringly open. I realise that I must say something both witty and redeeming. But I am unable to.

"Is this a rival party or a cop-out?" she asks.

"She was about to have a tantrum, Margo," I say.

"So?"

"I thought it advisable," I continue. "A distraction."

"Really," she says.

"Once round the block and she's human again."

The subject of our conversation has found a place in the circle and is comparing ice-creams with the little boy on her right. At least hers is the only one which has a golden wrapper.

CHAPTER SIX

With George Weir's binoculars William could scan the land from the farmhouse. (Two months earlier, he realised, he wouldn't have been able to do so, because of his unsteady hands.) A luxury was to do it from bed, in the early morning, his transistor tuned to classical music. It was late summer, the land parched and hard, the slightest wind raising clouds of brown or yellow dust (which, through the binoculars, looked like part of some vast obliterating storm).

Most days, alerted by these clouds, William got ready to do his job. But just occasionally – little holidays – he couldn't be bothered. Then it was the bushes and the trees seen through the glasses that engaged him. Or the hamlets. Or the sky. But above all it was the birds. These he watched intently: crows, plovers, curlews, pheasants, wrens, finches. Watched as they pecked at the dry earth: a deadly dryness, frustrating instinct. Watched as the smaller ones flew off to try again twenty or thirty yards away. Watched as they went round in circles, many barren patches tried in an hour. Watched with pleasure as the bread which it became his habit to scatter on the ground was flicked from beak to beak, eaten.

Otherwise he scanned the land carefully, made regular tours of inspection (his adjutant's walk less apparent, though, after his meeting with the captain and the lieutenant). But day after day he had nothing to report. Week after week, nothing. Nothing. Another might have been reassured, concluding that, like nomads, the enemy had gone elsewhere, or lost interest. But for William the silence was ominous. The longer he waited, the more he felt there must be something he was waiting for. That was how it presented itself:

something. A word without hint of form or feature, teasing the imagination but not yielding to it. Vandals deriding him; the Territorial Army advancing on the farm in the middle of the night; Sheila Weir arriving with fruit and vegetables: it was above such obvious threats and consolations. Towards evening, weary, his hands starting to tremble just a little, he had occasionally had the fancy that in a particular dust cloud, arising more suddenly than usual, apparently without wind, he had found what he was looking for. But no dust cloud lasted for more than fifteen seconds.

His transistor went with him on his rounds now, jostling for position with the binoculars on his chest. There were concerts and plays and cricket commentaries and talks on the political scene. He felt extraordinarily remote from them all, however, walking in the fields. It wasn't just the great silence of the countryside, in which as from other eras almost, he would hear a Mozart symphony, be told a cricket score, hear of some terrible event in Africa. Nor was it the occasional poorness of the reception, the moments when it went altogether. What seemed to be measured as he listened was the length of time since he had last concerned himself with such things. The years of his indifference; the extent of his ignorance. He had slipped from the world for a decade. By what path had he come back? What had enabled him to recover the simple pleasure of lying on dry grass under a blue sky? The complex one of listening to music at dawn? The ability to ask such questions?

His mother's murder. The only path he could see emerged from that; emerged from the shallow grave between the rhododendron bushes. He permitted himself the thought – they were the words in which it came to him – that she hadn't been butchered in vain. He spoke it aloud, slowly, carefully, as if testing himself for infamy. The burden the words placed on him was great: he wished he hadn't spoken them. But he had; he had held them up to the light. And the place where he had done so – the steading of the second hamlet – would have the power – always now – to admonish or approve. And might become memorable.

Many of the names he heard on the transistor would have been familiar to his mother. But they meant nothing to him. Some of them, however, would be his contemporaries. He was discovering them in mid-career, their stride lengthening. Reputations. Household names. Positions. Who, for example, was this speaking from Whitehall with such studied earnestness? Who was this making forecasts about mortgage rates? Why was he so given over to the subject? Who had taken over in Uganda, and why had human heads and torsos been found in fridges in his palace? He would have to inform himself. He would have to catch up with his era, its local and international celebrities, its opinions, whims, barbarities. That meant newspapers. He hadn't read one for years. The piles of them in the general store, so neatly laid out (so suggestive of comprehensiveness), had affected him oddly. They were for those who had remained loyal, who had kept going. You read them if you were in the world, doing its business or discovering good reasons for not doing it (proposing a higher business). But if, neutered, you crawled from the world, you had no need of reports, opinions. And returning, waiting in the wings (was that what he was doing?), you had to be careful. Newspaper readers were comparatively tough. How did you know when you were ready to rejoin them?

"Not even the hermit or the nun," a voice on the transistor had said one day in the yard of the first hamlet (its dead acoustics framing the utterance), "is without politics. Not even they – whatever they may say to the contrary. "I am political," he had therefore written, in the summer dust on one of the tractors. "How though?"

The programmes he couldn't bear were the ones about

family life. He would come across them – there always seemed to be one being broadcast – on his way from one programme to another, and he would give them a moment's horrified attention.

"The children of gamblers are apt to see the world as a lottery, to be won or lost by chance, not by serious endeavour. Such children ..." "The families of drug addicts have higher anxiety levels than ..." "The children of working mothers, during the critical hour after school, tend ..." "Families who go to church together score more highly on the happiness scale than families who ..." And women's problems: he couldn't bear to hear about those either. It wasn't just the fact of their sufferings that upset him; it was the way they were presented. The women-experts announced their findings so angrily and then gave advice so confidently. Sometimes he was afraid to change stations in case he came across a clever London voice theorising about premenstrual tension, post-natal depression, menopausal resentment, the superiority of orgasm by masturbation. Yes, in his world dominated by the transistor, women and the family were the dark spots – into which he feared he could be easily drawn. They had the power, he noticed, to make him shake again, curse and stumble in the dry fields, even weep. (Sheila Weir, it was true, had had a baby and left hospital after three days. But that was a simple fact. It hadn't been claimed by the gurus, doctored; it didn't rebuke him.)

He never returned to the farmhouse with the transistor on, however, always entering it in silence. The bareness of the place meant that its silences were grave, still. Sometimes, crossing the threshold after one of his tours of inspection, he had felt exceptionally light, as if to open a door on silences like these was to be promised something. What? Perhaps he believed that by circling the house and then very gently pushing open the front door he might happen upon some intoxicating truth. Emptiness rather than silence, however, had met him. Apparently it was not up to him to take the initiative.

Forty-four years of age, his face in the cracked mirror evenly tanned, his eyes, even when looking at themselves – searching for traces of yellow – reasonably steady.

The dark, circular dust cloud in the vicinity of the second hamlet struck William as a harbinger of winter. Was it the last day of summer? He ran, arms held low, binoculars jumping, thinking only that he must find out how it had arisen. It circled the hamlet almost entirely. It was as though the earth was breaking up, being drawn upwards, thinning as it went. Near to the ground it was brown, but about twenty feet up white, white and beginning to drift in the direction of the farmhouse. Looking at it through the binoculars, William had the thought that it was the summer going wrong: it had been too long and too hot. He had heard of small whirlwinds, under such circumstances, storms so localised as to have the appearance of omens. He ran on, more crouched than before, left arm swinging across his body, right hand restraining his binoculars. Between a phenomenon to be explained and a sign to be read he saw it, moving outwards in slow possession of the land, a vast graininess. It would be upon him if he went further; and he was going further. He folded his handkerchief in a triangle and tied it across his mouth. His eyes had begun to smart.

He ran on, into wind and dust and gathering darkness. He was running mainly with his eyes shut, which would account for the sense of darkness, but even when he opened them, there didn't seem to be much light. One moment he believed he was running in a straight line, the next that he was going round in a circle, a widening circle. He was also aware of a sound of moaning and determined to find its source, for it was definitely a sign of distress. Then it came to him that it was himself, moaning behind the mask of his handkerchief.

What surprised him was that this discovery didn't make it any easier. As if utterly separate from himself, the sound continued. Powerless to subdue it, to stop it, he ran on, moaning as the disturbance around him spread. Sometimes he was conscious of a wind in his face, sometimes there seemed to be no wind at all. He lost all sense of where he was, all sense of boundaries. The dust cloud might have been enveloping the whole county; there might have been birds caught up in it, small ones and large ones, darting about him in terror …

Then he heard that the moan had become a scream. He was screaming as he ran and apparently running round himself at the centre of the turbulence. Again he was powerless to subdue the sounds which came from him. It was as if he was inhabiting a stricken being as it ran towards the limits. The fact that the being was himself was astonishing. In thrall to himself at his most abandoned, rushing towards a place where light returned fitfully, if at all, and the land fell away into greater emptiness still.

He realised then that the scream had stopped, torn from him as though forever. There was gasping now, his own gasping. He was tugging at the mask to free himself, but feared for a moment that it wasn't happening, that the mask was entering his mouth, to choke him. He heard himself, as from a great distance, addressing someone, then understood that the someone was himself. He was talking to himself, simple instructions, reassurances. "It's all right, William." "Take it easy." "You're not far away now." "Soon you can rest." "Here, here."

He managed to tear the mask from his face at last, the same moment as the light returned, or not so much returned as seemed suddenly to have been there all the time, though not quite, for behind him a low dust cloud was receding, darkening the landscape as it did so, the same vast graininess he had entered some time ago, how long ago he couldn't have said.

He sat on a rock and saw that he was quite far now from the second hamlet. He had travelled a surprisingly long way. He would just sit here, he thought, not so much surveying the land as attending to it gratefully, resting his eyes, listening to the silence.

Eventually he walked towards the second hamlet. It had welcomed him before. It welcomed him again now. What he did then he knew to be absurd. A parody of housework. Stooping, he began to blow dust off one of the machines, and then, standing back, standing back and taking aim, he flicked at the dust with his handkerchief. Thus occupied, blowing and flicking, he passed about quarter of an hour. It was as if he was just one of many on the farm with a small task to perform.

Now – as if the last day of summer was to be one of apparitions and riddles – an old lady was coming towards him. First, in the morning, the dust cloud and his terror, now this frail shape, her gait alternately weak and obdurate, tottering and stiff. (Little puffs of white dust, raised with each step she took, seemed to linger, patiently and watchfully, after she had passed.) At first William mistook her for a man, so well-worn were the trousers, so nearly bald the head. And even when he saw her as a woman he could, with just a little effort (as though the marks of gender grow less with age), see her as a man again. Her right hand was pressed to her side, in expectation of pain rather than in pain, her mouth was open, and her eyes had a hollow look, as if in her final years she had given up hope of finding anything agreeable to look upon. And regularly, as at flies or midges, she swept her left hand across her face – a definite movement, very definite. It was its very definiteness, in fact, which made William suspect that it was involuntary, a spasm of old age. Watching her through the binoculars, he wasn't sure whether what he was seeing was senility momentarily transcended by insight and remembrance, or clarity passingly shadowed by senility.

He had been dozing, but was now fully awake. (There had been drunken dreams, once, from which it had been difficult to wake, which had set the mood, with some terrible image, for the rest of the day. To realise that this wasn't one of them was an immense relief.) He was steady, and out of his steadiness he moved towards her, calling out gently, "Hullo! Hullo there! How are you?" She didn't respond, so he waved, but again she didn't respond. Oblivious, she came towards him, the definite movement – a kind of swipe – happening every five or six steps. He had time to notice this. Time, also, to notice that her head was set at a strange angle: chin drawn upwards and slightly to the right, as from years of traction. It gave her an air of slightly crazed expectation.

He saw that he would have to make a joke of it. He placed himself in her path and, when she came up to him, still unseeing, he grasped her quietly by the wrist. It was the hand which had been making the swiping movement and he felt the frustrated spasms.

"Now then," he said, "you must be tired. To be out walking on a day like this! It's too hot even for me, and I'm used to it. Come in. I'll get you some tea."

"How very kind of you," the old lady said, her voice, as from years of over-scrupulousness, cracked and pedantic. "I'd forgotten about tea. Is it teatime, or have I missed it? Have I missed it?"

"Our teatimes are movable here," William said, leading her into the farmhouse. "Don't worry."

She allowed herself to be lowered into a deckchair, watching him closely as he helped her, watching him as he put on the kettle, made tea. Her manner was that of one who, entirely passive, hopes to get by with a kind of ingratiation: now trusting, now grateful, now pensive, now resigned. Faces for all occasions, but whether the faces of vacancy or of rich old age he didn't know. He discovered a tact and subtlety in himself, however, which he hadn't known since he had been with his children. He improvised. First he fanned her lightly with a newspaper, then, because she was unable or unwilling to hold the saucer or the cup, he fed her the tea with a spoon. After each mouthful she smiled, or made a movement with her lips which might have struck William as a smile had it not been so unvarying.

"Was that the gong?" she asked.

"No, my dear," William said, sure now that she had wandered from the Montgomery Nursing Home nearby. "You've walked a long way, you know. Three miles at least."

"I used to love walking," she said, her eyes clearing, her air briefly that of one affectionately familiar with her past. "But they don't allow you to walk much there. And some of them can't walk at all."

She had a habit of dropping her voice at the end of her sentences, as though she had long since despaired of being found interesting. Mumbled self-address. It distressed William.

"Will you stay for a meal with me?" he asked. "You're very welcome to. Stay till you're quite rested. I've promised myself a ham salad. We can share it."

"I know no one now really," the old lady was saying. "No one really. No dogs either. They don't allow pets there. Fair enough. I suppose. Can't have their mess. We're messy enough."

"What time did you set out?" William was standing above her, half believing that if he could ask the right questions in the right spirit she would come to herself again.

"When did I ...? Many years ago. When I was twenty, I think, Or was it eighteen?"

"Where were you hoping to get to?"

"The moor used to have the most beautiful views. But I can't remember which I liked best."

She smiled, and William smiled with her, but it was apparent that they weren't smiling at the same thing – they weren't smiling in accord – and this too distressed him. It was as if, to relieve him of the need to talk to her (or herself of the need to talk to him), she was beginning to make a show of her forgetfulness.

"A stupid question," he said. "I couldn't tell you what my destination was either. This house; these trees; these fields."

"And very lovely too," the old lady said, yawning. "The trees especially, only one can't remember if it was the ash or ..."

She fell asleep so suddenly that William wondered if she had taken ill. But her breathing was regular and her face more composed than when she had been awake. Touched that she had fallen asleep here, with him (as if it wasn't accidental where one fell asleep), and remembering the times when the children had fallen asleep with him (touched by that too), he went from the room and phoned the Weirs. Sheila Weir said that she would ring the home and then come over. She also said that she thought she knew the old lady: a Mrs Craig, whose husband had entered the home with her, only to die after just two days.

William sat in the back of the car with the old lady as Sheila drove to the nursing home. She was distressed now, crying and shaking her head. He held her hand and remarked on the beauty of the countryside. But they were soon at the home, driving up to the front steps, which were set grandly between Corinthian columns.

At the bottom of the steps, on the gravel, stood the matron, and halfway up two nurses, all three so still they might have been there for some time. They were wearing white uniforms, but in the beautiful evening light these seemed unpleasant, emblems of disease and enclosure. The old lady had to be persuaded by William and Sheila to get out, and, when she did, she went her own way, which was not up the steps, but round the side of the house. One of the nurses, respectful of her distress, followed slowly, the other went inside.

They were left with the matron who, smiling politely, thanked William for his help, explaining that because the Montgomery was understaffed such escapes were occasionally to be expected. Then, as if suddenly embarrassed by what had happened, she shook their hands and turned away, going rapidly up the steps.

September 19th, 1978

I was the one who suggested there should be this annual meeting of educational publishers (it is the third year we have met), and that it should be held in the Lake District. Sometimes I think I just wanted an excuse to come here. It is the same hotel as before, though a little shabbier, I fear, than last year. The proprietor's wife, ill when we last saw her, died over the winter, and this has noticeably slowed down the staff. Because of her death (confident, anyway, that things will be back to normal next year), we don't complain as we surely would have done otherwise: tepid coffee, cold bacon and eggs, sometimes an absence of towels from the bedrooms. The splendour of the setting makes up for it however. The glistening expanse of the lake invades all the rooms which overlook it, turning the light towards crystal, making the air vibrant. On my bedroom ceiling there are movements of light which are also movements of water: exalted refractions. I could watch them for hours.

I may well be watching them for hours if we have another meeting like the one we had this morning. It was my idea, but it didn't go well. Perhaps I didn't put my points across clearly enough; I have long thought, you see, that we ought to do more than just serve the educational establishment. We ought to drop hints, take the initiative, be pioneers. Instead of turning out standard textbooks year after year, we ought to be producing books which, sold to schools and colleges, would shed light, enrich the curriculum, loosen prejudices. A book can have more character than anyone who teaches it. That is the trouble. I often feel that it is the short-term welfare of unformed and insecure minds that determines what books are chosen – and I don't just mean the minds of the pupils. The young are bored by such choices; they end up by dismissing books altogether. But if we could entice the teacher with new books and new enterprises, if we could persuade them to take risks, then our risks would be justified. We would be a force in education, not just a cog in the wheel of its conservation. We would be helping to draw up the menu, as it were, not just to serve unappetising meals.

These poetry anthologies, for instance. I have long suspected that those asked to compile them are told what to choose by the headmasters. They are only apparently independent; behind them are the headmasters, with their fond traditional tastes. They are flattered, though, these editors, and well paid and they don't quite know what is happening. Is it any wonder that the young scorn poetry? In my opinion, we should commission poets directly to compile anthologies. It is with them that we should collaborate, not the headmasters. The headmasters shouldn't come into it.

I am told that my view is shaky. It isn't always the case that the headmasters are responsible for the anthologies. May I not be slightly paranoid in thinking so? Have I not got a thing about the educational establishment? Still respected by my colleagues – though occasionally suspected – I defend myself vigorously. The session ends with me being accused of a fondness for unacceptable risks. I remember a line of poetry and quote it – "Old men should be explorers" – adding that that should go for the middle-aged and the young as well (adding, too, a line of my own, "It is the young we should be serving, not their enemies"). I am hushed, then, made to feel (I quite often am these days) that I am overstating my case, pushing too hard, building up a head of desperate steam. It is perhaps true, but in the face of inertia what is the alternative? The listening face that is not really listening – doesn't it have to be vexed somehow?

Over lunch, I am as usual complimented on my drive, my originality. You'd think I was the king of them all, rather than the flawed prince. It never ceases to amaze me how boardroom disapproval, enmity even, can in an unofficial context – the pub, a stroll, an aeroplane – become its opposite – admiration, high respect. I am incapable of this myself; I am all of a piece, the same in the pub as in the boardroom. No wonder I am so popular; I satisfy my colleagues' need for continuity. I am the peacemaker still. In me the different games with their different rules become the one game (though I'd be hard pressed to explain the rules). What of those who play many games, however, whose behaviour here is contradicted by their behaviour there? Who will tell you on the twelfth tee that schoolmasters should be ignored, but who then, the very next day, write earnest letters to these same creatures? What is one to make of them? If it was a case of hypocrisy I would understand, but I don't think it is, for hypocrisy involves the condemnation of what one essentially favours, and these people don't, so far as I can see, essentially favour anything. Where is one to locate them – the bedroom, the boardroom, the golf course, the garden, the church? I am no philosopher, but it sometimes seems to me that the man for all seasons has, not a complex reality, but no reality at all. He is mostly between games (I see hunched figures scuttling across alleyways in the rain) and between games there is nothing. Nor am I any kind of historian, but I'm inclined to think the Scots are worse in this respect than the English. Too long inferior, subordinate, a nation for ever on the verge of becoming itself, we assume whatever forms our masters (whoever they might be) require of us, our endless talk about independence, tradition, nationhood no more than an attempt to persuade ourselves that the reality is otherwise.

Anyway, tired of their capriciousness, I go for a walk after lunch with Jennifer. She is an editorial assistant who joined us recently. She does her work well, without making any kind of fuss about it. (Why do so many young women make a drama of their jobs?) It might even be said that she does it well without being particularly involved with it. I like this about her. She does it with the air of one looking beyond it. Has she a lover somewhere? Is she hoping to find one? Is she leaving or joining the church? Writing a book? She is very amiable, doing what she's told, not because she has no ideas of her own but because she doesn't think that anyone will want to hear them (a justifiable suspicion, I'd say). One reason she likes me is that I am interested. I often ask her what she thinks, and she always smiles, as if honoured that I should ask. To begin with, though, she doesn't reply, as though uncertain of my sincerity or hoping that her friendly smile will be enough. I prod her however and eventually – with an enthusiasm she occasionally checks – she talks. But we do have a pact: I am never to ask her what she thinks during a meeting. It is to be kept private. I don't mind; it means, not just that I have an excuse to seek her out, but that, when I do, there will be (as now, strolling by the lake) this delightful sense of isolation.

I am awed that the still surface of the lake should be able to trap so much light. I ask Jennifer – but casually, as if, really, there are more important things to talk about now – what she thought of my morning performance.

"You were right, William. Maybe too sweeping, though. Are all headmasters cultural conservatives of the most deadly kind? But what would they do without you? How would they know what they thought without you to contrast themselves with?"

"True," I reply. "I am the rock they love to dash themselves against. Like all good rocks, however, I'm on the edge of the cliff."

It is time to go back for the afternoon sessions. The subject is mathematics textbooks. I have my opinions on these too, but suddenly, as Jennifer and I go through a wood between the lake and the road, as the sun falls on her hair and on the path, I can't be bothered. I can't be bothered. Jennifer cautions me, but I'm resolute. I tell her that I'll meet her in the bar at five. She hesitates for a moment, then goes off. I admire her walk, as modest and vulnerable as she. She turns once and smiles. I smile back, mimicking the drink we'll have together at five. It is apparent, however, that she suspects that I've had a brainstorm.

I return to the lake and just stand there. What else can one do in perfect autumn weather before a lake like this except stand? The afternoon sessions do not exist for me. All this light and stillness is an invitation. I am terribly excited.

CHAPTER SEVEN

William heard on the transistor that a low pressure front was approaching from the west. And that night it began to rain. It kept him awake until dawn – the unfamiliarity of it, the relentlessness – when he fell asleep, sleeping later than he had done since coming to the farm. It was still raining at eleven o'clock, and he realised, getting dressed, that he didn't have the clothes for such weather. It had been a summer to persuade the unfortunate that in some ways they were not so. But now it was over. Looking west from the kitchen at the settled greyness, he couldn't believe that yesterday it had been otherwise. Another country. He had eaten his lunch in the yard of the second hamlet, resting in the sun until mid-afternoon. Apart from the machinery, making the odd ticking or cracking sound after so many months of heat, it had been silent. Now the hamlets, landmarks throughout the summer, were barely visible, and the only sound was that of rain obliterating the lovely susurration of summer.

He stayed in the house until the rain stopped. That was not until the evening. Then he tucked his trousers into his socks, like a cyclist, and set off for the first hamlet. The paths he had made during the summer (he had grown proud of them, he realised) had already turned to mud and he slipped frequently. Once he fell, cursing, soaking the left leg of his trousers. A curse sotto voce, though, for he feared ungovernable cursing fits, the sense they had given him of being consumed, reduced to a pair of crazy lips uttering senseless words. Rather than curse he would slap his thigh and pause. He would turn on the transistor. (Rather than curse he would weep.) He found however that the transistor too had been affected by the weather. Stations which hadn't failed him during the summer were indistinct now, remote behind rushes of static. Alarmed, he held the transistor at every conceivable angle. Occasionally voices would rise from the roaring silence before being claimed by it again. Fragments of information. "It has been decided, following a meeting of the coal ..."

"Arbitration has been considered but ..." "A lioness in a private zoo in Wiltshire has ... more seriously than ..." "An adequate contract, leading to the decision not to ..." "the party ... South Africa ..." "Looting and burning, therefore, is expected for ..." "Prayer can take many forms ..." "Three hundred and two all out ..." "The silkworm, given the correct ..."

He walked on, gesticulating with the transistor, mimicking its broken communications. "The Queen Mother, keeping wicket for the Irish Guards ..." "A bomb where all roads meet ..." "The starving ... the banquet ..." "The grave ..." "The presbytery, discovered in knots, claimed ..." "The notoriety of the unknown drunk was such ..." "There will be squalls and more squalls ... disturbances ..."

Nothing was to be gained from looking through the binoculars, either. What he seemed to see were the elements of obscurity. Vapours. A landscape without lines. Objects as abstracts of themselves. Green under grey under grey. Grey. The world's inconsequence.

Ear and eye denied, he pulled the transistor and the binoculars round (truly as if he no longer had need of them) until they rested on his right side.

It was raining again when he reached the first hamlet. Was it one of those jobs which is bearable only in good weather? He looked across at the farmhouse, half a mile distant. The rain was getting heavier, slanting in from the west, now and then blowing into the barn where he sheltered, chilling him.

Why had he imagined that the heat would last and that he would prosper with it? (The conditions of recovery couldn't be that simple.) Brooding, perplexed, he did what he hadn't done during the heat, climbed onto the high seat of one of the harvesters. There was more shelter there, but he was close to the corrugated iron roof, the loud drumming of the rain.

Already the rain had kept him awake, made him miss three tours of inspection, destroyed his paths. What other gains would be eroded? What other gains had there been? High on the harvester, feeling that he had been put there for the amusement of children, he fixed his gaze on the gap between the roof and the ground. He could see twenty yards of mud, and he could see that it was becoming deeper: from soil to subsoil, remorselessly. So what, though? Why should it trouble him so?

It was perhaps because his position on the harvester suggested a patient and dutiful worker that he felt, after about ten minutes, that something was being expected of him. Was he to speak? To go away? To attend to one of the machines? To … what? It was like the long silence – that silence which need never end – which follows a difficult question. He felt there was another presence – whether an individual or a group, he didn't know – and that, yes, some account, some explanation, some demonstration … Immediately, too. The pressure was horrible. He shifted on the seat of the harvester, sat very still. He climbed down from it and stood at attention. A night and a day of rain and he had come to this. He walked out of the barn, collar up, hands in pockets. It was as if his temper had been a creation of the summer, his sense that he had built up reserves an expression of languor. A child of the climate; a mere organism.

The deep silences of the farmhouse had gone, banished by the drumming of the rain, and the rooms were no longer cool, but damp. For some reason he got it into his head that he should write to someone. "Dear friend," he said aloud, "the long-expected rain has come at last …"

The rain continued. It got colder. William gave up his tours of inspection and stopped scanning the fields with his binoculars. His summer conscientiousness began to seem so ludicrous that on the fourth day of the bad weather he burst out laughing. From room to room then (as in search of the object of this sudden mirth), striding like one who sees that it is because of its vastness that he has not recognised his folly. Except that it was not really folly of which he felt he had been guilty. He couldn't define his error – he couldn't even be sure that there was one – but he was determined to hold himself responsible. At a stage like this wasn't it either laughter or imprecation? And didn't the latter presuppose fate and lead to emptiness? So long as he could be sure that fate didn't have a stranglehold on him, there might be dignity even in loud and endless laughter (otherwise it would be the laughter of the damned – really, a kind of cursing). But it must not become endless laughter. Not yet. He found that he could stop it or at least modify it by turning on the transistor and writing a commentary on whatever he heard. His good days became those on which, for some reason, the programmes didn't fade into the roaring silence which seemed to lie at the back of things, his bad days those on which that silence (words, phrases rising briefly like salmon from a river in spate) was dominant. He could amuse himself, but he could also alarm himself. (He could do both at once.) After a discussion of current events, for example (chaired by one who gave the impression of being embalmed in the present), he wrote: "What happens to an event when it isn't current? Can it only be discussed if it is current? As it fades from currency, don't we need historians? Are there no historians on the radio these days? Don't we want their deadly revealing dexterity anymore?" Sometimes, startled by them, he would read his words aloud to himself, walking from room to room, but sometimes he couldn't bring himself even to whisper them, so acid and indisputable did they seem.

When the rain stopped at last William set off for the village, for if he was to live on the farm in the winter he would need an anorak and gumboots. Outside too he was troubled by mirth. Hands in pockets, elbows pressed to his sides, he bent double, straightened, twisted this way and that, all the while walking. What kind of vagabond would he appear to be, to someone passing? He defended himself against the rawness of such a question by considering the signs of autumn, everywhere apparent after the days of rain: the chill, the leaves turning, the dank undergrowth, the birdsong – light, unsettled – hinting at migration. The colours in particular made him grave, as grave as he had known himself for days. And it was in a grave mood that he entered the village and approached the store. He understood his gravity, though less than he had understood his mirth. Was it simply a defence against laughter, its further reaches? Here he was, a man about to buy an anorak and gumboots (gloves too, perhaps) in order to make himself feel that the winter could be commanded, that in the driving rain and the freezing silences he could be significantly busy. Clothes as theatrical aids. At least in anorak and gumboots he could make new paths, paths to which the frost when it came – as it would, as it would – would give an illusion of permanence. He recalled his idea that he should have a small vehicle: that would make tracks of another kind. And if he had a camera as well, he could take pictures of all these tracks, make records. Why not? Did the store which he was approaching so gravely and uncertainly (the only movement in the street that of the wind on puddles) sell cameras? Why hadn't he thought of it before? He quickened at the prospect, his hands – as though it was a well known camera shop and not an obscure store that he was approaching – coming eagerly from his pockets. He had denied himself the liberty to comment on what he heard on the transistor until confinement and despair had driven him to it. And he had denied himself the liberty to photograph his world until a vertiginous loneliness had compelled him to attend to his own tracks. There would be the traces and prints of birds as well, of course, and of animals. Even of animals long gone. A photographer of trails and traces, obscure residues, starts and false starts.

He emerged from the store with a blue anorak and a pair of gumboots. But he emerged also with a bottle of whisky, telling himself that it had been an afterthought (bought so suddenly!) but so horribly embarrassed that he had to admit that he might have been planning the purchase behind his own back. Standing quite still, he held the bottle by his side in a carrier bag, fancying that it had the meaningless weight, the irrelevant gravity, of a dead animal. Fancying, too, that it was perhaps for another. The terrible rapidity of such dodges. He watched with disgust as, like ants, the lies and evasions came and went, came and went: "A present ... George and Sheila, the baby." "Smash it on the first stone."

"One drink only ..." "Take it back ..." But still he carried it, approaching the newsagent's where he had been told he might get a camera, the presence of the bottle, though, having destroyed all sense that he had a right to a camera. "I will leave it in the shop," he said, entering the shop, light from the resolution. "I will leave it here." The thought of a bottle of whisky exchanged for a camera, however, brought back his mirth. A bargain struck in darkness. Shaking, caught between the two scales in which he was weighing his imaginable future, he had a whispered consultation with himself (not quite muffled entreaty, not quite sobbing either), turning the bookstand vigorously so that its loud squeaking would conceal his crisis.

The storekeeper was right: the newsagent did sell cameras. While William looked at one, a Kodak Instamatic, he manoeuvred the bottle of whisky with his feet into a gap between two crates of lemonade, all the time talking to the newsagent, who talked to him in return. He saw a pile of *Glasgow Heralds* and said that he would have one of these as well. He was tempted to add that it was the first newspaper he had bought in years, but after his performance at the bookstand (at one point, he had nearly overturned it) he thought that his reputation as a crank was high enough. Holding the camera, looking through the viewfinder, trying and failing to keep it steady, he suddenly had the feeling that the moment had been suspended. His gesture and he suspended, fixed, frozen. As though for his own contemplation. He was holding the camera with pride, he believed. And, indeed, surely he had won? How could he retrieve the bottle of whisky now without it seeming as if he was trying to steal some lemonade?

He left the newsagent's and began to walk back the way he had come. A wind was getting up (heard in the trees before felt on the face), bringing spots of rain. Out of sight of the village, he stopped and put on his anorak, easing himself into the stiff material. High up, wheeling, touched by the sun that had deserted the earth, there were gulls and crows. William watched them for a moment, struck by the way the gulls' spiral enclosed that of the crows. Then he walked on. He reckoned that he had owned the bottle of whisky for no more than ten minutes. Had he bought it, maybe, just to prove to himself that he could relinquish it? He had relinquished it. Indeed he had! He laughed out loud. It wasn't the same as his recent laughter, however. If that had aspired to embrace the unbearable – his mother's murder, the possibility that he had come to nothing again, the fact that he hadn't seen his children for years – this was entirely of the moment. The bargain struck in darkness bringing light. Cunning against cunning. (Cunning against cunning against cunning, even.) His several selves. To trick himself in the process of tricking himself. A little triumph. It was no wonder that he felt tired, and that he stumbled slightly as he walked into the rising wind.

He was about a mile out of the village and walking briskly when he heard a car behind him. He moved onto the grass verge to let it pass. But it didn't pass; it drew level, the driver sounding his horn. It was a green van, and after a moment William realised who it was. It was the newsagent. With one hand he was steering and with the other he was holding up William's carrier bag with the bottle of whisky in it. He was also smiling. William made a gesture of disbelief and went on walking. The newsagent followed him in first gear, still (William was sure) smiling and holding up the carrier bag. He walked with an image of the helpful smile for about fifteen yards. Then the horn sounded again and he turned: the newsagent was looking puzzled now. Pretending surprise, habitual absent-mindedness, William reached through the window of the passenger door and received back the carrier-bag, thanking the newsagent in a low voice. With a wave the newsagent turned and went back towards the village, watched by William until he was out of sight. It was then very still. Even the wind seemed to have dropped. The gulls and crows still wheeled – spiral within spiral – but no longer touched by the sun, no longer drama-tised in the mid-sky. William was looking down, swinging the carrier bag slowly backwards and forwards, very slowly, almost as though, unable to work out what he should do now, he was seeking peace in the simplicity of the pendulum.

A mile distant, almost midway between the village and the farmhouse, there was a clump of rhododendron bushes. William decided that when he reached them he would close his eyes, turn round in the road three or four times and, entering the bushes at random, place the carrier bag on the ground and withdraw. Eyes still closed, he would walk away, and after about seventy yards or so he would have no idea which bush hid the carrier bag. (He was as likely to look for the bottle after hiding it, he reckoned, as he was to buy a second after smashing the first.)

He carried out his plan with a vengeance, turning about several times in the road and then blundering into the bushes and abandoning the carrier bag. His face was scratched and his trousers torn and he feared for an instant that he wasn't going to be able to find his way out again without opening his eyes. This made him desperate and desperation gave him great strength: he crashed out onto the road, steadying himself by waving his arms about, then staggering off in what he trusted was the direction of the farmhouse, behind his closed eyes a world of red darkness and white stars.

He feared that in the hierarchy of bargains with himself this abandonment of the whisky in the rhododendron bush came quite low; but he walked as if it wasn't so, as if the appearance of the newsagent in the green van had been an illusion and as if strenuous walking would confirm this. But the result, he knew, was a walk which was almost crazy – arms and legs careless both of one another and of the space through which they moved. (If it is possible to walk as if trying to convince oneself that there is a space to walk through, this was William's walk at that moment.) He saw it so clearly that he stopped and, bowing, holding out his camera and gumboots as though to an audience contemptuous of such things (he could have abandoned them easily, without qualms), he fell to cursing. It became one of his ungovernable fits, at its centre a creature without a will, shaped and reshaped quite arbitrarily from moment to moment, to each shape corresponding a curse, the shapes getting smaller and more pitiable, the curses more venomous therefore. He cursed until he had his feeling of having become a pair of mad lips. And even then he cursed – at his collapse into cursing – his final curse (he was bent double now) having itself by the throat.

He returned, walking with deadly slowness, to the rhododendron bushes, entering them – as in parody of his earlier ruse – with his eyes shut. He kept them shut. One stoop however and he had recovered the carrier bag.

He thought again how it had the irrelevant weight of something dead. It was a rabbit, eyes bulging with myxomatosis. It was a diseased salmon. It was a huge rat (he had killed it in the always inhospitable third hamlet). It was a lump of mud seething with white worms. It was excrement.

Such fancies might have continued (leading him, as his curses had done, to the very edge of himself) but for the sound of a car behind him. He had the thought that it was the newsagent again. Back in his shop, he had trained a telescope on William, had seen what had happened and, moved to pity, he was about to offer to take the whisky back again. It seemed almost likely, for the vehicle, as before, was reluctant to overtake. It drew level, its horn sounding.

"You look done in, William." It was Sheila Weir. "If I take you home, will you give me some tea?"

"Sure," William said, getting into the car and leaning back. "With pleasure."

"I've been to the doctor with the baby," Sheila explained, moving off. "She's not been feeding well."

"Nothing serious?"

"No, just colic. And you? Anything serious with you?"

"I'm desperate, it seems. Is that serious?"

"Probably. And you're bleeding. Why?"

"I fell into a bush," William said, still disposed to regard her impatience with mere chat as a sign that she was unusually sympathetic. "Congratulations on the baby, by the way. I should have been in touch. I'm sorry."

"There she is behind you. Take a look."

The baby was in a carrycot on the back seat, tightly swaddled and wearing a white bonnet. All that William could see was red skin, a mouth for sucking, closed eyes.

"What's she called?"

"Karen," Sheila said. "Tell me, though, how you came to fall into a bush? Have you been drinking?"

"No. I just tripped." It was not quite a joke, not quite an evasion. He grinned, massaging his chin.

"I can't imagine what you've been doing."

The baby woke when she was being carried into the farmhouse. Sheila sat down and gave her the breast, watching William as, very deliberately, like one declaring himself, he set his purchases on the table. He made no kind of reference to the whisky but spoke instead of what he hoped to do with the camera. He hoped, he said, to photograph sunsets, trees, the brilliance of snow under sun, birds, the tracks of birds, stormy dawns. Sheila listened with amused attention, as if wondering when the list would end, head cocked above the sucking infant. William continued, speaking more and more excitedly. Every environment, natural or urban, deserved records, he said, deserved witnesses.

"I quite agree," Sheila said. "Far better a photographer or a naturalist than a caretaker."

"Yes ..."

"There's no doubt. You do realise, don't you, that in the winter there's virtually nothing to do here? You'll be wasted."

"I feared so. But there's no alternative."

"I don't know. You could extend your knowledge of the elderly."

"How?"

"Well, as you saw, they're badly understaffed at the Montgomery. I could fix a post for you with matron, I think. I've some connections with the place, some influence. I'm due there this afternoon, in fact."

"That would be extraordinarily good of you." He said it very quietly, sitting down, as though suddenly exhausted. "Extraordinarily good of you."

"Not at all. I'll ring you tonight."

"Would you do something else for me?" he asked, still in the same spent voice.

"If I can."

"Would you, you and George, accept this bottle as a present? To mark Karen's ...'

"I'd be glad to, William. Thank you."

"A small token ... long overdue ..."

"Thank you."

"A pleasure."

"Now you mustn't feel," Sheila resumed, taking the baby from her breast, grimacing slightly, "that you're walking out on the job. There's no job to walk out on. Really there isn't. George knows it too. It's no skin off his back. Anyway, you're not a caretaker."

"No."

"That was kind of you," she said, musing. "The whisky."

February 4th, 1979

It would have surprised me, I think, had I been told that I would actually have an affair with Jennifer. But when it happened I wasn't surprised. I seemed to have been waiting for it. On the face of it, it is an irresponsible and dangerous thing to do. It jeopardises my marriage; it might even be said that it jeopardises my job. How to explain it then? Well, I might start by saying that I've always wondered (I who have neither) at the coolness and ingenuity of those who have affairs. Where to meet, when to meet, how to meet, how to lie. How to lie: that is the most taxing part. I'm not at ease with my lies, though I have confidence in them. They work, they are effective, but with each one told – I sometimes fear – I undo a little more of myself. Not that I have to tell many, for it has always been my habit to work late two or three nights a week. Now, instead of working late, I go back to Jennifer's flat. She lives nearby and it is simple. How could Margo find out? There are no lines to the office after five and should she pass and see the lights out I could say that I was on my way home.

Why has it happened, though? Am I not still in love with my wife, still fascinated by her, still awed by her family? I am, and I must say that the more I am unfaithful to her the more she fascinates me. She is so much more complex and sophisticated than Jennifer, so much more highly charged, so much more difficult to satisfy, and I don't just mean sexually. A crude way of putting it would be to say that Jennifer is a holiday from Margo. Or a trial run for Margo. That is sometimes what I feel. I can make love to Jennifer without the sense that her being is a labyrinth, significant parts of which I haven't had the imagination to enter. Almost always with Margo the parts I've failed to reach are the parts which apparently on that day in that month ought to have been reached. She never says so – she's too considerate for that – but I feel it. I lie back with a deep sense of having failed her, of having lost my way in the foothills, fallen to my knees. True, I have sometimes thought that it is because she is my wife that I feel this – that I would feel it with anyone who was my wife. A reflection on marriage, that's to say, its way of waterlogging relationships with vows, duties, obligations, rather than on Margo? It's a theory; but I'm less and less convinced by it. I think that Margo will always be too much for me. Even in old age, with her belief that the days should be intelligently ordered (over the breakfast table, all options are reviewed), she will daunt me. She thinks, you see, that I have the makings of a lazy man. She says that if I don't watch out I will become slack, then slacker, then unable to make any kind of impression at all. I'm troubled by this view, naturally, even though I don't think I've done anything to deserve it. I've always worked hard at my present job and she knows that I'm held in high esteem there.

Well, I'm not working quite as hard or effectively as I used to. It's not just that the time which I previously spent catching up, getting ahead, briefing myself, I now spend with Jennifer. It's that even during office hours I'm not as decisive as I was. I hesitate more. (My double life interfering with the springs of action? The man I am with Jennifer and the man I am with Margo at odds, creating a kind of stutter in my approach to things?) One evening, as though trying to clear my head, recover my singularity, I worked late again, but the thought of Jennifer just round the corner was too much for me and after about an hour I gave up. The result is that I'm always slightly behind now. My boss, Geoffrey Archibald, realises it and no longer relies on me for instant information. I joke that it is premature middle age, but since he is distinctly middle-aged and I am not this doesn't go down well. (His face has a shrunken look, as if he has long lived in expectation of being hurt, and his shoulders are hunched, as if this expectation has included a fear of actual physical hurt.) I repeat my joke, however, in one form or another, because I couldn't possibly give the real reason. "Mr Archibald, Geoffrey, Jennifer and I are having an affair ..." "Working together, close colleagues for some time, Jennifer and I have become involved. You know how it is." Unthinkable. There can be no playing about with the immemorial sanctities where Geoffrey is concerned. A Protestant right down the line. Clean fingernails and tired hair.

I don't think though that I'm more involved with Jennifer than I was when we were simply friends. Sex has not uncovered new emotions, I'm afraid, nor intensified old ones. She senses this and doesn't like it, for it is not so with her. Each week her hopes and expectations increase, and there are times when this makes her as difficult in her way as Margo. A few times I've even found Margo a relief by comparison. She is so fiercely verbal, my wife, always aware of what is troubling her, always alive with explanations. Explanations! She is at her most intense when she cannot choose between two or three rival ones. Until she decides she is terribly restless. Then she will tell me why x or y is the most satisfactory one, the most imaginative. These moments of triumphant choice are usually marked by strong sexual desire: it is as if she enjoys a rush of energy each time she understands something and, generous as she is, seeks to share it even with one who may not quite have grasped the original dilemma, never mind its solution.

Jennifer by contrast tends to be listless in the face of her problems. She allows them to silence her. I have to provoke her into admitting them, and even then she does so in a way that exasperates me. It's as though she can't quite bring herself to accept that they are hers; as though they are problems which have been assigned to her by mistake, as a debt meant for Smith might be incorrectly assigned to Brown. I venture to explain her to herself, for which she thanks me, though she doesn't like the fatherly tone I apparently adopt at these times. In truth my tone is Margo's: not its vitality, perhaps, but its directness. The irony of this doesn't escape me. Inspired by my wife's intelligence to try and explain my mistress to herself! Am I that helpless? In the pub before I go home – the neutral ground between Jennifer's flat and my own that can strike me as preferable to either – I look into my whisky and wish I could feel that there was a significant and enduring "I" in all this.

CHAPTER EIGHT

The Montgomery Nursing Home, like so many homes for the elderly, had originally been a country house. Next it had been a hotel, then a mental home, before finally, ten years ago, acquiring its present character. The matron then was the matron still, Alice Macrae (known to her staff as "the moth", on account of her way of appearing, soundlessly and immediately, at any crisis). She took in a maximum of thirty patients, charged a hundred and ten pounds a week, and as well as insisting that the elderly be continent and ambulant if they were to be admitted, she let it be known ("we don't have an intensive care unit here, you know") that she wouldn't put up with them indefinitely if they ceased to be so. (This may have been why, once a week, a keep-fit class of sorts took place in the home. Mournful occasions. Limbs without memory of suppleness or vigour. Wretched grins.) At the time William came to be employed there, there were twenty-five women and five men – about the average ratio. Married couples were sometimes admitted, but it wasn't something matron was keen on, believing as she did that the married thought they had more rights than the unmarried.

The full-time staff usually chose to stay in the Montgomery, for it was thirty miles at least from the nearest town. Their quarters – matron had a cottage in the grounds – were in the west wing. There were three assistants, called nurses by the old folk but actually untrained, a cook, an odd-jobs man, and some occasional helpers. That was all. The local minister, a close friend of matron's, was a regular visitor, handling the Montgomery's accounts, but at pains to point out that his province was really elsewhere. Each afternoon and suppertime, however, he and matron could be seen walking in the grounds – under a golf umbrella if the weather was bad. (Mealtimes matron left to her assistants: they weren't exposed to complaints about the food, or, if they were, they didn't think that anything was to be gained by passing them on.) Sometimes he held a service. And sometimes he stayed the night.

It was by matron and the minister that William was interviewed. A bright autumn evening, the minister's light blue pipe smoke drifting in the rays of the setting sun, matron sitting forwards at her desk in her uniform, hands clasped. Their questions were casual, their tone condescending, but their need for a replacement for the last odd-jobs man – he had left one Saturday night and never returned – was clear. William had been well briefed by Sheila: he said he could drive, cook, garden, light fires, do carpentry, mend fuses. About his past she had advised him to be vague. Would anyone who simply wanted an odd-jobs man be particularly interested in his past anyway? He doubted it. Even on good days it came to him obscurely. It was as if, so long a source of shame to him, it had taken to presenting itself in riddles. (Not even dreams of it could have been stranger.) Incidents came to him either stripped of their contexts; or with contexts which rendered them peculiar; or in sequences which made little sense. And his mistakes, his failures: they too had lost their individuality, appearing to be manifestations now of the one essential failure, whose character, he sometimes feared, would always elude him.

The Reverend Walsh, however, was an inquisitive man, red-faced and overweight, his breathing, the rise and fall of his chest, like the rhythm of curiosity itself (his nose for weaknesses, indeed, might have been the main reason he was present). His pipe, as though an aid to enquiry, he held while speaking just to the right of his mouth, and his voice was deep, an actor's or an orator's voice. It had the effect, after some moments, of making William feel that here was a man practised at appearing taxed by ultimate questions, taken over by them, made sleepless by them. Before speaking, and often mid-speech too, he rolled his eyes a little, which made his words (a mixture of the colloquial and the high-flown) seem more carefully chosen and ambiguous than they were. William, unused to company, was watchful, fearing interrogation. Might they (these strangers with leisure) hunt him after all where he was least able to bear it – in his past? Oblige him to scour it, be precise? (The Weirs, gracious and forbearing, had spoiled him.) He bowed his head, waiting for the minister to finish.

"So if I may say so, Mr Templeton, you seem to be a man of some culture. I know these are times of bad unemployment, but how do you come to be applying for a job like this?"

"I had a job on a farm, as a caretaker. The possibilities seemed limited, particularly with the winter coming on."

"Sure, sure. But how did you come to be doing that job? It was presumably not a lifelong ambition, not a ..."

"No," William said, remembering his line with Captain Jenkins and Lieutenant Jackson. "I had reached a stage in my life where I wanted to do some writing. It seemed to me that such a job was ideal for that."

"That job, yes," the minister said, "but this one? What makes you think you'll have much time to write here? You'll be kept at it, let me assure you. You may even have to do a little nursing."

"One shouldn't be too isolated," William responded, roused by the minister's pugnacity. "I had no community. All I had were the fields and ... tracks, traces ... Also, I've always been affected by the elderly. Or, to be more honest, by the fact that I know less about them than I should."

"What if you find that you don't like them?" matron asked, smiling. "It wouldn't be unknown."

"I don't think I'll find that," William said. "I'd regard it as a failure, as …"

"…unchristian?" the minister asked, taking up matron's smile.

"We will grow old ourselves," William said. "What then?"

"Are your parents still alive?" matron asked.

"No. Both dead."

"Could I ask you," the minister pressed, "if you had to nurse them at the end? Had you to show yourself patient and faithful before their varying and difficult demands? Before God also, of course?"

Matron looked at him as if she feared that she was about to lose his drift. (Even she, his intimate.) She had curly silver hair which now and then – a gesture of excitement – she would fastidiously ruffle. She did it now, and it might almost have been the minister's words or voice – though in no obvious way – that had excited her.

"No, I didn't nurse either of them. My father died in hospital, and my mother came to an unfortunate end."

"For some, of course, death is an unfortunate end however it occurs," the minister said. "Was your mother's end …"

"She was murdered," William said.

"Oh, I'm sorry. How hard are some of our trials. How hard."

"Yes," William said, looking at him closely, wondering if his lack of surprise was genuine or affected, "you could say so."

"As far as I know, the murderer hasn't been found," he continued. Would he here, before strangers, in this home for the elderly, be overcome? He would stick to the bare facts: the bare facts consoled. "And probably never will be. Apparently there were no motives. Case just about closed, I'd imagine."

"I am sad to hear it," matron said. "Such a violent world. Was she old?"

"I never thought of her as old. Late sixties."

"She'd have been a youngster here," matron said, brightening. "Most of our patients are over eighty. What would you say the average was, Alan?"

"Eighty-two," the minister replied, as if it was just one of many figures he had at his fingertips.

"How is the old lady who walked over to the farm?" William asked. "She seemed a vigorous eighty."

"She was. But she died shortly after that. It's often the way, isn't it, Alan?"

"Yes, you often find it, Mr Templeton," the minister said. "There's an extreme gesture of some kind – a bid for freedom, an outburst, an assault even. Then death. Death. Funny."

"An assault?" William asked.

"Yes. Assault and die seems to be the impulse."

There was a silence. William had the impression that the minister and matron wanted to look at each other, but were refraining, out of politeness. He could tell nothing from their manner. Had he acquitted himself well or badly? Struck them as erratic or trustworthy? Were they prepared to set aside any such misgivings because of their need for an odd-jobs man? An odd-jobs man. To pass the time while they deliberated – silently, looking in opposite directions, as if they were summing up a house they'd just been shown round – he played about with his title. Odd. Jobs. An odd man. Jobs for the odd. Jobs. Odd. Time gathered about the words and was treasured. The silence deepened.

At last matron looked up.

"We're pleased to offer you the post, Mr Templeton," she said, ruffling her hair. "Start whenever you want. There's a room for you in the west wing. Don't worry: you'll slowly pick up what's required."

She stood up and shook his hand. Suddenly jovial, the minister did so too, pressing his left hand on top of their two clasped right ones, a gesture which, neither caution nor benediction, struck William as almost meaningless. Ecclesiastical good form, he supposed, nothing more. His smile wary, he struggled to say something appropriate.

"A sherry, Alice?" the minister suggested.

"Will you join us, Mr Templeton?" matron asked.

"If you don't mind, I'd rather not. I don't drink. But don't let me ..."

"Quite right," the minister said, first leaning with his left hand on matron's desk, then, with his right, opening a drawer halfway down the side of the desk and taking out a bottle of sherry. "Sure I can't tempt you?"

"Sure."

"We'll show you round," matron said, sipping her sherry. "Let you see for yourself."

Supper had been over for half an hour, but still the impression given was that the elderly were journeying, slowly journeying, from half-finished puddings to their appointed lounges and favourite chairs. From a point which no longer existed (the puddings would already have been thrown out, or given to the dogs, or recovered for the next day) to one which some of them may have feared they had forfeited by their absence, however brief, they fanned out, as best they could. A quitting which seemed to be getting slower by the minute, too, more enfeebled. Most were too absorbed in the act of moving – many with the help of sticks or zimmers – to be in a position to attempt anything else. Who was next to whom, therefore, was determined not by affection but by mobility. Arch-enemies, for all William knew, went side by side because they hadn't the strength to be anywhere else. Such conversations as there were were more apparent than real – unsteady monologues happening to dovetail for a moment. "They give me ice-cream an awful lot." "I don't like jelly." Matron, approaching from behind, addressed them all by name; but as though afraid that they would fall if they tried to address her in return, she didn't linger, and didn't appear to want the minister or William to linger either. And indeed there were few acknowledgements of her passage – fewer than there were farts and groans and belches. (To fart, William noticed, the elderly stopped altogether, leaning on their sticks or zimmers and looking straight ahead.)

Walking almost normally, though stopping now and then, was a Miss Anderson. William was introduced to her. "Our new helper," matron said, as if William had been chosen from hundreds. There was a cluster of black hairs on Miss Anderson's chin, her cheeks were a high colour, and her eyes, as from a lifetime of scheming and frustration, were angry and scornful. She told William that she hadn't enjoyed supper at all and that she hoped he would get to work on the cook. Then, cupping her left hand where her left breast would have been, she stood back and admired William. Boldly admired him. She was still admiring him, still holding the memory of a breast in her quivering cupped left hand, when he said goodbye, following matron and the minister down some stairs. He walked without effort these days, head and eyes steady, hands steady too. And today he felt youthful as well. He supposed it was a common experience for newcomers: a sense of increased vigour brought on by so much evidence of decline. He noticed the firmness with which matron descended the stairs, using the bannister for effect rather than from necessity, once looking back at him, quickly smiling, tossing her head.

"There are some characters here," she called to him. "Will we be as interesting at their age, Alan?"

"Of course, Alice," the minister replied, so that William, following, had the impression that it was an exchange which had occurred before. "Some aren't dimmed by age at all. Look at Miss Baxter: at crosswords she leaves me standing."

They passed an old lady in an overcoat lying slumped in an armchair, one arm trailing from her zimmer like a rope from a rowing boat, her stockings round her ankles. She was snoring loudly, her lips curled back over ill-fitting false teeth as though not even in sleep would the habit of contempt leave her. Would it leave her in death? William wondered. Would it leave her then? And had she missed her supper?

By the time they had completed their tour William had identified the smell of the place. Fish and urine. It was everywhere, though stronger in some parts than others. Not even the disinfectants and air-purifiers and vases of flowers which stood on table after table could banish it.

"Now let me show you your room," matron said.

The west wing was cool by comparison with the rest of the house, and it didn't smell. Efforts had clearly been made to establish it as the staff quarters. The doors, for example, were locked (otherwise the elderly would stray in there, matron said, and wet themselves), the furniture was bright and modern, and there were posters on the walls. Even the light – lucid and even – struck William as different.

"Even I find this a haven," the minister said, "and I ...'

"...don't even work here!" matron laughed. "Yes, it's a pleasant complex, with pleasant rooms. This is yours, Mr Templeton introduce yourself to it and then – visiting hour is upon us, I'm afraid – just let yourself out. We'll be pleased to see you whenever you choose to start. When might that be?"

"I'll start the day after tomorrow, I think," William said. "All right?"

"Excellent," matron nodded.

"So long, Mr Templeton," the minister said.

Alone in his room – matron was quite right, it was a very pleasant room, a room in which you could sit or read, write long letters to distant friends, sleep well for the first time in years – William walked to the window. The sun was shining, the colours were autumnal, and between the oaks and beeches there were broad paths, secret and silent. Round a bend in one of the paths then, came, very slowly, an old man and a nurse. Mainly the old man's look was of extreme delight, but every ten yards or so – as though the very extremity of his delight unbalanced him – his left foot got stuck and he became distressed, giving himself up to the nurse. Dextrous for both of them, the nurse nudged the old man's calf with her instep until his leg moved again. William watched closely, drawn by the nurse's patience. Exemplary gentleness. Young and dark, she might have been thought naively forbearing but for her determined air. They combined oddly, in fact, the forbearance and the determination. (Too much one way and she would have had no presence, too much the other and she would have been overbearing.) William was made particularly aware of it because at one point – as though taking a moment off from her ministrations to remind herself that in spite of all it was a comparatively young world through which she and the old man were moving – she looked up and saw him. She didn't smile, but her look wasn't unfriendly, either, "Who are you?" it seemed to say. Simply that. It may not have been a question William could have answered, but nor was it one which at that moment – standing back slightly from the window – dismayed him. It was not with shame that it pierced him.

July 22nd, 1980

I am to meet mother at the hospital at two o'clock. Father has had a serious heart attack. After three weeks complaining about the heat he keeled over this morning after breakfast, grabbing at the tablecloth as he fell, pulling cups, plates, the teapot down on top of him. Mother is very distressed, naturally, I rather less so, I'm afraid. And not really surprised. A lifetime of tension and grumbling was bound to lead to something like this. It is fitting, really. I ask myself am I heartless as I walk to the hospital through bright July. Father and I have never got on. Never. I sometimes have a dream in which as a baby – but a baby with a sophisticated consciousness – I am lying behind a mosquito net or something of the kind. It has apparently been put there by mother to protect me from father. He glares in nonetheless, whenever he can. His famous gaze: a flat white face, terribly flat, straight hair brushed severely forwards, eyes which – as though limbering up for a shouting match, a coup – seem to be doing exercises. He looks in and is gone. Looks in and is gone. And I, helpless on an arrangement of scented pillows, look left and right for mother. But mother is not there, or is there but silenced, dying perhaps.

Mother has been at the hospital for three or four hours. I meet her in the large cool entrance hall and she tells me that father is very bad. I touch her on the arm and she looks at me with one of her quick smiles. Even in grief she does me the honour of recognising that I have reason not to feel as she does. (Her journeys into the lives and personalities of her son and daughter have been remarkable, I realise.) She says that father is in the intensive care unit and that, though conscious, he is exhausted and behind an oxygen mask. The visit will be brief, conversation neither possible nor desirable. As we go up in the lift, I try to imagine what father will think of our appearance, healthy birds in his chamber of death. I cannot do so. He will hope that Marion, alerted in New England in the middle of the night, will make it in time. Or does he see himself recovering, walking perhaps with a stick, leisured at last, enjoying gardens? No. I think he has vexed himself to the grave.

He manages to raise his right hand a little above the sheet. For once I am sure that he is as weak as he appears. Too weak for show. On an impulse I go round and touch his hand. It strikes me as alien, not a part of him, not a part of him at all, and this frightens me. What do I mean? It is his hand. Have I not touched it before? Emotional in the death chamber, I am aware of mother behind me, smiling, unsurprised by my state, ahead of me as usual in these desperate matters. She motions me to sit beside her and we agree that father looks rested. Is it tears behind his oxygen mask or perspiration? Perspiration. Mother rises to wipe it away, leaning gracefully over the bed, smiling. (Will I ever know what enables her to smile when I – such are the shadows – can hardly breathe? When what I hear is a kind of grinding?) She has managed, I notice, to dress both for the day and the occasion: a summer frock, but with the quietest of colours. The quietest.

A nurse comes in, checks whatever it is they check at such times, smiles quietly, and goes out. Again father's hand lifts a little, drops. This time it doesn't have the air of a terribly reduced greeting, but of something involuntary. Maybe it was involuntary the first time and my feeling that it wasn't really his hand had some truth. Is he gone already beyond the bounds of his body? Is that what mother's smile means?

After twenty minutes mother whispers to me that we should go. Father is sweating badly. I touch his hand again. It is clammy. There is no response. I should be used to this, but I am not. Mother wipes his forehead. Then kisses it.

I tell mother she can't wait around all day. She says nothing. She is going to a friend's, ten minutes from the hospital, because the friend hasn't heard the news. I accompany her, her walk no less vigorous than mine, if mine can be described as vigorous anymore. The pavements are baked, the parks and gardens parched. I think we both have a sense that what is going on outside the hospital has nothing to do with father. It is both a comfort and a comment. Although he has lived in the country, I wouldn't say that he has been a lover of nature. I wouldn't say that he has been a lover. These trees would not have been noticed by him.

Mother asks me to come in with her to her friend's, but I decline, pleading work, saying I'll be back at the hospital later. I have no desire to work, however, I will take the afternoon off. If I hadn't done my work so well over the years I'd still be striving, maybe. But, as it is, it has little left to offer. I have mastered it, maintained my mastery more or less, become a kind of hub in the educational publishing world. A reputation of sorts. But now? Now? One can't stay in the same place forever. It would be boring to try. The path downwards, to foothills in some other range, is more appealing than the same summit, month after month, year after year. How many people can summit hold anyway? There are younger men coming up.

I drive to a pub in the country which I discovered in the days when I went birdwatching. Now I hardly even notice birds, I'm afraid, far less watch them. Can I understand why I had the passion? Never mind. The courtyard of the pub is quiet and white – bright July indeed – and I drink beer. I hear behind me somewhere a circular saw and now and then smell pine sap. It must be a thick trunk – a thick trunk or weak men – for the saw labours and there are pauses. Sometimes there are shouts: perhaps they aren't sure after all where the tree will fall. I imagine it coming down across the courtyard, crushing me. Father and son departed together. Poor mother. Poor Marion. Would mother go and live in New England then? A visit, maybe, but not to stay. Away from her country she would wither, her eyes alone telling those with eyes to see that she had once been otherwise. But why am I thinking about mother when it is father who is dying?

I get the impression that the tree is about to fall, for the saw is going fiercely and behind it I can hear shouts. When it comes, though, the fall is less impressive than the preparations. It is as if it is occurring in slow motion: light sounds, feathery sounds, a kind of whispering, at last a clump. Then, in the following silence, twigs snap, snap as in afterthought, casually. And go on snapping. I imagine dust and flies above the torn earth.

Slightly drunk, I approach the fallen tree, and notice that not only has it been cut down but, as though diseased, uprooted. I am greatly impressed by its roots, too healthy to be out of the earth. It is an offence. Where are those responsible? I cannot see them. They have gone. More time must have passed than I thought. I am – I was about to say "we" – for the fallen tree seems to be a presence – on the edge of a forest. It is entirely silent now. I lean on the tree for support, and notice, coming from the earth that clings to its roots, ants and slaters and earwigs, hundreds of them.

CHAPTER NINE

When he woke in the Montgomery on his first morning, William was confused by what he heard. They were strange sounds: he hadn't heard anything like them before. Sounds as of air escaping or being compressed. Sighs – but too extended to be human. He slept again, retreating from the strangeness, as though a patient himself, and dreamt of a hazy dawn in the Mediterranean, of the sounds and sights of a carnival. All the colours in the world were there, and young men and women were dancing. He himself was on a high bank with others, watching. When the carnival procession passed by many of the spectators ran down and joined in. William's feeling was that if he could do that he would instantly become young again. But he stayed where he was. And was quite happy.

He woke again. This time they were sounds he recognised – doors banging, plates being stacked, trolleys rumbling, voices enquiring, requesting – and knew that a routine was starting up, a routine, a day, in which he was to play a part. But still he lay, reluctant to rise. On the wall opposite him, the shadows of trees danced and were still, danced and were still. Or was it the pattern of the curtains that did so? Whichever it was, they seemed to matter more to him than the sounds of gathering purpose. Some of the elderly, he supposed, would be up and dressed before him, converging already, with that dry and musing slowness, on the breakfast room. Each at his own pace from dawn to dusk. The life of the place seemed suddenly clear to him: it was as if he had lived through it many times already. He dozed again, unable to overcome the feeling that he was a patient too, here to rest in pleasant surroundings, to complete a recovery, to have it recognised that his path had not been easy but that he had done well.

There was a knock on the door. They had come to remind him that he had duties. He propped himself on one elbow and called, "Come in!" The door opened slowly, almost teasingly: it was the nurse he had seen with the old man. He had been introduced to her and the other nurses the night before, and had thought her much the kindest and brightest of the three. She was called Sophie Mackay. Of the others, May, in her fifties, was aggressively offhand, as though, with infirmity on all sides and death a more regular visitor than some of the relatives, she believed that a crude attempt at levity was better than none at all. The third, Margaret, was the same age as Sophie, but ill at ease with almost everyone. The impression given was not of a lack of kindness, however, but of imprisoned kindness. (An impression which, with William, had taken a strange form: such was Margaret's pallor and thinness, she would one day look into a mirror and barely see herself.)

Sophie entered, opened the curtains an inch or two and sat on the end of William's bed. Breakfast had started, she said, but there was no hurry. None at all. She didn't seem surprised at finding William in bed, and she didn't seem surprised at his continuing reluctance to get up. She didn't seem surprised at anything, in fact. It gave her the appearance, this unsurprised alertness, of looking boldly beyond the rim of the normal, of being on good terms with risk, challenge, adversity. Whether it was an expression of unusual naivety, however, or of painful experience, William couldn't tell. Given her age, it was perhaps the former; but given the frankness with which she regarded him propped on one elbow, the ease with which she appeared to disdain – as out of a respect for what waited in the shadows – the more obvious features of the scene before her it was perhaps not. And was she smiling or not? He couldn't be sure about this, either. All he knew was that with her brown eyes, brown hair and thoughtful mouth she was pretty.

"You look as if you want to stay there," she said.

"I am staying here," he smiled. "Hasn't matron told you? I'm one of your patients. The oldest young one in the place. What's your treatment?"

"All right," Sophie said. " I'll check you. Lie back and keep still."

Because he didn't lie back immediately, Sophie placed her hands on his shoulders and pressed him gently downwards. And because, when lying, he didn't lie still, she placed his hands together on his chest and indicated that he should keep them there. Then she felt his forehead, took his pulse, pulled down his eyelids, looked at his tongue. There were no signs that she was treating it as a game. No signs that she even noticed the little smile with which he submitted to these unexpected attentions.

"You can get up," she said. "You're a bit bleary, but you can get up. Don't you know you look well?"

"My tan? It was a good summer."

"I'm not a real nurse, by the way," she said thoughtfully. "Matron is the only real one around here."

"Why don't you become one? You'd be good."

"I'm thinking of it. The trouble is I have so many plans I can't choose between them."

"Too many futures? That's a luxury, I can tell you."

"Well, are you going to get up?" she asked. "I think you'd better. And don't forget to put on your white jacket. It'll make you look like a dentist, but we're all in white here."

"Except the minister," William said.

"Except the minister. He's in black."

"Okay I'll be along in a minute. What should I do, though?"

"Talk to them, help them to their chairs, read to them, help them to the lavatory."

But even after Sophie had gone, William didn't get up. From his bed he could see his regulation white jacket, with its little epaulettes, on the back of a chair. He didn't want to wear it; it would indeed make him look like a dentist. When had he left the farm? Only yesterday. Already, though, it seemed distant. His shoes; his trousers; his cracked mirror; his razor; his transistor: he could see them all from where he lay – he itemised them, in fact, now in one order, now in another. But it didn't bring the farm any closer. Could he not even hold on to his recent past? Did he not really care about what passed through his hands? His hands: slowly – as if he had never done so before and feared what he might find – he raised them until they were level with his eyes. Some of their lines were strong, strong and forked, some indistinct, vanishing in the middle of the palm, but what held him was the submerged blue of the veins at his wrist. Evidence of persistence, of mysterious stubbornness.

There was another knock at the door. This time however he didn't call "Come in!" because the knock had been so sharp, so imperious. He hadn't heard any footsteps, and he didn't hear any now. Indeed he was sure that were he to open the door there would be no one there. He got up and started to dress, proceeding hastily and without pause for fear that the knock would come again. Dressed and shaved, he checked himself in the mirror above the wash-hand basin. It embarrassed him to see himself so trim and ready, so defined. A second-rate dentist in a colony of the dying. A spoiled sub-urban vet. An attendant in a mental home. A waiter without a restaurant. All and none of these. He looked away. And found that he had lifted his hands again (as if sensing that he would have particular need of them in this place) and was turning them, palms in, palms out, slowly.

He locked the door of the staff quarters behind him (everyone who slept there had a key) and set off down the corridor. It was hot and silent and the smell this morning – possibly because they had had it for breakfast – was of fish rather than of fish and urine. On the walls, dingy with age and hanging at an angle, were Constable and Turner prints, and arranged on a low table, as though for sale, were nine or ten pot plants. They had recently been watered, and William wondered who the gardener was. Further on, there was a small fish tank on the wall, brightly illuminated and making a purposeful bubbling sound, but either empty of fish or with sleeping fish.

It was when he turned into the next corridor, unlit for some reason, that William began to feel anxious. And began to worry about his walk. How should he proceed along these distressing corridors? Enter these blighted lounges?

His adjutant's walk was unthinkable, for combined with his white jacket it suggested self-satisfied super-efficiency. A rangy walk suggested that he was chafing to be outdoors, digging ditches. A quiet stroll that he had no more than a casual interest in the place. A fast excited walk that he expected to find someone dying round the next corner. Was he a man without a walk? And was such a man a man without a point of view? He tried to remember how he had walked in his twenties, but – like trying to remember how the world had seemed to him then – it was impossible. Coming to the end of the corridor, he realised that he was stumbling slightly. Was this his walk, then – a species of stumble?

Breakfast was over and the elderly, against a background of bright sunshine and blown leaves, were already on their way. Standing by the dining room door, William had the fancy that they were going round and round – out this door, in another, in and out of tables, chairs, out this one again. Fatigues for the fatigued. Bending forwards slightly, hands behind his back, he waited for an opportunity to present himself. Some of the patients paid no attention to him, others looked at him as if they thought that they ought to know him. He smiled at them all, not just out of pity, but out of a sense that he must not misjudge this first presentation of himself. As well one as another, or should he wait until the spirit moved him? (What else moved here but the spirit and wasted bowels?) The eyes, hinting at no past and at no future beyond the next four steps, gave him no help. The set of the mouth, where a mouth remained, was a better guide. This mouth, for instance, seemed to be savouring a delight which only the old lady in question knew would never die. Eagerly William put his hand under her arm and asked could he be of any help. She didn't seem to know or care, however, where she was going.

"The north lounge, William," Sophie said, overtaking him. "That's where she always goes. Isn't it, Miss Black? Along to the end there, then left, then first right. Get her to show you; she really knows."

"Good morning, William," matron said, also overtaking him. "You've missed your breakfast. We have tea at eleven."

"You've missed your breakfast?" Miss Black said, as though she couldn't make up her mind whether to do so was an act of daring or madness. "You've missed your breakfast! Bad luck. I didn't miss mine. I had fish, I think, or was it eggs?"

Her voice was low and slow, always failing, and it had the effect of making William want to bend low beside her as he walked. Once, in fact, he did so, but it appeared he was about to pick her up in his arms and run for the nearest exit, and so he desisted.

It took him about ten minutes to get her to the north lounge and about three to settle her in her chair. She said then that she would be all right. Looking back at her from the door, however, he saw that she was staring straight ahead, fingering the hem of her skirt. He couldn't bear it.

"Can I read to you, Miss Black?" he asked, bending over her, noticing that she hadn't registered that he had gone. Her voice in its abandoned lowness had the quality of dust settling.

"That would be nice. Thank you."

The only book he could find in the lounge was *Prester John*. He began to read it, his voice quiet and firm. Once he looked up. If Miss Black was not actually listening, she was not ignoring him, either. Her parched skin, he oddly felt, would have received the morning if it could have done and her dry lips spoken a refrain if she could have recalled one. He read on, as encouraged as if she had placed the book in his hands.

"She's not listening, William," matron said, suddenly above him. Absorbed in his reading, he hadn't heard her come in. He read on, fearing that if he looked up he would see her – hands taut, birdlike – preparing to ruffle her hair. Or could he hear her doing it already, a dry, abrupt sound, irritation and excitement in equal measures? "There is the garden. It is beginning to let us down."

"At the end of the chapter, matron," William said.

"Very well. But she isn't listening, you know. And remember to leave your white jacket indoors."

"Yes, matron."

By the end of the day William was exhausted. After reading to Miss Black, he did some gardening, and after this he talked in turn to Miss Watson, Mrs Walker and Mr Clow. Then, after some more gardening, he read to Miss Parsons (*The History of Mr Polly*) and helped serve tea in the north lounge.

It was part of Sophie's faith, he discovered, that if you didn't talk to the elderly or read to them they would sleep. If you talked to them they ate more. They read more. They were more inclined to go for little walks. They lived longer. What was the point of the long afternoon sleep so reminiscent of death? The lounge that matron was in charge of was full of slumbering figures, apparently. Sophie called it the lounge of the sleepers. Whenever she could, she slipped in there and woke them, talking to them, telling them stories, reading to them. A few times, she said, she had found that the long afternoon sleep had passed over into death without anyone noticing, and this she took as proof of her theory. William was shown this lounge, standing with Sophie outside the glass doors, feeling the force of her will as she silently regarded the sleeping figures, the sacrificial throats and necks.

"They could have been sleeping for years," William said.

"Exactly. I'm sure that's what some of them feel."

"Isn't matron very busy, though?"

"You could say so. Her accounts are endless."

"Isn't that the minister's job?"

"They work at them together," Sophie said, starting to smile. "He checks her figures, she checks his, God applauds."

He had managed to encourage some reminiscences in the course of the day, and to follow them even when they wandered, as they often did. He seemed to have a talent for it. With his own past shifting and oblique, he was well placed to understand what was happening. Miss Watson told him that she had been born in Brighton in a large house and that she would soon die there. Brighton to Brighton – she saw it as a perfect circle. On her way, she had nearly been married three times but had always held back (her bad breath, her unreliable eyesight and her fear of the black stick). She had worked as a secretary in Paris, a minor diplomat in Marseilles and a fashion designer in Nice. William remarked that her French must have been perfect and she said that it still was, giving him a demonstration in English. A dashing inconsequence ruled her memories. William listened affectionately, encouraged to find that there were others who moved from moment to moment, event to event, with little regard for links. Now and then, therefore, on this first day, this day of initiations, he recalled episodes from his own past, sometimes sharing them, sometimes not. Conversation among the elderly, he saw, was more a dovetailing of reminiscences than an exchange of impressions or ideas. The best moments were those when, side by side, memories vindicated each other. Similar coins on the windblown slope. Miss Parsons, for example. She had worked with Girl Guides until she was fifty and on one of her weekends with her girls there had been a thick mist. She remembered the penetrating silence and how no one had felt that she should break it. William understood, for once, out birdwatching, he had been caught in just such a mist. He remembered his feeling that the mist would lift if he could only keep still. "That's it!" Miss Parsons said. "I told us to draw our legs up and sit tight." And Mrs Walker: she had been a drinker too, it seemed, particularly after the death of her husband. She had a nice turn of phrase, telling William that she had entered the Montgomery on a tide of gin which, once out, had unfortunately never come in again. "I am beached, William, beached with obscure companions." The word "obscure" she spoke very carefully, as if just discovering it, or as though persuaded that, perfectly spoken, it would release her somehow. William hung on these attempts at the triumphant pronunciation, speaking the word inwardly (thinking how he had lost touch with too many words) as the old lips humorously pursed themselves. "Open wide and keep still," Mr Clow had to say four times in his high-pitched voice before William realised that he was in the presence of a retired dentist. It explained the shining envy in his eyes: he wanted to be allowed to put on William's jacket. And, eighty-eight years old, he did so, bending over William and telling him that his teeth were rotten, his gums even worse. Behind, playing the part of the dentist's assistant, was Sophie. "Pull them out, dentist," she said. "Pull them out and make him start again."

"Terrible neglect," Mr. Clow muttered. "Terrible. You're too young to have a mouth like that."

He had been in the garden for about forty minutes – feeling his teeth with his tongue for evidence of the decay Mr. Clow had spotted and working at one of the rockeries with a hoe Sophie had found for him – when matron approached.

"It's been months since anyone worked at the garden," she said. "Months. Your predecessor wasn't keen on it and then of course he left so suddenly. But if you're determined you may make it again one of the most beautiful gardens in this corner of Lanarkshire. In the days when the Montgomery was an estate, you know, this garden was famous. Distant days!"

She was wearing a blue cape and brown leather boots. It was drizzling slightly and William realised that she wasn't on her way anywhere but had come out especially to see him. Holding the cape at her neck, she looked as if she was protecting more than just herself. And the word "protectress" came to him. It was part of her idea of her role, apparently, that she should try, now and then, to turn herself into a symbol. It was one of the things that made dealings with her awkward: these switches from the personal to the impersonal were unpredictable. She moved a hand out from the cape and ruffled her hair, but lazily, looking at William as if to say she was only doing it because he was taking so long to speak.

"Matron?"

"Yes?"

"Is there a lawnmower?"

She turned, smiling, and walked to a hut which stood against the high wall which surrounded the Montgomery. She had the key to it in her pocket – one of many on a huge key ring – and William noticed that, using it, she was careful to keep the other keys from jingling together. The hut smelled of oil, grass and dampness. He was invited to look inside. There was a selection of gardening tools, two lawn-mowers, a large hose, a folded trellis fence and a wheelbar-row. He stooped to inspect the lawnmowers, while outside, holding the door to stop it from swinging shut, matron made another remark about the garden's former glory. Down on one knee, William ran his forefinger along the blades of the lawnmowers and stood up.

"I'll oil them," he said, "and cut the grass when it's dry."

They returned to the rockery, where William took up the hoe again. It was her impression, matron remarked, that he had created quite a stir. He would be popular. He smiled, working with the hoe, wondering what it was about her manner that prevented him from being more pleased. He didn't speak. There was a knock then on a window behind them. Matron ignored it. But William could see that it was Sophie, holding up a cup of tea, mouthing between smiles that he should come in out of the drizzle and enjoy it.

"Young Sophie," matron said without turning. "The drizzle is certainly getting heavier."

April 2nd, 1982

I'm on holiday this week. I can't quite understand why, but I am. Was it perhaps suggested that I take a break? Possibly. My work has been ragged, I have to admit, but no more so than that of others. Anyway, I'm on holiday, whether it was my choice or not. It may be that the distinction between free and unfree acts can no longer be drawn in my case. That might be a comfort. Let it slide!

Margo is in and out, which is just as well, for I'm ill at ease. And then, at the end of the week, Kathleen is off school. She was sick in the night, apparently, four times. The doctor is called, but it is not I who see him. Margo is better at describ-ing symptoms, crisper in her sense of what is wrong. I have a tendency to exaggerate symptoms, even to invent them. I stay out of sight until Dr Purvis has gone and then offer to go for the medicine. Margo says that I can combine it with a trip to the school to fetch Kenneth. Believe it or not, I haven't done this before; I have always been working. I note the fact with acute resentment: I have always been working!

It's a pleasant day, early spring. There is a pub across the road from the pharmacy and I sit there for more than the twenty minutes I've been told the prescription will take. I have had a good lunch, so I will not become erratic. On the contrary, by the time I rise to leave I am steady, steady and as if on a summit. There must be some way of fixing oneself at such a pitch. (All these pills and drugs, and the fearless moment, the moment of unabashed friendliness, cannot be maintained?) The girl in the pharmacy asks me my address and after a pause – a pause filled by my smiles (licked by them, one might almost say) – I give it. She smiles back as she reaches the medicine in its white paper bag over the counter to me. Perhaps it's as simple as this: one customer in every ten is a phenomenon of some kind, to be smiled at or grieved over. This girl sees that I'm not to be grieved over. And that's good. That's as it should be. As any sensible girl would have it.

Ten minutes early for Kenneth, I station myself at the entrance to the playground and wait, wondering how he will react when he sees me. Sees that it is me and not his mother. I hope he'll not be embarrassed. Probably amused at such a departure from the normal. At worst, smilingly suspicious. I'm rather awkward with him, so it's well to be prepared. I rehearse questions and jokes and observations – enough to get me through three such meetings – and find that, doing so, I've grasped one of the railings and that rust has come off on my fingers. It's a long ten minutes. I look at my watch rather like one of those elderly people you see: that haunted preoccupation with something whose function is no longer quite grasped. They're not so much looking at the time, it seems, as for an explanation why there should be time-pieces at all. I'm glad – if this is really how I'm looking at my watch – that there are no other parents about yet.

A bell rings and I hear, for quite some moments, sounds of muffled preparation. The huts in which the children have their lessons are below me. My vantage point is perfect. I have a momentary anxiety, though, that in the press and crush of excited children I'll miss Kenneth. I make myself conspicuous, therefore, lounging at the side of the gate, an attitude of jovial readiness and responsibility. I enjoy the attitude; there may be something to be said for acting. I even have the impression that were the children to appear now I would be able to be a convincing father, inspired by my pose, persuaded by its implications. A well held pose, I reflect, may be a launching pad of sorts. Ought I to act more then?

The children don't come. Why am I the only parent up here, anyway, enjoying the spring breeze? It's all very silent. Maybe there will be a second bell; maybe not. I go down a flight of steps and approach the huts. A teacher comes out. Trotting towards her with my hands in my pockets (my pose has not entirely deserted me), I ask where are the children. She says they've gone, pointing away from us, in front of us. I thank her, as if I'd fully expected her to say this, and, still with my hands in my pockets, trot round the huts and into what I now see is the main playground. Sweetie papers and crisp packets and orange-juice cartons (almost as if they too are packing up for the week) retreat before the breeze, making a light scattering sound, and teachers in twos and threes move towards the main gate. The main gate! It is where I should have been all the time. Why wasn't I told? My hands come from my pockets. Was I told? I am suddenly distressed and, outside the gate now, begin to run. The trouble is that I don't know which way Kenneth has gone. I run and run, looking into side streets, looking into lanes. I run until I can run no more. Such foolishness! It all comes from not being prepared. I call Kenneth's name, or rather a cry with his name in it is wrung from my throat. The sound alarms me: I run again – run until, almost crying, I enter our street.

Reaching the front door, I hear laughter, and opening it, I see Kenneth. "Where were you?" he asks. "Didn't you see me?" I reply. "You weren't there," he says simply. Margo comes into the hall and asks if I was at least able to get Kathleen's medicine. I hand it to her, saying in a low, apologetic and suddenly broken voice that I waited at the top gate. Looking at me closely, she says that she can see that I'll not make the same mistake again. (I have to say that she never rubs one's nose in one's mistakes. If you want to discuss them, she'll do so; but if you don't, she's happy to say nothing. Fierce with herself when she fails, she's not so with others.) She says that she and Fiona Gardener, the mother who kindly brought Kenneth home, are having tea and asks me to join them. I don't want to, but I feel that I deserve to be made uncomfortable. I sit silently while Fiona tells me about comparable mistakes made by her husband. She finds them terribly amusing. Poured out soup thinking it was dishwater; bought rice instead of flour; forgot where he'd parked his car; put damp sheets on the children's beds; took his son up a mountain in the summer without food or drink; locked himself out of his house and his office on the same day. She would have gone on – on into outright scorn perhaps – had not Margo lifted a hand to silence her. I do not deserve such loyalty and consideration from my wife. I am careful not to show my appreciation, however, for in some of its forms it excites her contempt. Recently, for example, she asked me who was writing the script for my life these days – a social scientist or a superannuated priest. (A reference, I suppose, to my fatalism on the one hand, my curious moralising and

135

philosophising on the other.)

Eventually I excuse myself and go upstairs to find Kenneth. Some kind of apology is called for. But he is showing the Gardener boy his computer. I'll speak to him later. His eyes tell me not to worry. Or not to fuss. Or not to appear again until I have found another level. His eyes tell me many things.

CHAPTER TEN

To those unfamiliar with such personalities, the Reverend Walsh's behaviour in the Montgomery would have been hard to understand. His heavy juddering walk down the long corridors suggested many things (as his personality seemed to come at you, in obscure flashes, from many angles). One who has just heard it rumoured that all, himself included, are damned, and is looking for a party with his fellow damned. One who has just heard a joke that unlocks the riddle of existence and is looking to see if others have the wit to appreciate it. One who has just heard that a charismatic stranger has been and gone and left his mark, and is resentfully wondering what he has missed. One who is confident that his pride will allow him to survive every abandonment. Doors he knew to be the doors of cupboards he opened and, after a cursory glance, shut again. (The doors of the lounges too he was in the habit of opening and shutting in this way.) At the intersections of corridors he often stood musing, as though the fact, the idea, of intersection was growing in symbolic power for him. In the lounges he sat reading or writing, paying no attention to the elderly whatsoever, exhausting them with his indifference. Or he came in with his hands behind his back and addressed them on a wide range of subjects, exhausting them with his enthusiasm. With visitors he fancied he would stroll in the grounds, diverting them with tales of local history, even (who knows) with tales of life in the Montgomery. He was frequently present at reunions and reconciliations, grandparents and grandchildren, parents and children, coming together in his presence (smiling gratefully – sometimes sentimentally – for hours afterwards). His services at Christmas and Easter were famous for their mixture of tact and vigour, humour and elevation. He seemed to know what it was like to be very old, or, if he didn't, he was able – from his makeshift pulpit in a corner of the large east lounge – to conceal his ignorance very convincingly. He had had a small book of his sermons, "Sermons for All Seasons", published privately, and copies were available at all times on the oak table in the entrance hall. He delighted in signing it for anyone who bought it, and each time he did so (leaning heavily on the oak table with his old fashioned fountain pen), he would remark that had he not been a minister he would have been a writer of some kind. He had been overweight all his adult life, but he exploited his portliness so that it seemed the source of his strength. (One old lady, who had been wasting away for years, said that when the flesh left her it went straight to the Reverend Walsh.) Each year he went on holiday with matron to France or Italy. And generations of patients – a generation of patients being eighteen months – had suspected that on these holidays he and matron slept together, goring and refreshing each other in turn.

Newcomers to the Montgomery fascinated him; he would talk to them until satisfied that he could learn no more.

William knew that the minister was hoping to corner him. Now he heard him about twenty yards behind him in one of the corridors, brogues thundering and squeaking. Now he saw him about twenty yards before him, starting to smile. So far he had been able to limit their meetings to brief exchanges: there had always been a patient to help, a tray to carry somewhere without delay, a trolley to return to the kitchen. There was one thing though which he couldn't do anything about: the minister's habit of playing the part of the supervisor and sitting nearby while he talked or read to someone. He overheard much of *Prester John* in this way, and the beginning of *Mansfield Park*. Sometimes he appeared to be listening intently, sometimes to be abstracted. But he was there. His arrivals and departures, like matron's, were abrupt and unannounced. There he would be, smiling enigmatically in the doorway. Or already seated, humming. Or standing up to go, brushing at his trousers as if he couldn't rid them of crumbs. Once William read a whole chapter of *Prester John* to Miss Black while she slept, knowing that by the time he came to the end of it the minister would have gone. And once, for the same reason, he questioned Mrs Roberts endlessly about her love of butterflies.

Was it fear? Why should he be afraid? He wasn't afraid of matron, though he didn't like her – her deviousness a corruption of sensuality, her bright remoteness, her aspirations to a command beyond ordinary command – but he did think that he was afraid of the minister. Was it because he was educated, cultured even, and it was years since William had spoken to anyone like that? (Talking to him, he would have to think clearly, carefully.) Because he was disinclined to accept a person's account of himself at face value, having – or priding himself on having – a nose for lies and evasions? Because he regarded the Montgomery as a most significant terminus? (Why had Sophie, Margaret, William, the others, all ended up there?) There were many questions. So although, head down with his duties, William was able to avoid the minister, he was affected by him nonetheless, running up against him in his mind, shadowed by him in spirit.

It was clear that May and Margaret also feared him. They helped each other out when he was around. If May was detained by him, Margaret would say that she was required elsewhere, and vice versa. William didn't know them well enough to speak to them about him. He could only speculate. Once, though, he had noticed the minister with his arm round Margaret's waist. Even from thirty yards away and from behind her distress had been obvious. He had rescued her, running up and saying that a patient was calling for her; and then, still running, he had gone off himself on an invented pretext.

Sophie alone did not fear him. She was impertinent to him – an impertinence he expected and, indeed, was at pains to provoke. He didn't have any other way with her. Passing her in the corridors, he would say: "Well, Sophie, what should I be doing today?" or "Well, Sophie, where have I erred today?" Sometimes she didn't bother to reply, but, when she did, she displayed the sharpness and calculation of the licensed rebel. "God has work for idle hands to do, Reverend. Don't tell me you don't know?" "Is this how you take your exercise, Reverend, walking the corridors?" "You could pray for the soul of Miss Jackson in the south lounge, Reverend. You may not have noticed, but she's fading." "Which lounge do you plan to die in, Reverend?"

Watching Sophie with the minister, William was ashamed. That was how it should be. She might have youth on her side (he, William, was too old to be anyone's pet subversive), but her aggression was admirable. It wasn't easily managed, though: the line between licensed abuse and outright abuse was indistinct. Several times he held his breath, wondering if she was going to overbalance, draw blood at last. She always caught herself in time, however, though it was apparent that she saw less and less point in doing so. William would come upon her in a corner somewhere and notice a dark puckering (as from suddenly intensified purpose) about her mouth and eyes. And he would be moved, knowing that she knew she was about to come of age.

But the minister caught up with William eventually. It was after lunch one day. They were in the west lounge, but there was no one else there, and William could think of no excuse for leaving. The minister was tapping a newspaper against his left hand and looking round, scrutinising the empty chairs, as though from the disposition of the cushions something significant could be learned about how the elderly had passed the morning.

"You won't be finding much time for writing, William," he remarked. "Whenever I see you, you're working. And matron confirms my impression that you're commendably diligent and industrious."

"It doesn't matter," William answered. "I'd come to a halt anyway."

"Writer's block?"

"Something like that. Even with the best the spirit sometimes freezes."

"Indeed." The minister nodded, sitting down.

"Not that I'm classing myself with the best. Oh no ...'

"You looked bloodless when you came for the interview," the minister said, smiling, but whether at his own forwardness, the impression he thought it would make, or at the memory of William on that occasion wasn't clear. "Do you know that? In spite of your tan, you looked bloodless."

William had guessed that this would be the minister's way. Either you accepted his theories as part of a robust game he never tired of playing, or you were roused, you took exception to them. Even as he was considering the first option, William found that he had taken up the second. Or that it had been chosen for him, for it was as if, at the last moment, an impulse of equability and tolerance was overtaken, arrested, by one of outrage. He gave up pretending to rearrange the cushions and, sitting down, faced the minister. His mouth was dry.

"Bloodless? That suggests many things. Ill health, indecision, cowardice, apathy ..."

"It wasn't any of these I had in mind when we saw you

that day," the minister said, speaking – as out of a sudden judiciousness – very slowly. "The impression I got was of a man who had been stalled, who was merely going through the motions of finding his way. Let me not talk of the blind leading the blind, for clearly no one was leading you, but that was how it appeared. You looked as if you were proceeding on trust, step by step in almost blind faith. It was most touching."

"And did matron find it touching too?" William asked. He had hoped to sound sarcastic, but it came out sounding more forlorn than sarcastic.

"I dare say she did. Not that I can vouch for her."

"Why don't you try?" William suggested, wondering if he had been avoiding the minister until he felt that he was ready for him. Did that mean that he was ready now? Would this mixture of baldness and hostility be enough? Or was the minister, a tactician in debate as he was in the lounges and corridors, only allowing him to think that it was? "Go on."

"Why should you want me to? Do you have doubts about how your little story came over?"

"My little story?"

"Well, there was such delicacy. You told us, you will remember, that your mother had been murdered. Now I don't need to point out that it's not every day that one meets someone whose mother has been murdered. Matron was astonished, I know. So why not moved, also?"

"It makes for a certain bloodlessness, I suppose, having one's mother murdered," William said, speaking so quietly that he might have been addressing himself.

"Sure, sure."

"A certain bloodlessness," William said again.

"Do you think it's any coincidence that you've come to work here?"

"You'll have to explain yourself, I think."

"As I think I said before, you're a man of some culture. Given, then ..."

"What if I told you that I'd not read a book in years? And that it's an effort to read newspapers?"

"It wouldn't surprise me. Such a suspicion was implicit, in my description of you as bloodless." The minister was smiling again. "A bloodless man doesn't climb mountains, doesn't read, doesn't write, doesn't have love affairs. But can I go back to my question? Your mother was murdered; and now you're here. Any connection?"

If he had not then been assailed by scenes from his mother's final years, William might have answered immediately and in the negative. He was suddenly sure, however, that he had visited her only once towards the end. And his feeling was that this was because she had been too tolerant. Too forbearing. Had she been less so, he would have visited her more often. Regularly perhaps. Might he even have tried to stay? For the whip, to be derided? For a true picture of his fall? Was this why he now pictured her as he did, or why she now came to him as she did: in pain, in wrath, drinking and accusing? Why had he the illusion of eavesdropping on a woman he had never allowed himself to know, or who had never allowed herself to be known? From the scenes, which as if from some bitter alternative biography came to him and played themselves in his mind, it appeared that sometimes she took herself out of the house and out of the garden, even, and into the fields – the far fields, too, where there were copses and crows and strange boulders – there exhausting herself with cries and curses.

"Are you all right, William?" the minister asked, leaning towards him. "Yes," William said, speaking then in a rush, as if inspired and concentrated by these scenes from the life his mother might have led. "To answer your question ... I assume that what you have in mind is penance. I am here to do penance. My diligence – which you've been kind enough to remark on – is a form of expiation. But for what? Here I don't think I understand you. I don't think I understand you at all. If there's blood on my hands (isn't there blood on everyone's hands?), why assume there's any connection with my mother? So why should I be wanting – except in the most general way perhaps – to do penance? It's straightforward: my job on the farm was unsatisfactory, and so, when Sheila Weir suggested the Montgomery, I responded."

He had hoped to discount the minister's theory about penance entirely, but he didn't think he had done so, and made a gesture of irritation.

"You're putting words into my mouth, you know," the minister objected. "Of course I don't think you had anything to do with your mother's death. Blood on your hands? What blood? I wasn't talking like that. Not at all. What I feel is this: there's a sense in which we should all be helping the elderly. We all fear death, and so, as our parents approach it, we inwardly – and sometimes outwardly – abandon them, leave them to it. We may deny we're doing this, but we're doing it nonetheless. It's almost a law. In working with the elderly, though, we can try to make up for this betrayal. And, who knows – though I personally doubt if success is ever possible – we may succeed. That's all I was trying to suggest."

"I see," William said. "It's possible, I suppose. So that's why you're here so often?"

"My ministry drives me into many dark and challenging corners, William," the minister replied, deepening his voice and raising his hands. "For instance, there's an old lady here, a Miss Friel, who hasn't left her room for years. Almost the last thing she said was that the flesh which falls from her is instantly claimed by me. Now that disturbs me. What a terrible thing to say! I've been to see her, but it's hopeless: she won't talk. It's the same when matron tries – and she tries often. Sophie and Margaret, I believe, can get a smile out of her – especially Sophie – but no words. I'd like it if she would talk before she wastes away entirely. It's not right she should die with her account half made up. You're a new-comer, William. Mightn't it get your blood going again to visit her? To try to get her to talk?"

"What method of interrogation do you propose?" William asked. He had intended to make light of it – he could have sworn the clown in him was trembling to be released – but, once again, he surprised himself. A deeper response; a darker thrust. (It had happened several times this afternoon, and it was perhaps why – the great relief involved was perhaps why – he suddenly felt like banging the arms of his chair.)

"That's unnecessarily nasty," the minister said. "Perverse, in fact. We aren't torturers of the elderly here. You've abso-lutely no right to think so! Now: will you meet me outside Miss Friel's door at four?"

"All right," William said, standing up. "At four."

The minister had stood up also. He was slapping his news-paper against his thigh. Then, abruptly, he held it out.

"Have a look at this until your charges return. You can give it back to me later. In fact, if you like, if it's not too much of a strain, you can borrow my paper any day you want."

"Thank you, Reverend," William said.

Glancing at the headlines, he read: "Famine Area Spreads".

When William told Sophie what the minister had asked of him, she said that she couldn't believe it, that it would be better for the minister if Miss Friel never spoke again. She wouldn't explain what she meant by this, contenting her-self with saying that Miss Friel never had any visitors, had not spoken for over two years, but would sometimes smile, and had once, memorably (at something Sophie had said), laughed. She read, however, and even, Sophie suspected, kept a diary.

The minister was at Miss Friel's door before him, talking with matron. William approached slowly. It was his third week at the Montgomery, but he was still uncertain of his status. Sometimes it seemed to be on a par with the nurses', sometimes distinctly below it. Today, elected by the minister and matron to approach Miss Friel (were all their decisions combined ones?), it was as high, he supposed, as it had ever been. He handed the minister back his newspaper (he had glanced at it merely) and nodded, ready for his adventure into the extraordinary silence that lay behind the door. On the door, in fact, was a notice, erratically printed in blue biro: "Silence, Exam in Progress". William pointed at it – silently, as it happened – and was told by matron that Miss Friel had three notices: "Silence", "Silence, Exam in Progress" and "Silence, Court in Session".

Matron took William in and introduced him, withdrawing immediately. His last sight of the minister, as matron closed the door on himself and Miss Friel, suggested that he might be in awe of the old lady. And no wonder. Alone with her in the small room, sunlit today and with a hawthorn tree moving outside the window, William was immediately in awe of her himself. Using the flat of her hand, she gestured to him to sit down, and then, still with the flat of her hand, she made a gesture as of one trying to compose and redeem an unsteady situation. In her lap, open, was a book, and from her neck hung a pair of spectacles.

She was wasted indeed, and sallow, but she bore her emaciation haughtily, as if it was as inconsequential as speech. The main smell in the room was of milk puddings, but on the fringes of it somewhere was another smell, of excessive and troubling sweetness. How did she regard him? Tugging at his white jacket (some stains on it already) as he sat, William thought that he wouldn't be able to make much headway until he understood her expression. To begin with he had the feeling that it was a familiar one, but he couldn't understand why he felt this. Then – as though, the more it aspired to be known, the more inscrutable it became – he concluded that he had never seen anything like it before. She was over eighty, but the steadiness of her smile – and it was steady, not unnervingly fixed – made her seem younger. He asked her if she minded if he spoke, but she didn't reply, and only then did he actually believe in her as the silent Miss Friel. To the other questions he couldn't help asking in the first moments of their relationship she didn't reply either, but slight changes in her smile, and in the tilt of her head, told him that she was listening. He wished that Sophie had warned him that she smiled so much, and that her smile didn't seem to mean happiness, or hope, or welcome particularly. If he felt anything about it at all, it was that it expressed certainty – a certainty that the world would continue to mean what Miss Friel in her dying days had decided it should mean. The meaning of her expression; of his presence here; of the minister's desire that Miss Friel should speak again before death; of the movements of the hawthorn tree outside the window; of the world in which all this was happening: it was the clamour of these questions, as well as the conviction that Miss Friel was a good listener, that made William start speaking. He spoke to lessen their awful weight, and he spoke in a voice – at once trembling and strong – he hardly recognised. He also saw, lying at the foot of Miss Friel's bed, the notice "Silence", and experienced it as the most wonderful compound invitation or sanction. "Silence, Welcome, Let Go."

"As matron just said there, my name's William Templeton. How do you do? This is my ... seventeenth day in the Montgomery, and certainly my strangest. I've really no idea why it should be thought so important to get you to talk. You've a right to stay silent if you want to. It's all the same to me. Anyway, silence is golden. Let sleeping dogs lie. You've a nice room here, I must say. If I ever get round to reading again, I may ask to borrow some of your books. I see you have several on birds. I was keen on birds once myself. Does that hawthorn tree attract birds? I'm sure it does! I was once many things, actually – husband, father, publisher, lover, friend to more than a few, peacemaker. I'm now either none of these, or some of them in name only – husband and father, for instance. I took to drink, you see, though I still can't entirely understand why. Any giving of reasons seems to fall short of the real reason. The real reason ... I sometimes feel that that will only become apparent towards the end ... (Look! There are some sparrows and blackbirds!) So I'll not talk about how it became too easy to get bored; how there were no tests or challenges left; how my wife was too clever and vigorous for me; how, eventually, I seemed to be aiming at a kind of invisibility, camouflaged because I was in pieces, a human being in name only; how, failing in this. .. Oh no, I'll spare us both that ..."

As suddenly as he had started, William stopped. The hawthorn tree was scraping thinly against the window, a sound weirdly tentative, midway between silence and actual tearing, clawing. And Miss Friel – or was it himself? – seemed to be holding her breath and rocking gently. He went on:

"Another thing: my mother was murdered. Oh yes, quite recently too. The spring. By whom and why will probably never be known. But her being done in seems to have brought me to my senses. I wouldn't have been touched, you know, had she died in bed. Afraid not. Probably wouldn't even have gone to the funeral. The murder inspired me. Oh, I know I don't look inspired – the minister thinks me bloodless – but you should have seen me before. Well, I got a job as a caretaker on a farm near here. My first job for years. It was very silent there. Much longer and I'd have been speaking to the fields, the machinery. Or, like you, not inclined, to give tongue at all. One day someone escaped from here – a Mrs Craig, perhaps you knew her? – and I brought her back. How long have you been here? I'm sorry, that's none of my business, forgive me. I've been here seventeen days. But I've already told you that. Oh dear ..."

By now William was distressed. Would it have been easier or harder had Miss Friel suddenly spoken? He had no idea. All he knew was that he couldn't go on speaking without a more definite response than he was likely to get. Why had he imagined that it was all right to say these things in the first place? Miss Friel, no longer smiling now, was probably still a virgin. Had possibly never taken a drink. Would surely have had the remotest acquaintance with murder and murderers. He stood up. Miss Friel stood up also. She was still not smiling. He stood very still, looking at her, aware again of the excessively sweet smell that lay just behind that of milk puddings. She was perhaps just a cracked and stupid old lady, silent out of perversity and using what histrionic skills remained to her to try and make nothing look like something. But then, her smile returning (almost as steady as before), she took his right hand in both of hers and moved it slowly up and down. Approval, encouragement, commiseration, farewell?

Turning to leave, he saw "Silence, Court in Session" on the back of the door, hanging on the overcoat Miss Friel had apparently resolved never to wear again.

He went straight to his room then, where, sitting on the edge of his bed, he wept with bitter patience.

November 4th, 1982

I walk about the house in my dressing-gown waiting for Margo to come back. She has taken the children to school. I have a hangover and my relation to space and time is strange. It wouldn't surprise me if there was an explosion in my head and

I came out with a stranger one still. One so strange that no one could understand what I was talking about. Since losing my job, I've delayed getting dressed. I walk about like this or lie in bed drinking coffee. Today I am uncharacteristically angry, because for the first time in our married life Margo has seen fit to change my underwear. It wasn't on the chair where I'm sure I left it last night, and when I went to look for it I found it in the laundry basket. I can't see that this vest and pair of pants is particularly dirty, particularly smelly. I've taken them back to the chair, but I won't get into them until I've asked Margo to explain herself. I'd say that although in some areas my judgement has proved tired and mistaken, in this matter of my underwear I'm as reliable as ever. A man should be king of his own underwear. Give over that right and one will be bound and gagged, led by the nose to a table where the right victuals are. Victuals? It's another of these fragments which come into my head when I'm hungover. "Spartan disguise" was perhaps the most unusual one. "Henceforth I'll go about in spartan disguise" I heard myself say, following the loss of my job. Why does it happen? I can't quite say. It's as if the hungover brain as it turns from disease back towards health (health?) throws off sparks, which appear in my head as these verbal fragments. A kind of cerebral crashing of gears, or skid. "Victuals", "Spartan disguise", "The long path that strangles itself", "The window without a pane lets fall its brains": these and other oddities dance into my hangover – or dance at me from its depths. It's no wonder I drink to calm myself. As I drink now, waiting for Margo.

The front door bangs. Margo has gone to the kitchen to unpack the shopping.

I sit where I am, waiting. The underwear waits with me. A cistern goes. I hear Margo coming up the stairs then. From the measured slowness of her walk I can tell that she is looking for me out of duty alone. She doesn't come swiftly towards me anymore. No wonder. I don't blame her. The door opens and there she is, still in her coat, her face pale and her dark eyes very alert.

"Why did you throw out my underwear?" I ask.

"Because it was dirty."

"Is that underwear dirty, would you say?"

"That is the underwear I put in the laundry basket," she says, lifting and dropping my pants. "It's as dirty as I thought."

"Are you calling my underwear dirty?"

"I'm afraid so. I only hope I'll not have to call you dirty one day."

"In what way?"

"Dirty in body, dirty in spirit. The sin of sloth."

"Are you telling me you think it's coming?"

Before answering, she crosses the room and sits on the sofa beside me. Her walk is painfully formal.

"You've already had your first drink, and our first conversation is about dirty underwear. Tell me before it's too late – before you go out, coming back to sleep or collapse in the lavatory – whether you think that a day that starts like this can be saved."

She is sitting beside me, but my feeling is that she is circling me. Her hand is on my arm, but I only know this because I can see it.

I'm visited at this point by the following: "The twins in disrepair abandoned". Nothing else is in my head and so I speak it, crouched low on the sofa, for all the world like one who fears that his role is to be a medium for such senseless utterances. (Only a drunk would be deceitful enough to describe them as riddles.)

"You're talking nonsense, William. You do realise it's nonsense, don't you?" She speaks very quietly, eyes on the carpet and as though hardly breathing.

I stand up and announce that I'm going to get dressed. I also promise to pull myself together before it's too late. But since, saying this, I'm slipping on my pants, it savours more of an evasion than a promise. Margo doesn't move; doesn't speak. She has the air, with her coat still on, of one who doesn't think it matters what she does, what she says, where she goes anymore. I am now in the underwear she thoughtfully discarded, but I have nonetheless the sense, the very odd sense, that I can see myself – in my dressing-gown again and terribly bored – sitting on the sofa beside her. That I can see us, wife and husband, Margo and William, fixed in poses of lament and wretchedness respectively. Though I dress noisily, my balance being poor, I am sure that I can feel the unutterable silence of this seated couple.

At last Margo stands up and walks slowly to the door, where she turns. I can see that she has been crying.

"Do you remember who's coming for lunch?"

"Don't worry," I answer, mock-alert, "I'll be there."

Her father and brother are coming for lunch. (The son is a repeat, with minor variations, of the father, but the result isn't boring, for the father is splendid, rich enough to be repeated.) I'm fond of them both and out of their fondness for me they are concerned. I am to be invited to join the family business. In some menial position, of course. A salary will be paid me for putting in a daily appearance. It is the safety net I've always known is there. Margo's money. (Has it played a part, by any chance, in my undoing?) I know what my in-laws think. They think that so long as the money is there and I unemployed I will drink it. The choice therefore is between drunken leisure and a lowly job which may lead somewhere. The son-in-law; the brother-in-law: there he is in office number five learning his new job. His jokes are better than his work, though. That's the trouble. He'd make a career out of his jokes if he could. A pity there aren't such posts: the industrial joker, the commercial clown ... But what about the intervals between the jokes, and what if the jokes only come if there is a glass before me? "Undone by his jokes": not really one of my fragments, for I understand it. "Undone by his underwear" neither, for I understand that too.

I go to the bannisters and call down to Margo in the hall. She is still in her coat, and has been crying again.

"What is it, William?"

"D'you think I'll be the first man to be undone by his own underwear?"

She's not amused. I don't blame her. She walks away. I'm left leaning on the bannisters.

CHAPTER ELEVEN

One night at the start of winter William was wakened out of a deep sleep by Sophie. He was slow to recognise who it was, but, when he did, he made a joke of it.

"I'll move over. Right away."

"Listen, William: Miss Bethune has just died." She was still shaking him as she spoke. "She's in the south dormitory. We must get her out before the others wake. Can you help please?"

She stood by the curtains talking about the death while William got dressed. She had spoken to Miss Bethune at one-thirty, she said, when the old lady had remarked that she hoped the turkey would be properly stuffed this year. Then Miss Bethune had slept. When she checked her at three o'clock, however, she found that she had died.

"In her sleep and with stuffing on her lips," William said. He felt erratic at this hour; unable to get his bearings; as though coming at the world from a peculiar angle. The hallucinatory strangeness of the hours before dawn. What was this delicate smell of soap about Sophie? This darkness suddenly flooded by moonlight? These shadowy objects? And what was this talk of death but an old tale in an improbable setting? Closer, he felt, to a fabulous sense of death than to death itself, he splashed cold water on his face, slapped himself on the cheeks.

"Better than with a curse," Sophie said.

"Right. I'm ready. Let's go."

William hadn't seen the Montgomery at this hour before. Blue and yellow bulbs were on in the corridors, their light so weak that there were hardly any shadows. The usual smells, of fish and urine and ancient sweat, were fainter than during the day, so that it was possible – as if they bloomed only in darkness – now and then to smell the flowers. The scents might almost have been released by the silence, though, it was so vast and deep, seeming to include the land beyond the Montgomery as well as the Montgomery, land and institution, as by some law of night, flowing into each other. If, troubled by a dream, one of the elderly had risen and walked the corridors, William doubted that he or Sophie would have stopped him, for terminal wanderings, in such a light, such a silence, would have been as natural as rain from a black sky.

As they walked, Sophie explained what would happen. The essentials of corpse disposal. She had parked the mobile stretcher outside the dormitory. They would move it to the side of Miss Bethune's bed and lift her onto it. This was easier said than done, though. Miss Bethune was a large woman, but, even if she hadn't been, it would still have been difficult. The important thing was simultaneity: they must lift her at exactly the same instant, he at the feet and she at the shoulders, or the other way round. If the legs were lifted first, the head and neck would loll badly; if the shoulders, the legs would appear boneless. Once, Sophie explained, she had tried to lift a corpse by herself, thinking that the old lady in question would prove as light dead as she had done alive. But dead weight was different from living weight, apparently. The body had fallen between the bed and the stretcher, and Sophie had fallen with it.

"Shouldn't matron be told?" William asked.

"She doesn't like being wakened unless it's absolutely necessary. 'What can you say to a corpse?' she once asked me."

"Truly?"

"Yes. Don't worry, though, when we've laid Miss Bethune out in the billiard room, I'll go and wake her, whether she likes it or not. What it'll mean to her is that there's now a vacancy."

"The waiting list ..."

"Dear Miss Smith," Sophie mockingly intoned. "A place awaits you in our Montgomery Home for The Elderly. A place, a slab, a memory. Yours truly, The Moth."

They spotted the stretcher outside the dormitory. At this hour and in this light it had the air of an object which had got there by itself.

Sophie stopped outside the dormitory and listened, indicating that William should do likewise. He didn't know what he was supposed to be listening for, but he cocked his head nonetheless. Silence. Sophie seemed to hear what she was listening for though: very gently, she pushed the stretcher into the dormitory where three slept and one was dead. Though almost soundless, their appearance roused the three ever so slightly: they turned, their breathing changed, there was a minute or two of snoring. Sophie had obviously expected it, for under cover of the snores she manoeuvred the stretcher into the required position.

Miss Bethune was lying on her side. It would be necessary to roll her onto her back before she could be lifted. William looked on as, with a gentle whisper of "Come on" to the dead woman, Sophie surely did this, the head following the body, the mouth open, the eyes staring, saliva across the chin. Speaking then swiftly and definitely – as if she had appointed herself his instructress for the time – Sophie said again how it was harder to move the dead than the living. If you turn the sleeping, the head comes with the shoulders; if you turn the dead, the head comes last, if at all (this was how some deaths were discovered apparently: the body wouldn't go with the hands of the living). Then she nodded, going to the shoulders, indicating that William should take the feet. Still in emphatic whispers, still with the air of one giving him lessons in death, she said that he should grasp Miss Bethune firmly under the knees (adding, with a kind of tender casualness, that this shouldn't be too difficult, Miss Bethune having been knock-kneed).

Though dressed for the part – his white jacket recently pressed, an air of sober readiness – William didn't feel it. To meddle with the limbs of the dead, to prepare them for burial or burning, he felt as though he didn't have the experience necessary for the task and this was entirely his own fault. Sophie was already at work, he saw, crouched behind Miss Bethune, holding her up as if to allow her to vomit. And looking at William. "Come on," she whispered, nodding at the legs. The legs. Miss Bethune's legs. He stooped and clasped them, but there was something altogether wrong, he knew immediately, about the way in which he did so. He seemed to be expecting a favour from the corpse; expected it to ease his dread a little. Laying down the head and shoulders, Sophie moved to the legs, pushing William aside. First, she did what he hadn't done (wouldn't have dreamed of doing) – she pulled up Miss Bethune's nightdress in order to get at the knees more easily; and then, exploiting the fact that the knee is a joint, she held them – bent, the ankles dangling – against her breast, looking at William over the top of them, in her look now a cluster of questions. Do you see? Can you manage? Will you learn? Why so ill prepared? What to fear? Who are you anyway? Who?

Who indeed? Shamed, William grasped the old knees as if, given time, he might learn to embrace them. There was a strong smell of urine, and, as the corpse was lifted onto the stretcher – expertly by Sophie, woefully by William – there was a fart. William looked at Sophie, who whispered that this was quite normal: the dead could fart for days.

"Celebrating their release, d'you suppose?" William said.

Sophie laughed, pushing the stretcher out of the dormitory, pushing it then slowly, almost playfully, for all the world, William thought, like one trying to divert a patient before an operation.

"You're used to this?" he asked.

"Soon you'll be too."

"Had she any family?"

"A sister, I think," Sophie said. "She was a peculiar shape, you know. Thin arms, long legs, knock-kneed, but an enormous stomach. Did you notice?"

"I never got to know her."

"Just now, I mean. Did you notice then?"

"I can't say I did."

"Ah."

It was still a lesson in death. These were apparently the sort of details it was unfortunate to miss. William had missed them because he had been too aware of his instructress. Diverted by the living, you weren't drawn down to the dead, to corpses, with their smells and their uselessness. It was perhaps inappropriate, he knew, to be so aware of Sophie at a moment like this, but he didn't care, for it allowed him to contemplate the laying out of the corpse without dismay or dread. If this was his way, so be it. It was with a kind of sensuous gratitude, therefore (as if, aroused by the living, he had begun the long task of making peace with the dead), that he entered the old billiard room.

The table was covered by a white cloth on which there were dark stains. They lifted Miss Bethune onto it and Sophie arranged a sheet over her, leaving the face uncovered. The lights above the table were bright, and showed a face so lined and sunken that it was difficult to see it as having any expression at all.

"I'll get matron now. Can you watch her for a minute? She'll not bite, only fart."

She smiled, turned, and was swiftly gone.

The only other things in the room were two wooden chairs. They had been placed on either side of the table, as for the convenience of those who wanted to contemplate the dead in profile. Not wanting to do this, William stood about twelve yards back, in the area of shadow that lay beyond the central pool of light. Miss Bethune's eyes were still open – was it matron's responsibility to close them? They appeared to be staring deeper into the lights above, or deeper into death, than anyone had done before. Left on his own, William felt almost nothing; but thinking that this was weak, a betrayal of his mood of some moments before, he began to circle the table, stopping now and then to see if the face, viewed from this angle or that, affected him at all (saddened him, sickened him, alarmed him), but finding that it did not. After a while it seemed a pointless thing to be doing, but he didn't want to stand still again and he didn't want to turn his back on the corpse. To see if dawn was breaking he glanced over his shoulder. It was not breaking. The darkness and the silence – as if conspiring in the interests of his, William Templeton's, appreciation of death – were intense. Round and round he went, therefore, tiptoeing exaggeratedly, until he could imagine the vigil becoming endless. And until, without quite knowing what he was doing, he had fiddled with the light switches, first plunging the room into darkness, and then – overtones of the dead watching the living, now, rather than the living the dead – having the table and the corpse in shadow, the rest of the room brightly lit.

Eventually, lulled perhaps by his orbit about the corpse, William felt calmer. He walked over to the table and looked down. He had never read to this woman, not *Mansfield Park* nor *Prester John* nor even one of the ladies' romances (*Celia of The Heights*, *Clarissa's Return*, *The Maid of Menteith*) that were so popular in the Montgomery. Whatever she had read in her eighty-odd years, it didn't show now. Nothing showed now.

The dead stare, the lips slightly parted, the curled old tongue, the toothlessness, a remote gurgling, as of gastric juices settling for the last time, a smell of dried sweat: all this he was able to notice. And the long legs? The thin arms? The enormous stomach? Astonishing himself, he sought her hands under the sheet and discovered that dead fingers couldn't be kneaded. His knuckles brushed the enormous stomach. Enormous and cold. Enormous and old. Enough. He withdrew his hand and held it, clasped in his other hand, before his chest, like one who wonders if he has been guilty of a violation. Then he stepped away, back into the area of shadow, knowing that he was not guilty. To search the dead for their secrets, he understood, was ridiculous, for they had none. To touch their hands therefore was simply to say goodbye. As he had done. The point, the consummation of his vigil.

When matron and Sophie entered, matron walked straight over to the table, first confirming that there was no pulse, then, with the surreptitious deftness of one leaving a tip, closing the eyes and pulling the sheet over the face, her pride in these final acts greater, apparently, than her dislike of being wakened. Sophie stood silently beside William. It was his impression that she and matron had been arguing.

"I could have closed the eyes," William said. "Now we are all up at four-thirty."

"It's not four-thirty," matron said. "It's five-thirty. Time flies with the dead. No, Sophie was quite right to wake me. The fact that nobody else does under such circumstances is neither here nor there."

"The others close the eyes, then?" William asked.

"No I do – in the morning," matron said.

"Ah," William murmured, more knowingly than he had intended.

There was a silence. Sophie was not going to break it, and William felt that he had said enough.

"You might as well go back to bed, William," matron said, ruffling her hair. "And you, Sophie, might as well go off duty; you've only another twenty-five minutes left."

"Thank you, matron," Sophie said dully.

She hurried away, not bothering to wait for William, letting doors swing back in his face which normally she would have held open. At first he was tempted to let her go; but then, grave and curious and pitying after his vigil with Miss Bethune, he went after her.

"What's wrong?" he asked, catching up with her. "What have I done?"

"Nothing."

"Then why are you so angry?"

"Matron. It's usually matron."

"All right, tell me."

"I don't know where to start," Sophie said, her anger, now that she had stopped hurrying, giving way to distress. "And I think I'm too tired to try and explain."

"That's feeble," William said, aware that they were approaching his room. "Come in for a moment. Come in and explain."

She gave him a look in which curiosity and exasperation, appreciation and doubt were combined. Then she nodded.

"All right. I should say, though, that I'm a bit annoyed with you too. Why shouldn't matron, whose place this is really, check them at the end? Do the final honours? Why did you offer to save her the trouble?"

"All I was suggesting was that she could check them in the morning. Let others …"

"But they don't decide to die in the middle of the night, do they? And they don't die every night. The time of death should be respected; and the time of death isn't five hours after it."

"Was she annoyed at being wakened?"

"I wish she had been," Sophie said, sitting down on the edge of the bed. "That at least would have been normal. But she's never normal. Have you noticed that? All right if you say so, Sophie, but I can't see the point. Another of your games, Sophie, which I'll play because otherwise you're so useful, but really it's rather a silly game. That's not anger; it's contempt. Don't you feel it, William? It's everywhere – in the corridors, the lounges, the notices, the furnishings, the food, the silences. It's even in here, as we speak. Don't tell me you've not felt it?"

"How old are you, Sophie?" William asked after a pause. Although not as disarmingly as he would have done in the old days, when confidence had given him charm, and charm confidence, he spoke as disarmingly as he could, for he wasn't so much looking for an answer as trying to gauge if Sophie was likely to understand him. "I ask because, since coming here, I've been struggling to keep going, though it might not have been obvious, I know ... Well, the trouble with that kind of struggle is that it narrows your vision. You tend to limit what you take in, believing that if you take in too much you'll sink. You can't afford to suspect too much. And you reduce the intensity with which you have your suspicions. I used to have many more, I think. Yes, many more."

It was apparent that they weren't quite getting through to each other. As though to admit it, make light of it, begin the move beyond it, they both laughed. But the following silence was an awkward one. William felt that he ought to be able to do something about it. (As the older of the two, didn't he have responsibilities?) Standing behind the chair looking down at Sophie – she was sitting on the bed with her back against the wall now, an attitude of willed alertness – he took off his white jacket (it smelled of Miss Bethune, it smelled of death) and cast it from him. As though this would help him to think more clearly. But he knew that no kind of gesture would make any difference: he had lost the art of making himself plain. The new art (if there was one) was one of brave approximation. Too much had happened for it to be otherwise. Twenty-one, twenty-two, twenty-three, twenty-four years old (she had never said), Sophie remained silent, as if to give him a chance to explain himself further. It looked like patience, but, as was evident after another moment of silence, it was not: it was strictness. It had happened between them before, though never so sharply: just when he thought her young, she would appear experienced, experienced, she would appear young. Either way, the effect on him was the same: he felt challenged to extend himself (tales for the girl; explanations for the woman).

"So you're not especially disturbed by matron?" Sophie looked at him, looked away, as if offended by any kind of hesitancy. "Of the two," William said, leaning on the back of the chair, "I'm more disturbed by the minister."

"Can you separate them? Are they not one?"

"How d'you mean exactly?"

"They stand or fall together. They're a team. Anything he lacks, she has, and vice versa. The place is in their grip. I can't imagine what we could do to remove them."

"Literally remove them, do you mean?"

"Yes," she said, looking at him directly. "Yes."

"Are there any crimes you know for certain they've committed?" William asked. "I mean, particular crimes in which you think we might be able to interest a board or tribunal? Impressions and suspicions won't be enough, you know."

"Would you be prepared to write a letter, William?" she asked softly. "A letter to the papers, a letter which will make influential people sit up? I'm no good at letters, but I'm sure you are."

William wasn't particularly good at letters either, but for some reason he allowed Sophie to think that he was. And this meant allowing her to imagine other things about him as well, such as that he had once had scholarly leanings, modest literary ambitions, a talent for quiet advocacy. She was smiling at him now, head cocked, one hand on the bed beside her, the other lightly caressing her ankles. Was he desired (to his surprise, he thought that he was desired) for his own sake, or because she was beginning to see him as an ally, a fellow subversive in the dimly charted world of the Montgomery? Was it he, William, who excited her, or the thought of what they might achieve together – the sort of team they would be, faced by the unfathomable deviousness and malice she obviously found in matron and the minister?

"You're very charming, Sophie," he said thickly.

"So you'll not write letters?" she said, pretending to pick a thread from the coverlet.

"But what offences can I mention? I'll have to be specific, as I said. I'll have to be able to say, for example, that on the tenth of January last year the minister strangled an old lady in her bed, and that a week later matron allowed someone to starve to death. Have there been such cases?"

"No," Sophie said quietly. "No, there haven't been."

"Then what can I put in this letter you want me to write?"

Head bowed, Sophie lifted a hand to the back of her neck, as though there was tension there.

"There have been no offences as such, neither major nor minor. But that's not really it. No. It's not so much what they do as what they are. It's their spirit that's wrong. They don't care about the patients, and they don't care about death. They don't care."

"Possibly I'll come to agree with you," William said. "But you must realise that I can't say that in a letter. We'd be laughed out of court. They may be as terrible as you think, but it would be libel to have it printed."

Sophie's head remained bowed, as if she was painfully familiar with the story of what couldn't be done.

"There must be a way," she said. "I hate them, you know!"

She looked up, her eyes even angrier and more frustrated than her words.

"Do the patients hate them?" William asked, looking at her closely, wondering if there was something perverse in this youthful passion.

"Those that can still hate, do hate them. They make that clear. To me at least."

"They tell you they hate them?"

"Not in so many words. But I can see it."

William was silent for a moment, searching for an agreeable way of suggesting to Sophie that she might be painting an unjustifiably dark picture. "How do you know it's hate? They may simply rather dislike them."

Sophie's face was suddenly twisted with impatience.

"Have you always been as cautious as this?"

"What I'm trying to suggest …"

"Answer my question!" she repeated, banging the bed beside her.

He had managed to be frank with Miss Friel because she didn't speak and possibly didn't even listen. He had been lulled by the elevated obscurity of her silences, treating her – who might, if she ever spoke again, talk with remorseless triteness – as someone venerable. Why then shouldn't he be frank with Sophie, who might become famous for her honesty and daring?

"I've been open with Miss Friel …"

"And what were her last words," Sophie interrupted, "heard by Margaret, May and me? Eh? 'The flesh which falls from me goes straight to the minister.'"

"Words of hatred, I agree," William said. "No, I've not always been as cautious as this. By no means. I was once famous for my lack of caution. My devilry, even. It may be hard to believe now, but it's true." He sat on the edge of the bed, looking down. "If you can guess the truth about matron and the minister, I'm sure you've guessed it about me. A familiar story. I'll not tell you now though. All I'll say is that I've not always been like this. And what I was, I can hardly believe I was. Or I can hardly believe I'm now this. If one's past and present are in tension, totally different countries, one of them can seem to be an illusion. Sometimes it's as if I was that – oh, definitely was that – and this is a kind of epilogue, a dry run towards death, full of illusions of recovery and balance; or I am this and that was mere chaos, unreal, pointing nowhere. For one lifetime to have had two such selves … No, I've not always been cautious."

It was apparent that Sophie was riding her intuitions, invigorated by them. The effect on William was challenging. Did he share these intuitions or not? Was it enough scrupulously to gather evidence for or against the view that someone was bad? Acceptable to have a view even although you couldn't support it, referring instead to the triumph of intuition? If you couldn't support it, was that a sign that it was perhaps wrong? If there was water divining, could there not also be a divining of souls?

He had to admit that in the presence of matron and the minister he had been aware of a certain balefulness. He had had a sense – not that he had ever been so proud as to consider it an intuition – that over the old or the innocent they might lunge suddenly forwards, either the one or the other or both together, and that the lunge might then seem to have been inevitable, expression of some deadly earlier calculation.

He felt tossed about between suppositions as Sophie regarded him, waiting for a fuller answer to her question. He knew that she wouldn't have any patience with vexed distinctions of any kind. She was in the full flood of youth and he, if he had even known that, was well beyond it now, compelled to ask himself if there could ever be any virtue in uncertainly.

He leant back against the wall beside her. She was smiling at him, but he hardly noticed. Suddenly, as though lowered by something in his own words, some shadow of pain or disaffection, he longed for rest and silence.

"You're the man I've been waiting for, William," Sophie said, putting on an American accent and chuckling.

"Do you mean you're hooked on failures, and I'm a prize example?"

"No. You've come through. You're ready for the next round."

"With you?" he said dryly. "Against those two?"

"Something like that," Sophie said quietly, laying a hand on his arm.

Just as he was wondering what to do or say next, William saw that Sophie had stood up, without giving him a glance, and was undoing the buttons down the front of her white nurse's uniform. So casually did she do it, with such a dreamy unawareness of time and place, that he wondered for a moment if she had forgotten that she was not in her own room and was preparing for bed. She took off her slip in the same way, and then her pants. Only then, naked, did she look at him. She was smiling.

It was years since he had made love to a woman. What he had done with Sandra Mclehose could hardly be described as that. Either she had been too dry and tight, or he too limp, or both. Bestial nuzzlings merely.

But Sophie was not dry. And it was this more than anything else – the simple fact that he was desired – that aroused William. That and the extraordinary patience with which Sophie stood there, hands on his shoulders, as he undressed.

She was as swift and easy in love as she had been in undressing, crying out in painful modesty at her climax. There were cries from himself also. Low ones, as in wonder at the deathlessness of instinct, of desire. He heard them as though they were the cries of another. Risen in hope from broken regions. Risen; subsiding.

"That's better," Sophie murmured. "It's been a long night."

They lay in silence. Dawn was breaking. In the distance somewhere a door slammed.

"It was my first corpse," William said.

"I thought so. Poor soul, she looked the same dead as alive. So better dead. Better dead."

"But better this than dead," William said.

"Sure," Sophie responded. "Sure."

January 8th, 1983

I'm on my own now. Nothing else for it. A pleasant enough room. And I've found I don't need much. Most of what I own (owned?) I don't need. A mistake to believe otherwise. So I was mistaken for years. Oh I know it's said that drunks need only one thing. But still I think I have a point. The clamour of one's possessions! Better a silence like this, spaces like these. I've little to do either, but, even if I had, would I rouse myself? I doubt it. To do nothing well: that's the thing. Not to feel it's ignominious, that there's help just round the corner. Perhaps I'm too far gone to be able to see how I might be rescued, by whom and for what. For what? I've no profession to return to, under whose coat-tails I might start again. (Start again!?) But, even if I had, wouldn't I soon be sickened? To cling to such coat-tails for all to see – or for all to see who've long since climbed them – is not my idea of fun. And if I fell again, fell worse than before?

My love of exile, of expulsion: it may well be perverse, as Margo says. And I may well spend too much time telling my perversities how splendid they are, how promising. Oh I may, I may. It's true a lot of my talk is self-justification, and that I talk to myself cockily in the dark. (Cockily in the dark? What else?) Where was I? The longing for expulsion, the perversity of this. Maybe. I'm sure Margo has thought it through, taken advice, read books. But it's not the whole story. What the rest of it is I don't know. It tantalises me that I don't, but I have faith that I'll find out. Whether I do or don't, however, I must avoid playing the part of the visionary exile, seeing all from beyond the grave of his first life. I've not been drawn from my family, my friends and my job by a vision, its unsettling force, but by drink. Let me not pretend otherwise. But is a drunk merely a drunk? Is that all? Oh God is that all? If not, what else is there? Here we are again – this matter of the rest of the story.

The future as it becomes the present will be fouled, fouled and fouled again. Poor future. Flowing into the stagnant pool of one's desperate habits, how could it be otherwise? So there's no rest of the story. But then (an instant, this, between the lifting of the glass or bottle and the drinking) I think it's not so certain. The future may surprise me with chances and possibilities. It's part of the bounty of life that it should be so. I may be swept from the low ground of my foundering to high ground somewhere. My steps may not always be in a narrow circle in a dead neighbourhood.

My steps today are towards the dole. I've found myself without money, you see, since leaving home. Did I expect to be supported? They're not a mean family, Margo's, and I can see their point, but I'm a little offended nonetheless. Better to drink with their money than the state's. (Apart from anything else, there's more of it.) As if, reduced by the dole, I'd stop drinking! Sobered by disgrace! My arse! My habits will get worse and worse. At home – oh I'm not saying I'd have pulled myself together exactly – I'd have tempered my excesses a little because of the children. Here there's no reason to. None at all. Absolutely none. See what I mean? Families should stick together. I wouldn't have thrown Margo out if she'd become a drunk. But of course she's always had money and so I probably wouldn't have thought of throwing her out. Money gives even the broken and wretched status, bargaining power. That's what's wrong with me. Imagine the most wretched man alive: imagine him first with money, then without. No comparison. The drunk with money is always a somebody; he glitters with his gold. Without, he's a nobody.

A nobody. There are nobodies on the dole. The Law cannot help them (though it hovers, I do assure you, over the line of those waiting to sign on) and I cannot help them. Always as I wait my turn I look upwards, as though examining the yellow ceiling, and address The Law. And almost always there are assurances: he who tries will be given a hearing; his words will be patiently listened to; pains – yes, pains – will be taken to interpret them as charitably as possible; in due course there will be a ruling. It is this, in fact, this rather fantastic notion of The Law, that prevents me from feeling a nobody too. How would I define a nobody? He is one who doesn't look to the side, doesn't look at the ceiling, doesn't look down. (Who doesn't look at all, one might say.) He never starts a conversation in case he finds (as he surely would) that he has nothing to say. He often apologises, but for what and to whom is not clear. His walk alternates between a scuttle and a pathetic imitation of resolve. He has a squeaky cough. He wears tight gloves which he fumbles to remove when he has to shake hands or sign on. If – God knows how – you were to get him talking, you'd find that he believed in everything and nothing. To get a job, he'd betray his best friend. Only he has no friends. Or enemies.

I brood about nobodies because it helps me to feel that I'm too sly and arrogant to become one. Having signed on, I pocket my dole card and, lifting a hand to The Law to show that I know It's there (but that it can't be buttonholed – oh never can be buttonholed), I leave the office of The Department of Health and Social Security. Have I said that I'm rather drunk? Well, I am. I proceed with caution because of the snow and ice. And then I see him. So perfect an embodiment that I doubt my senses. A nobody. He is supporting himself at the entrance to the grounds in which the dole building stands. There are two pillars there, joined by a wrought-iron arch with an obscure golden crest. (Most of the entrances to hell, they say, are fancy ones.) Against one of them, still with his gloves on, he leans. Is he drunk? Ill? (I wonder suddenly if a nobody is beyond even drink.) I go to his assistance, enquiring sympathetically if I can help. He nods, but so briefly that I don't know if he's dismissing me or admitting me. I stay. He stands stock still then, not even leaning against the pillar. In his unseeing eyes there are tears, but that could be the cold. Then, suddenly, he is bent double and vomiting. Unsteadily I put out a hand to steady him, telling myself that I've helped my children and my wife to vomit (Margo vomits grandly, waving her hands in irritation). Soon there's a pile of multi-coloured vomit on the snow, steaming a little. Still unseeing, the nobody apologises and walks away. To scuttle away from one's own vomit – isn't that a terrible thing? I think so. It is probably what makes me feel suddenly sick myself. If only he had cursed! I curse him for not cursing. But still feel sick.

I may vomit too, in the next fifty yards, but I shall do so grandly, waving my hands in irritation.

CHAPTER TWELVE

Leafless, the trees no longer protected the Montgomery from the imagined gaze of the world. A relentless gaze (or so the encircling silence, reaching right up to the walls, lapping against them, suggested). On clear days, William could see the farm, even some of the hamlets, a place, he now appreciated, in which he had moved, however faithfully, in decreasing circles. Another few weeks and he would have been stalled utterly. Mired. How had he passed his time there? He could hardly remember, so crowded were the hours in the Montgomery, so varied the challenges. All that remained was an atmosphere: heat, silence, waiting.

His relationship with Sophie continued (several times, and always in a funny voice – as if it was a joke or a riddle – she said that he was the man she had been waiting for), and he was refreshed. He walked the corridors with eagerness and elation, whistling for the first time in years (old tunes, but freshly conceived), singing, rediscovering the clown in himself. He clowned only in snatches, however, for extended clowning, he found, could exhaust the elderly. One morning, indeed, he discovered that he had it in his power to make them die of laughter. He got the ladies in the east lounge laughing, and then, with the same piece of clowning (an imitation of the minister eating porridge), those in the north lounge. But when he returned to the east lounge he found that the laughter had died, and that the old ladies were coughing, wheezing, distressed. Through laughter to desolation; and through desolation – a paroxysm or two away from it merely – to the grave.

He found himself, his popularity growing with his

happiness, reading several books at once in the different lounges. He would put down *Great Expectations* or *Oliver Twist* here and take up *Emma* or *Wuthering Heights* there. In the south lounge there was even a request that he read the one book – *Vanity Fair* – to everyone, but he declined. He didn't like the book and the thought of eight old people being read to day after day, week after week, upset him.

They weren't children, he pointed out, and they had individual tastes. Once he looked up from *Jane Eyre* to find Sophie, as if she had just understood the importance of stories, standing in the doorway, listening intently. It made him stop reading. A silence fell. At last a cracked old voice asked if William read to her too, at night, and there was laughter. Sophie said that that would be telling, but, laying a hand on William's shoulder and smiling, she told nonetheless. One of the old ladies got it into her head then that they would be leaving soon to get married and that they would never come back. She wouldn't be persuaded otherwise, weeping as William continued with *Jane Eyre* and Sophie held her hands. Soon her weeping spread to the others, who wept – it had to be assumed, for they were quite unable to speak – for husbands, wives, brothers, sisters, children, friends. Wept for the flatness of the land, even. For the frequency of the winds. For their childhoods, so much more present to them now than their middle years. For the hour of their death.

There were weeping sessions in all the lounges at this time (the elderly rarely sobbed, not having the strength). They were usually brought about in the same way, one of the patients, for no apparent reason, starting to cry, and the others, after an ineffectual attempt to comfort him, following. Once under way, the weeping couldn't be stopped, but had to run its course. (There was one afternoon, William could have sworn, when all the patients in all the lounges, as in response to some calamitous intimation borne on the wind, wept simultaneously.)

It was after one of these sessions that William – he had known that something was approaching, some storm of the body or the spirit – lost control. It was as though, after the weeks of happy clowning, of strange friendships with so many of the elderly, of lovemaking now diffident, now passionate, of the weeping sessions and the profound still silences which came after them, he had become too rich. Too expectant in spirit. Sometimes he could tell when he was about to be overcome, and he would withdraw, the fit of mirth or sadness taking place in his room. His lovemaking with Sophie had perhaps begun it all, but for all her sensuality and idealism she couldn't contain it. It went beyond her, sweeping some-times through the lounges, leaving the elderly as confused and awed as, weeks before, they had been entertained and delighted. Wondering if he was going off his head, William stalked the doctor on his visits. Should he consult him or keep his own counsel? Several times he was on the verge of addressing him, but always he passed by instead. How he did so was remarkable: with relief, waving his hands and smil-ing, as though, at the last moment, he had been sure that this neat and bespectacled man, fussy with himself and fussy with the elderly, wringing his hands more often than he used them, could tell him nothing he didn't know already. The seizures were a stage in recovery. The sudden spring after the long winter; the chaotic thaw after the deadly frost. A kind of delirious loosening. He explained to Sophie that this was how he understood it, but she was suspicious, uneasy, afraid that this middle-aged man she had become involved with was disturbed. So, not wanting to put her off, to lose her, he learnt to hide what he was feeling when he was with her. And soon the pretence that he had recovered himself was complete (even he himself occasionally almost taken in).

He had rarely known such extremes. Incomprehensible drives into mourning and celebration. There would be the sounds and smells of the distant past – a setting for grief; and then, as if a switch had been thrown, of the recent past – a setting for gladness and celebration. The impression was not of arbitrariness, though; it all seemed to be happening for a purpose, one of which he needn't be afraid. Should he visit Miss Friel again? An extreme creature herself, she might understand the purpose of extremes. Might even be moved to speak on the subject, if not on any other. He toyed with the idea, but always passed by her door (a new notice, "Silence for All Souls", had appeared), as he had passed by the doctor.

He spent more and more time in the garden (though he knew it wasn't the time of year for such work), because his new energy demanded outlets. And gardening allowed him to collect himself. He particularly liked digging, for with each thrust or cut of the spade he could call out, sing, laugh, curse, and there was no one to hear him. There was a long border, uncultivated for years, which he dug over again and again, and in which he planned to plant leeks and onions and sprouts. Here especially – piling the earth, shaping the border into a perfect rectangle again – he was able to convince himself that his strange new energies were subject to laws as agreeable and far-seeing as those which governed other tides, other cycles.

Just occasionally, though, the closeness of his behaviour to the most erratic episodes in his past alarmed him. Drink had done something like this to him once – that exhausting familiarity with the poles of his being – but now it was happening without drink. Was he damaged? Deprived of the ability to act moderately? Doomed for the rest of his days to move senselessly between woe and ecstasy? Thinking that he might have destroyed whatever made equability and moderation possible, he thought again of speaking to the doctor. Again however, nodding proudly, he passed him by. As if toying with his expertise in order to assure himself that he had no need of it. That his condition was not of the body but of the spirit. (Stages in the soul's descent, in its check and recovery: those wouldn't be the doctor's terms, William was sure, were he to stop him in one of the corridors and unburden himself).

Then he began to get better. And soon he was sure that it had passed. To those who asked, he gave conventional explanations: it had been difficult to adjust to so much old age and death; he had become overtired; his mother's murder had affected him belatedly. Conspicuously, the minister was not one of those who asked, though he had made it obvious, walking round William like an unsolicited consultant, that he knew that something was wrong. William had sensed that he had a diagnosis to offer, and that it would be as relevant, probably, as the doctor's would be irrelevant. But he hadn't wanted to hear it. Why consult a lover of weaknesses? A connoisseur of the fallen world?

As if, though, his excitement had subsided too far, he recovered his composure only to lose it to boredom. The place became too small for him. Perhaps, in his excitement, he had glimpsed possibilities for himself not to be realised in the Montgomery. He walked the corridors as if to show that they led nowhere. Sat in the lounges as if awaiting release, repatriation (but where was his country?). It got so bad that he didn't see why he should read to people who understood so little; help them to eat if they didn't want to eat – let them die instead; help them to the lavatory if they didn't care whether they soiled themselves or not; post letters for them if the letters were full of senile gossip and the recipients (if they hadn't died long ago) would be bored or distressed to read them. Surely he was intended for something higher? To be neither one thing nor another was to be insulted. Not

176

quite a gardener, not quite a nurse, not quite an entertainer, not quite a waiter: "not quite", he feared, qualified him almost entirely. Sure that he was meant for something else, he withdrew to his room whenever he could. When he tried to imagine the world beyond the Montgomery, however, the world in which he might do this something else, he found that he had lost the ability. What he pictured was a vastly expanded version of the Montgomery. The world as an institution, the poison of time in everyone's veins. Multitudinous debilities. In squares and corridors the sick tending the sick. In recesses, the dying. But this, he felt sure, couldn't possibly be right. Alarmed, he attempted, using each of his senses in turn, to recover the world he hadn't known he had lost. (What sights? What sounds? What smells?) But he didn't succeed; and so remained shut in, an exile; but an exile without an exile's memories.

Then he thought of a plan. He would get to know some of the visitors – influential-looking sons, for example – in the hope that one of them might offer him a job, or know of someone who might be able to do so. He would cultivate such visitors, relatives, assiduously. Almost all of the professions were represented, Sophie had told him. The cream of Scottish middle-class life (what else?) filtered through these homes. Senile ex-businessmen still discussed stocks and shares with their astute sons. Still got serious about shooting and property. Surely therefore he would find something for himself soon? He imagined the conversations he would have, the ways in which he would present himself, and he imagined a proud but unobtrusive departure. The thought of departure: it was this that relaxed him and allowed him to become almost himself again, attentive, amusing, industrious.

And Sophie? It was a measure of his distraction that he thought (if he thought about it at all) that there was a good chance that she would come with him. That she might find it possible to replace her passion to transform the Montgomery with some other passion. That a relationship which had arisen in the Montgomery – and might only be possible there – could be transplanted. Woman as helper, as ground bass for male achievement: it must have been some such notion, spawned by pride perhaps, that affected him at this time.

With the approach of Christmas, visitors appeared who weren't seen during the rest of the year, drawn by the season from the narrow circle of their charity. Some came with gifts, walking the corridors boldly and cheerily, as out of long familiarity with the place, others made no attempt to appear at ease at all, but stood apologetically in the entrance hall, or moved furtively, sometimes bearing flowers, in the corridors. Others still, performing for each other, acted as if they couldn't understand why they hadn't developed into regular visitors, as if their negligence was as inexplicable as it was inexcusable. And the regular visitors – those who came at the same time once or twice a week, with the same greetings, jokes and enquiries – became grand in their solicitousness. Strong in the belief that Christmas (this Christmas, next Christmas, some Christmas) could make a lasting difference, that the transcendent could surprise even the demented, they pulled up their chairs in the lounges or dormitories and smiled and smiled and smiled again. Sherries were poured, boxes of chocolates passed around, anecdotes (as if in this, if not in anything else, the Montgomery aspired to unity) carried from lounge to lounge. Family raconteurs got going, the elderly – straining often from an abyss of deafness or confusion – propped up so that they could hear how John or Richard or Betty had elaborated a favourite joke or story. (The day that Aunt Catherine sneezed her false teeth into a cake. The day the vicar fell from the pulpit. The day the garage blew away.) Matron produced a tape recorder and tapes of Christmas carols were played, neither so loudly that conversation was affected nor so softly that some insult to Christmas seemed to be intended. It was one of William's tasks to see that each lounge had its share of carols each day. An hour, he decided, would be enough. The hour up, he would come in to take the tape recorder away, with the air of one who, left to himself, would have organised Christmas very differently. (If he could not have said what the true icons were – could not even have pointed in their direction – he knew that, whatever they were, they were being suffocated.)

Another of his tasks was to put up the Christmas decorations. Unpacking the box in which they were kept, he came across, in addition, paper hats and crackers and plastic whistles. The paraphernalia of facile celebration. It could have been a children's home. Or a rugby club. Dismayed, he put some of the decorations up in the lounges and corridors and entrance hall, then put the box away in a cupboard and locked it. But matron said he had been mean. What was wrong with him? Had he no sense of occasion? Where were the orange suns and the silver stars and the lines of green and yellow ringlets and the bunches of plastic holly? He unlocked the cupboard and got the box out again and, bloody-minded now, put up everything he could find, including a huge plastic cross with jaded paper angels dangling from it. May and Margaret said that they had never seen the place looking so festive, but William, his feeling of offence deep, said that it looked to him like vulgar propitiation.

His plan to ingratiate himself with the visitors wasn't going well. He would wait until he saw a male visitor at a loose end, or at the end of his tether (it happened quite often). Then he would ask him if he would like a cup of tea or coffee, suggesting that he accompany him while he made it. Sometimes they came, sometimes they didn't, but whichever they did, William was dismayed, for he was either treated as a dedicated nurse, to be consulted about medical matters (a lot of the men suffered from dyspepsia, it seemed, and headaches, and one of them had piles), or as an eccentric handyman, a character, to be patronised. To a florid and overweight young man, for example, he confessed, as they waited for the kettle to boil, that he could do with a change. Time for a move. Oh yes. The florid young man just looked at him, however, as if the context of visiting in a home for the elderly made such confessions unintelligible. William repeated his remark, elaborating a little, but with the same result. Eventually, having finished his cup of tea, the young man wandered away. Exasperated, William smashed a plate on the linoleum floor of the kitchen, and then – as in some savage game for the frustrated and dispossessed – kicked the pieces about the room. At this rate, he would be as unpopular with the visitors as he was popular with the patients. Understood by neither, he would spin like a top, his idiosyncrasies would multiply, and he might finally be asked to leave whether he wanted to or not.

He made a few more attempts, this time working on the wives of the influential-looking sons as well as on the influential-looking sons themselves. Still without luck, however. He was made to feel a fool; a man who didn't know his place; one who was betraying matron's trust; one who, if this was how he was going to behave, ought to be cast into outer darkness; one who might even be a little unhinged. He began to dislike the visitors, soon extending this to the world from which they came. Their odours, ambitions, manners, clothes, opinions, gestures: weren't they horribly characteristic of that world? Sometimes he thought that the visitors actually stank of it. Stank of it as an animal stinks of the place in which it has been foraging. The perfumes, the aftershave, the cigarette smoke, cigar smoke, the gin. Odours of scented plushness, but rank odours, too. More smells than he could name. Smells he hadn't known in years.

And with this dislike of the visitors came a renewed pity for the elderly. With sons and daughters, nephews and nieces like these, who could blame them for cowering, losing their memories, fouling themselves, refusing to speak? A world well lost. He thought that his place might be with the elderly after all, exiles like himself, and with a sort of sentimental relish he turned to them conscientiously again, reading as before, joking, helping with the preparations for the Christmas party, even assisting some of the old men to the lavatory (a task he had previously shirked). Sentimental attentiveness: he suspected that he was indeed guilty of this, but wasn't it better than boredom and indifference, and mightn't it lead, if not to grace, then to a kind of constancy? To Sophie he joked that the terrible decorations had gone to his head. It was their fault: there were orange ringlets about his heart as well as in the lounges. There were all-purpose carols in his soul.

So he came to avoid the visitors whenever he could, ashamed that he had hoped to persuade them to help him.

One day, however, hurrying to his room at visiting hour, he saw someone he knew. He tried to walk past her, but he knew that she had stopped behind him and was wondering if it was really him, William Templeton, that she had seen. He believed that he was going to pass on, nonetheless, leaving her to wonder about this moment by a fish tank in an unlighted corridor forever, but to his surprise he found that he had stopped and was turning, slowly turning. And slowly, very slowly, like one about to float or dance – as if to meet someone again after a long time and in a strange place is to feel that you have cheated time, gravity even – she was coming towards him, quizzical, friendly, head slightly to one side. He didn't want to appear menial or ashamed; he didn't want to grip his white jacket and tug it downwards. But he feared that, as if he was a member of the Montgomery first and an individual second, he did just this. Her name, he recalled, was Lesley, her husband's David, and there were male twins, Oliver and Mark. The wondering slowness of her approach it was that allowed him to remember all this. He was even able to recall the timbre of her voice: gentle and low, very pleasing to the ear, encouraging. The memory of it relaxed him, made him glad. Might even have moved him to embrace her had he not been wearing the white jacket.

"It is William, isn't it? William Templeton?"

"The very man, Lesley. Back from the dead."

"I'm glad to see it. How long have you been here? And are you a nurse?"

"I've been here about four months. Not a nurse, no, but kind of. In a place like this, you could say, the intention is all."

"I see," she said, smiling. "I still see Margo, you know ..."

His wish was to be told only a little about Margo. What would he do with too much information?

"She's well," Lesley said carefully, "and will be glad to hear that you are. Are you well?"

"Yes. Now I am."

"I'll tell her so."

At this point the man he had remembered as David approached, sauntering. His name was indeed David, but William realised that he hadn't remembered him accurately. Or that, since their last meeting, David had changed, been corrupted somehow. He had a casualness, a blandness which seemed to issue from the belief that there were no limits of any kind anymore. That in the worlds of the young, the middle-aged and the elderly anything went. He didn't recognise William at all, couldn't get it out of his head that his wife was consulting him about something medical. When, mocking him openly, she pointed out who William was, he tried to hide his embarrassment by shaking William's hand, but simply communicated it more strongly. Then, his wife half turned away now, he seemed, as in an excess of idleness, to saunter on the spot.

For an instant, then, the marriage of Lesley and David was a meteorite from the world beyond fallen at William's feet. How could he avoid regarding it?

"We should really go and see Grandfather," Lesley said, as in retreat from her husband's foolishness beginning to move away. "Maybe you know him, William? Albert Clow."

"Oh yes," William said. "He told me my teeth and gums were done for."

David laughed loudly – a hollow booming laugh – and might have tried to shake William's hand again had William not been looking closely at his wife. Lesley appeared to walk off with David then, but what she did was to lead him away and station him at a distance. Then she returned.

"Things won't be the same again, William," she said, laying a hand on his arm. "They can't be. You know that as well as anyone. But do write to Margo. She's a generous woman. She'll be glad to hear from you. Goodbye."

"Tell her you found me, as young as ever, in an old folks' home!"

He stood where she had left him, under red, blue and yellow Christmas decorations which looped their way (rustling a little as they did so) like frivolous snakes towards the south lounge, and there – now like strands of hair under a clasp – came together beneath a huge paper bell. Weak sunlight came and went. A declining December sky. Other visitors passed him, the florid young man and his fat young wife among them. He paid no attention to them at all. Only when the last ones – speaking of bananas as the fruit for the elderly ("once they're peeled, of course") – had passed did he turn. And then he seemed just a little uncertain of his destination, as if, disturbed both by the Montgomery and the world beyond, he was seeking some other world.

March 3rd, 1984

I'm not proud of my room when I consider asking the children here. They're embarrassed enough as it is when we walk in parks, sit in cafes, go to cinemas. No longer a driver, I can't take them anywhere they'd find really exciting. A time may come, I fear, when they don't want to come and see me at all. But until then the arrangement (The Arrangement, as Margo, with regretful emphasis, calls it) will stand. She will honour it, I know, as long as she can.

Sixty yards or so away the car stops. It's not a car I ever drove myself, though I drove one like it. Kenneth and Kathleen get out from the back. Do they see me? Anyway, they don't wave. They are still talking to their mother, receiving instructions. I'd love to walk down and speak to her, but I daren't, it's not part of the arrangement. The arrangement requires me to keep my distance now. I stay where I am, hands in the pockets of my raincoat. A slight wind – slight but cold – troubles the space between myself and the children. The grass is pinned back on the bare earth. For some reason, I have an impression of approaching bareness everywhere.

They approach me slowly, my teenage children, hesitantly, talking to each other. Jokes? Mutual encouragement? Curses? I walk to meet them, suspecting that the bars of chocolate I've bought are melting in my pocket. The car has driven off (did Margo wave to me?) and the street with its severe little gusts of wind is deserted except for me and the children. Only sixty yards and yet they seem to take ages to reach me: I who used to say good morning and goodnight to my children in a variety of accents – French, German, American – am now at a loss to know how to greet them. I sway, I think, and fear that they notice, though I'm not bad today, not bad at all. Yesterday

I couldn't have managed it, though of course it might be claimed that had it been yesterday I'd have kept my worst for the day before, or for today.

I don't know how to greet them. Neither the tone nor the words.

"How are things?" I venture.

Kenneth, face pale, freckles prominent, speaks for them both, smiling as he does so. He has always had the habit of smiling while he speaks. It is as if the child's thrill at the fact and power of speech has never left him. Add to this the impression he gives of choosing his words with an exceptional awareness of those he is talking to and you can see why I'm charmed.

No less by Kathleen. She listens to her brother with admiration, as though what he is doing is bringing an approved script to life in a remarkable way. Now and then she smiles at me obliquely, her air that of one drawing attention to hidden depths in his words, depths she personally will be pondering for weeks to come.

He is giving an account of their week. I am glad of this because it provides me with the context I need if I'm to respond at all. When he stops it will not be so hard for me. Kathleen takes my arm (checking first to see if it really is an arm) even although we are still standing, and even although Kenneth is speaking more and more intently. He is describing the visit by fat Aunt Mary and suddenly, after he has said how difficult she finds it to stand up out of armchairs, suddenly we are walking. It is Kathleen who starts us off and then determines our easy pace, our rhythm. My son in charge of speech, my daughter of movement. One day they will have to be praised for this. How quickly we have come to the end of this street, where the gusts of wind are unsettlingly severe, and are turning into a warmer street, tree-lined and with untroubled houses set well back from the road.

Kathleen isn't really listening to Kenneth now. I realise that their plan is that he shouldn't stop talking. Always a good talker, he is exploiting his ability in circumstances they clearly consider to be desperate. To keep me speechless. But what might I say that would be so terrible? Or is it what I don't say, haven't said, can't say? Immediately I realise what they're up to I feel weak and can't think of anything to say at all.

By the end of our time together (one and a half hours, four o'clock to five-thirty) I notice that there are beads of sweat on my children's foreheads. I have exhausted them. Not by talking too much or by remaining fearfully silent (eventually I was able to mention moments from our past that I think will never lose their significance). I have exhausted them by being what I have become. What I have become but once was not. Once not what I now am. By being what I have become which is not sufficient and with hardly a hint of a comeback anymore. With this and doubtless with other things I have exhausted them, my children.

They leave me where they met me and go to the car. The door is opened from the inside – something horrible about this. They get in but – how strange! – they wave more feelingly than they get in. The car, as in consideration of my solitary station, goes the length of the street in first gear. Vanishes.

The evening of this day I'm bad again and going towards what used to be my home. Not even its lights, charging at me over the head of the pillar box, charging, receding, charging, are familiar. The gravel is hard to fall on but the lawn when I gain it is a delight. The fiercely lit rectangles in the house so high above me are all I need. For what? For what I can't exactly say, but it's preferable. To what? To what I can't exactly say either, but I'm here and here, tilting and drowning, tilting and surfacing, I'll stay. For haven't I stayed before – many more or less uninterrupted years and my wife grown more generous than ever? My wife. I've rung the bell, I realise, and, looped over the railings a little, I see that Margo is answering it. Everything inside is lit with a terrible, an insistent, an exclusive brightness. I think I see the children – poised as in eternal expectation of bad news – half way up, or down, the stairs. Bad news. The worst news. Am I not that again? Margo is saying "no" and "no more" and "not now" and I know from the tone of her voice that ... What? I stand upright, stand to attention, salute. My last joke for a time. Forever? I strongly suspect it but can't say why, which makes it seem more certain still. So the last joke is a line over which you trip, falling with the sounds of polite strained and appalled laughter behind you? Lines in both directions, though. As ever, choices. I had hoped, apparently, to cross one which divides here from there, there where Margo and the children are. How would it be if I were taken back? Terrible obligations! Ghastly pursuit of the gods of renewal! Maybe therefore it's just as well I'm being led by someone (who? oh who?) across the lawn and the gravel and then out. Out.

This is a lane now. The most backward of back lanes. And that is a full moon, blood red over the troughs of heaving refuse. There is surely a cat around. Yes, but I cannot rise to stroke it. As well, for it doesn't want to be stroked. Its wish is to forage. It is fat, it is gorged. On what? That I couldn't say with any confidence. I too was full but have been sick it seems.

CHAPTER THIRTEEN

On Christmas morning in the darkness William woke not once but three times, the first with dread, the second angrily, the third with a feeling of defeat. Three selves, three awakenings. And each time the wind howling and the curtains, as if addressing those in bed, appealing to them, seeming to billow insistently inwards. In the corridors such a wind – some freakish pagan pentecost – would agitate the decorations and, after a time, cause them to fall. All would fall and Christmas would be cancelled. There would be no such wind, however, no such cancellation. Christendom, standing to attention, would sing and pray as usual. He had wakened first, though it was Sophie who delighted in Christmas. Propped on one elbow, he stared at the door, listening. His apprehension about the day was extraordinary, its roots, he supposed, in some region of the spirit it would take him months to uncover. Gently he shook Sophie awake, amused at her excitement when told what day it was, but embarrassed that he couldn't share it with her. Couldn't share it at all.

"Christmas," she smiled, combing out her hair with her fingers.

"Yes," he said. "Christmas."

They exchanged presents, Sophie taking pleasure in trying to guess hers (a bracelet, bought where William had bought his camera) in the darkness. "Now get up and try on these socks," she said.

If it was more of a command than he was used to so early in the morning, William didn't mind, for today, Christmas Day, he would be happy, he felt, to submit to any authority that was spontaneous and vital. (Could he be sure of finding his way otherwise?) Naked by the bed except for his socks, he stood to attention and saluted.

"They fit beautifully," he said. "Beautifully."

But Sophie, snapping on the light and throwing back the bedclothes, banished his piece of clowning as though it should never have been.

"Get dressed," she said.

Such crossness from Sophie seemed to William uncharacteristic. He couldn't say that it was premenstrual tension, for it wasn't. It seemed deeper and more particular than that – Christmas had unsettled her too. It went before him into the corridors and lounges and dining room. It troubled the atmosphere. At one point he noticed that she had stepped outside and was standing in the garden, arms folded, looking up at the lowering sky (if he had been asked for a caption, he might have offered "rebel in chains"). He tapped lightly on a window to attract her attention but she didn't turn or look up. Later, he approached her with a cup of coffee, but she contrived to dodge away. He thought she might have responded to a bunch of flowers but there were no florists nearby and anyway it was Christmas Day. He could, of course, have pinched one from one of the residents, but all the flowers he saw that morning were wilting, past their best. He would just have to let her be, not allow her to seem to be querying him, the point or worth of his existence. It exasperated him that he had been so quick to think this – that it was because of some lingering insufficiency in himself that her mood had suddenly darkened.

It relieved him, however, to see that most of the elderly were as remote from the day as he was, but it saddened him too. (Relieved because it meant that he wouldn't be conspicuous, saddened because it rather suggested a community of the disheartened.) Those who weren't remote were not so much alert as agitated, struggling to recover whatever sense of occasion or festival they once had. And those who had to be told what day it was repeated the word "Christmas" slowly, either with a dawning sense of its significance, or, shaking their heads, with little sense of its significance at all. Such greetings as there were were aimed, William felt, more at the dead than at the living. This conspiratorial tenderness in the north lounge, for instance, this clapping of the hands, this low singing that was interrupted as though by a blow: hadn't it arisen with the dear dead in mind? Here and there, too, scraps of paper were produced on which, in childish aged hand, greetings had been scrawled – some of these for William and Sophie and Margaret and May, it was true – but some to be delivered elsewhere. Elsewhere. Anywhere. William stepped out into the corridor, therefore, waited for a few moments, and then, returning, announced that the messages had been successfully delivered, gratefully received. Knowing smiles – more knowing than any he had ever seen – were invariably the response to this.

There was to be a service at eleven, in the east lounge, followed by lunch at twelve-thirty. William took three of the patients to it in wheelchairs (amused at his ease and dexterity with wheelchairs now – he who hadn't been able to walk straight a year ago). For each he had a story, which he told in a quiet voice, leaning forwards. And each listened, as if this story was part of the service – the service itself, even. As if in the coils of William's narrative might be the good tidings long promised, long denied. For Miss Bruce he had a story from his childhood, an episode long forgotten. He was walking with his sister in the hills and before them, suddenly before them, was a man who could have been a shepherd or a poacher. He was kneeling, very still, as if he had held the position for some time. They were reluctant to approach, but the man beckoned to them, and when they came up to him they saw a sheep on its side, in labour. The man asked them to touch it, saying, "It was lucky to be touched by the bairns." William did so, feeling a violent tensing beneath the thick damp wool, but Marion, who was squeamish, turned away. At which the shepherd, looking up, leered toothlessly.

He came to the end of the story just as he was settling Miss Bruce in the east lounge. It happened with the other stories too – he finished them just as he was settling Miss Marshall and Mr Lawson, a coincidence of timing which greatly pleased him. In wheelchairs side by side, their heads not drooping now, but craning, expectant, three old people to whom he had just told stories, the stories as fresh to him as they had been to them. And all perhaps complementary. One about a lamb that wouldn't be born; another about the first fish he had caught – nine years old, he had cried for hours because it had been so little; the third about a time when, across swampland and into a copse, he had been chased by a mother swan.

There were those who refused to attend, however, remaining bitterly in their favourite corners, the reasons given being a dislike of Christmas, a dislike of the minister, a dislike of the sound of aged voices singing hymns, a dislike of prayers and of assembly. Matron made several attempts to round them up, but without success. Muttering about "impossible natures", she asked William to see what he could do; but, faced by such bitter obduracy and by rages so deep they made the patients and their chairs tremble, he could do nothing but stand and pity, stand and admire. The reverent submission to Christmas and this virulent resistance to it: he admired both equally.

Miss Friel was one of these. Though sure that she wouldn't go to the service, William was unprepared for the manner of her refusal. Smiling, she took him by both hands and walked slowly into the corridor with him, standing just outside her door. She wouldn't let go of his hands and, after a few minutes, he didn't want her to. Thus, like lovers unable to part – a sort of exquisite idling – they stood for some moments. At last, reluctantly letting go of his left hand, she shook him firmly by the right, still smiling (she might have been smiling since he had last seen her, weeks ago). And said, her voice thin, high and fading: "enjoy yourself." Only after a moment or two, though, when he was out of the room and descending the stairs – descending them with an obscure but deepening sense of purpose – did he realise that she had actually spoken. He stood stock still and seemed to hear the words again, louder now. "Enjoy yourself."

Standing at the back of the congregation, William whispered to Sophie, who was beside him, that Miss Friel had spoken. Had bid him enjoy himself. She looked at him in disbelief. But then, as matron and the minister entered, the minister in a black gown, matron out of her uniform, in a blue dress, she quietly slipped her right hand into his left pocket and began – at first as if trying to conceal her purpose – to massage his groin. When he looked at her, she raised her eyebrows and mouthed, in mock-ecstatic slow motion: "enjoy yourself." He looked down and grasped the back of the chair in front of him. In it was old Miss Adams, already half asleep. (Or was she ill? Dying?) As Sophie continued to massage him, William, in an effort to control himself, fixed his gaze on the back of Miss Adams' neck. Down from the neck would be the vertebrae, crumbling probably, and down from them the pelvis, a mere cage now for bloodless loins. But the back of an adult neck: wasn't it almost unchanged from infancy? Notwithstanding the yellow skin, the moles with hairs growing from them, the dead white hair? Desperately aroused (such a private excitement on such a public occasion), half trying to disengage himself from Sophie – who, each time he glanced at her, slowly mouthed "enjoy yourself" – William bent forwards. It seemed to him that he wanted to do one or the other of two things: press his lips to Miss Adams' neck, or tell her, whisper to her – deeply whisper to her! – a story. Could he somehow manage both, making the rhythm of his harmonisation (story with kiss, kiss with story) express some of this dreadful excitement that Sophie – her hand in his pocket as quick and deft as a tongue – was making him feel? No; mere craziness. Mere craziness! He turned his attention to the minister's words – his address had been under way for some moments – hoping that they would allow him to compose himself.

"… a special day, this day of the Lord's coming. And special regardless of our age, health and circumstances. You who are hard of hearing, or lame, or confused, can still know the richness of this day. The unique richness of its promise. To turn into the paths of redemption after a lifetime in the shallows of disappointment is, let me assure you, always possible. Always. There are no full stops in the spiritual life. All is possible, rich …"

The minister was standing at an old lectern on what looked like a polished segment of tree trunk. Now and then he leaned on it, as though it was a true pulpit high up in the corner of some church, and it creaked and moved. It didn't seem as if he intended it to move, but, when it did, he used the movements to suggest the precariousness of the Christian life, smiling tensely and wrestling with it.

"… we are always as though between the certainty of God and the certainty of His absence. We move uneasily, craving a deeper knowledge, a deeper certainty, but we move nonetheless. For movement with respect to God is not like movement in the world; it is not measurable …'

Sophie's hand had slipped from William's pocket. Glancing at her, he saw that, having been as aroused as he, she was becoming tense, angry. It was as if the minister's manner had killed their passion not just for today but forever.

"So however old and frail we may be, we stand an equal chance with God. Youth does not give us an advantage here. Youth with all its arrogance is not better positioned to receive God's grace. Oh no! If any are favoured, it is those who, with the years, have become purged of their egotism. So take heart on this day, and remember Christ."

The skin on the minister's face, William thought, seemed tighter today than usual. And the face redder. The skin tighter and the face redder and the words less controlled. The sermon did not seem to be his own. Did you labour in the pulpit if the words were not your own? He had begun by preaching with a sort of mannered quietness, but now he had become as though severed from his own words. The lectern rocked again and the minister's head jerked forwards, backwards, forwards. His words might have been jabs in the side, so strangely was he moving. And the words "arraign" and "arraignment" – grinding words, absolute words – came to William. Could you be arraigned by your own words? Brought low by your own phrases, metaphors? Cut down?

Behind the minister and to the left sat matron at the piano, hands in her lap, utterly impassive. There was only to be one hymn, William had heard, and only two verses of it at that; the congregation was not up to any more, apparently.

"So let us lift up our hearts in gladness on this day. He who has made it so that age can be as youth in matters of the spirit was born in a manger, in Bethlehem of Judaea. And in our gladness let us sing verses four and five of hymn number one hundred and ..."

Under cover of the sound of hymn books being shakily opened Sophie leaned over to William and asked why the minister wasn't in "a real church". In her flat shoes her toes were squirming with irritation. The elderly, dewlaps jiggling, grew long necks in order to look at each other before they rose (as though, to be able to rise at all, each had to be sure that he wouldn't rise alone).

A passion for oblivion could be heard in the singing, if singing it was. When William sang, however, it was with a defiant richness which surprised him. His baritone beside Sophie's eager soprano might have heartened the occasion considerably had they been allowed to sing more than two verses. Should he lead the congregation in another verse therefore? Make it possible for those who wanted to let go (to bleed or to praise) to do so?

"Let us pray ..." The minister's tone was sepulchral-majestic, but still he appeared to be wrestling with the lectern.

In the silence, then, Miss Adams, who hadn't risen for the hymn, fainted sideways in her chair. Quickly gathering her up in his arms, William carried her out and bore her as far from the east lounge and the broken muttering of the final prayer ("...father who art ...hallowed ... name ...") as he could.

At a point where two corridors met – a point where, because the roof was high and arched in order to join two wings of the building, there was unusual silence, resonant silence – he lowered her into a chair. And there, saying that she was too old for worship now, for the wheedling impatience of ministers, she eventually revived.

The idea was that the staff should eat separately; with some of the patients in need of assistance at the table, they wouldn't have much chance of enjoying their meal otherwise. William helped Mr Clow and Miss Adams, Miss Adams, smiling gratefully, finding enough strength to pop the occasional bit of turkey into her helper's mouth. It had been so, William remembered, when the children were young – that patient mimicry of the mouth movements you wanted them to make.

Young and old coaxed into sustenance. Open – close – eat. Open – close – eat.

Mealtimes in the Montgomery were invariably quiet, because the elderly couldn't do justice both to their food and their companions. But this Christmas lunch was the quietest mealtime William could remember. Now it was like the last meal before exile, now like part of some remorseless plan of matron's to sustain the illusion of festival, now like something so little desired by the elderly it had the appearance of sadism, now like a scientific experiment (how much turkey did people over eighty actually eat?) and now like an advertisement for some worthy but hard-pressed Home or Hospice. Many appearances, many faces, but the occasion dropping through them like a stone.

Soon turkey and roast potatoes and sprouts – a quarter eaten, half eaten, barely touched – were growing cold on twenty-five plates. Sophie, William, May and Margaret looked at each other but didn't speak, didn't move. Another course – jelly and ice-cream – was promised but it was as if the patients, by their remarkable silence, were declining it. Sophie, perhaps thinking that this might help to explain the general disaffection, sampled a piece of turkey. The collective pulse dropped. Dropped further. Further. The fluorescent lighting clicked and winked. Someone was heard to ask why they were still praying. May snorted. Somebody else laughed. Then – but for a low moaning, almost inaudible – there was silence again. Outside also it was still, still and grey. (The morning wind had died, leaving a ravaged unmoving sky.)

William's last thought before he stood up (knocking over his chair) concerned the relationship between the unprecedented silence and the unprecedented loss of appetite. Did the silence come from the loss of appetite, or the loss of appetite from the silence, or both from some other source – some profound instinctive obduracy?

He didn't stop to pick up his chair, but moved to a corner of the dining room where, arms folded as in ostentatious supervision, he stood with his back to the wall.

He was smiling, he knew, but he didn't understand why. From her occasional glances of approval, though, it was as if Sophie did understand. His feeling was that he had been divested of the usual responsibilities in order to assume some greater responsibility. Was he bearing witness? If so, to what exactly and in whose name and why did he bear it with a smile? (If he had a certain dignity, withdrawn in the corner, it was partly because he believed he would soon be able to answer these questions.) He received further looks of approval – not just from Sophie now – which made him feel even more strongly that something was being expected of him. Was he simply to mark the afflicted state of this particular community on this particular day, imprinting it deeply on his memory? Or was he also to act? How? And in what spirit? Unusually still – watching and being watched, smiling and being smiled at – he asked these questions of himself. That someone had to stand where he was standing – a threshold, surely – was apparent. The spot might have been marked out for just this kind of occupation, for just this kind of desperate readiness.

Then, with a bang, the dining-room door opened and the minister entered dressed as Santa Claus. He had a large sack of gifts on his back and walked with a kind of mock-benevolent stoop, leering and looking to left and right. Behind him came matron, smiling as if she had done well to find a Santa Claus prepared to enter the Montgomery, and clapping as one does to alert others to the slowness of their appreciation.

So it was for this that he had been waiting? To this that his strange smile had been pointing? A terrific smile, William felt himself drawn down into it further, into its remorseless-ness, its inspired disenchantment. And moved forwards, knowing a concentration of mind and body that was like a release from all faltering.

"So take heart on this day," he said half sardonically, "and remember Christ."

All the presents had been gaily parcelled and named, and all were so light that if the sack had been cast into the morning wind it would have blown away over the walls of the Montgomery. There were cheap biros and two-handled plastic mugs with mottoes in small red letters and toothbrushes and framed photographs of the Montgomery (taken on a day more promising than this) and calendars and sea-shells and plastic egg cups. It was apparently the minister's belief that he alone should be allowed to distribute them, picking them from the sack one by one. But he found that, following behind, were Sophie and William, and that soon they were picking presents from the sack before he could get at them, trying by the manner of their giving to redeem the occasion a little.

It wasn't easy. Even those with little sense of occasion seemed to William to register offence – if only by laying down their gifts beside their plates of turkey and staring into space.

He caught up with the minister outside the dining room, cornering him before he could hurry away to take off his Santa Claus outfit. All that he could see, between the top of the huge white beard and the bottom of the hood, were his eyes. Sweating eyes. Jealous eyes. The eyes of a master of ceremonies. First they showed surprise, then alarm, then annoyance at betraying alarm: William was as sure of the sequence as he was of the fact that many of the elderly who were being pushed or helped past him by Sophie, May and Margaret had wet or fouled themselves and on a normal lunchtime would not have done.

"So we're a lover of disguises are we, Reverend?" he heard himself say. "And we love acting it up with the very old and, I dare say, with the very young do we? I'll thank you to confine your dressing up in future to your dog-collar. Understand? And what about a bit of consultation? Or has that gone too? Condescension and tyranny! Condescension and tyranny right down the line! Screw the folks and screw your colleagues until the cows come home! Well I'm not going to allow it, Reverend, for eventually the cows do come home – not to mention the elderly – and there has to be someone to meet them. Not someone in disguise, either. Not some fraud."

"You're being very impertinent, Mr Templeton," the minister said, throwing off his hood. "Very impertinent indeed!"

Matron's office, high up in one of the wings of the Montgomery, had been converted by the minister for his own purposes. And they were peculiar purposes. Entering, William thought of it as a sort of coda to Christmas Day, a presentation of credentials, a declaration. Spread across the desk and on two tables beside it and pinned to all four walls were photographs of the starving. They were of many different sizes, some in colour, some in black and white. William hadn't seen colour photographs of the starving before, and he was horrified. By conveying weight and space and atmosphere so much more powerfully than black and white, by showing the effects of disease so much more vividly, as though for medical posterity, colour made it appear miraculous that the starving could stand or sit at all. Even as he looked – forced to acknowledge the photographs before he acknowledged the minister (of how many ceremonies a master?) – the limbs seemed to buckle a little more, the staring astonished eyes to become a little more sightless. One photograph in particular held him: in some hollow of the desert an old woman was dying, attended by a young woman with a baby strapped to her back. Behind them, darkened spray against the light, sand had been blown upwards from the rim of the hollow.

"More surprises from Santa Claus," William said, nodding, pointing. "Wind and death, I'd call that one. But what are you trying to say? I'm not ignorant of the world."

"I didn't imagine you were," the minister said, regarding the photograph William had pointed to. "I think you may be ignorant about me, though. You see me as one whose enterprises begin and end here, in the Montgomery. You see me as provincial. Isn't that so?"

"A big fish in a small pond, but one who has known bigger ponds," William said, trying to divide his attention between the minister and his photographs.

"And in what pond did you drown, William?" the minister countered. "I've always thought, you see, that you have the mark of one who has known drowning."

"Oh really," William said, as if the minister would have to be much more interesting than this if he was to hold William's attention.

"What you are trying to do, I'd say, is about the hardest thing one can do. Particularly in this culture." The minister had sat down, and William noticed that – as though it was to be worn again that day – his Santa Claus outfit was on the back of the chair. "Yes, to try and remake yourself in this culture is heroic, really. I take my hat off to you. Really I do! But observing you in the last few weeks I've thought … would you like to know what I've thought? I've thought you've looked cramped, as though you need more space, considerably more space, to complete your recovery. Many get so far and no further, you see. The last stages are the real challenge. Ah yes!"

"Are you trying to say that we don't have second chances any more? If you don't succeed the first time round, you've had it?"

Though he had looked away from the photographs to ask this, William appeared to be speaking from under their shadow. His left arm, as though to clear a space for himself, was slightly but insistently raised.

"There are second chances, but only the exceptional take them. The rest are broken." The minister spoke swiftly, summarily, as if any other manner might have allowed his words to get back at him. "But can I ask you – are you essentially the same the second time round as the first? Or very different?"

It was a question William had sometimes asked himself, and, as before, the answer took the form of a set of images, a reverie. He was in what looked like the garden of the house from which Margo had banished him. A tall fire was burning, and, in it, were his possessions. There were two presences, in the foreground himself, in the background a dark figure in the process of stealing away. His feeling was that it was imperative to identify the figure. But, awed by the fire in which most of what he held dear was being consumed, he couldn't move. A dark figure and himself watching it through the relentless fire. Sometimes (this time being one of them) he became able to move stealthily to the right round the fire; but the dark figure moved at the same time, always at the same time, into the shadow of some trees, where it paused as though awaiting him. At which he paused too. And so it remained: the fire burning and these two arrested figures.

"I sometimes think," William said, appearing to attend to the photographs again, "that the short answer to that is the only answer. The first time round I was a drunk; this time I'm not."

There was a silence. The minister seemed to be hoping for more, but William, wondering why he had spoken, said nothing. He had spoken as if to himself, but he couldn't understand why, for wasn't he in the presence of a lover of weaknesses – a spy, if you like? This was how you spoke to friends, or to a wife. He looked up defensively, to find the minister regarding him indulgently, as if he knew what William had left unsaid.

"Do not regret speaking, William," he said. "Your secret will be safe with me. Though it could be said that I knew of it already."

"Why, though, are we sitting here surrounded by all these photographs?" William asked, his manner as he stood up exasperated and challenging. But then he looked at them more closely, as if he had seen that the answer to this lay with them, if it lay anywhere.

"They hem you in?"

"One is aware of them."

"And so we should be – continually. They increase daily, the starving, did you know that? Or don't you have an opinion?"

"I'd have said, no, I'd not have thought they were increasing," William answered, made to feel that an absence of opinions on starvation was a kind of consent to it.

"The Church to which I belong isn't indifferent to these matters. It is widely engaged. And our emissaries aren't dressed up as Santa Claus either. There are other sides to our ministry besides the pulpit and Santa Claus. Oh yes! We don't just step from the one to the other and back again."

"I'm glad to hear it. Santa Claus was a mistake, if I may say so."

"You already have – very rudely too. One doesn't always attire oneself appropriately, I admit, but there are worse crimes than what you obviously regard as folksy sentimentality. Aren't there?"

"In my view," William said, standing over the minister, "Christmas has been ruined by two things – commercialism and sentimentality. A minister worth his salt should be saying so. Again and again. His pulpit ..."

"But I have no church, William," the minister said softly, almost appealingly. "That is my secret. I have The Church, but not a church. Parishes are at a premium, so why entrust one to a man in his late fifties and in poor health? I have blood pressure problems, you see. A giddy pulse."

Having said this, he appeared briefly to lose all interest, a kind of pained blankness overcoming him.

"High blood pressure?" William said slowly. "High blood pressure? I see."

For a moment he had the air of one who thinks he may be on the verge of a discovery. High blood pressure, alcoholism, amnesia, senility, heart disease: might there be an essential link between these conditions, light shed on one proving to be light shed on all? Himself, the minister, the elderly explained by the one law? He raised himself on his toes, lightly, as if to hasten such a vision. But then, appearing to see more folly than promise in it, turned to the photographs once more. As though to be chastened; instructed in the elements of a darker vision.

"It may not be as unrelated to the photographs as one might think," the minister resumed, coughing. "As I was saying, the Church to which I belong isn't indifferent to these things. There is a Commission, of which I'm a member. I've been a member for sixteen years. Indeed, I was one of the founders ... Once or twice a year we go abroad to apprise ourselves of what is happening. We visit colonies of the starving. We make reports. We give money and try to see to it that it is well spent. But we haven't been noticing improvements ... Did you know any of this?"

"No."

"That's because you've been too concerned with saving yourself. But let us assume that you are saved now. As saved as you will ever be. As intact. As ready. Let us assume that.

Now I have a proposition to make ... Engaged in remaking yourself, as you undoubtedly are ..."

Here, as though troubled by some impulse behind his words, he broke off.

"... undoubtedly are. Yes. But why stop here? In the Montgomery? Will your passion for the elderly endure, deepen? How d'you know you'll not weary of them, with their fads, their monosyllables and their smells? (Maybe you've done so already?) Is this really your vocation? How d'you know that in ten years time at Christmas you too will not be dressing up as Santa Claus? Anyway, how, I ask you, do you bring the gospel to the elderly, the confused, except by ..."

"Santa Claus today was an insult as I said," William muttered, as if his mind suddenly was on greater insults still. "And if I should ever find myself dressing up as Santa Claus ..."

"You'd take to the bottle again. Yes, you probably would, wouldn't you? But before then, before then – and I'm offering it to you because, with my uncertain health, I've been advised not to go again – there's the Commission. You could go as my representative. You could keep me informed. You could help a little, too; the understaffing is unbelievable. It'll make you or break you, William." Here the minister paused and looked away, giving William the impression that he might take as much pleasure in the thought of him broken as in the thought of him restored. "See it, if you like, as the final stage in the remaking of yourself. Refuse the offer and let me tell you that you'll understand what it means to be stuck. Stasis! Stasis! Santa Claus in a cul-de-sac awaiting you with open arms!"

"How long for?" William asked, feeling that he had been mistaken for someone else, that there had been a confusion of destinies.

"A few weeks." Then, suddenly smiling – one of those

smiles which, knowing it is not really a smile, postures in its falseness – the minister added: "But I should say that, if you don't go, it'll not be easily apparent why matron should want to keep on a bloodless assistant."

He started to roll up the photographs of the starving then, putting an elastic band round each of them, patting their ends – a pedantic dismantling of the scene which, William was now sure, he had prepared with angry relish. The scene in the garden came to William again, but this time the fire was dying down and there was apparently no reason to watch it anymore. Beside the trees the dark figure, always with his back to the concerns of the firewatcher, stood waiting.

"And so," the minister said, appearing extremely composed, "Santa Claus can give you the experience of a lifetime – can whisk you from this obscure corner of Lanarkshire to the fires of the desert and the moans of the dying. Of course, you can play safe ..."

"Oh no," William answered sharply, hoping to conceal the fact that, at that moment, his commitment was not so much to the starving as to the idea of commitment. "I'm on my way. Make the necessary arrangements."

November 15th, 1984

From nought to nought. That'll be it. A logical step, if step it is. To have come to nought, though? Had I another destination? Apparently. Can I say what it was, now I'm here? Apparently not. A craving to shed encumbrances – that has been clear. But for what? For what? To drink alone and with occasional others to my heart's content? No heart now to be content with. How to be content anyway after so much? Heartlessness: as well not to afflict others. Astonishing after the early signs of a fullness to come. Illusions, clearly. Tedious this. Tedious too the resolve to end it. Tedium out of heartlessness.

The landlord is away. I have the house to myself, or rather a back room in it to myself. Such a neglected back garden! It is as if the landlord's ambition is to be able to walk head high in nettles. I could lie down in the nettles rather than in my bed. Easier for them to find me there than in or on my bed. More appropriate too. His last bed one of nettles.

What clothes? Not much choice now. Wear what's to hand. What's not to hand is not. Sometimes in the mirror I've glimpsed myself dressing. A lunging figure who seems never to have dressed before. Lunging, plunging. When dressed and moving I note the scared way my feet fall. Part of my condition, apparently (peripheral ...?), but also fitting. To walk as if banned from the earth, every patch of it.

Notes? Margo, the children! Nonsense! "I thought it best ..." "No alternative now ..." "Too many mistakes, sorry ..." It won't surprise Margo; she once feared as much (or as little). To her nonetheless a note. Saying? Regrets too easy. Too easy. Anyway, what regrets? To kick the bucket without being clear about these – how irresponsible! Why bother though? Responsibly to try and account for one irresponsibility while the pills stand ready and the clock ticks – absurd.

The pills stand ready. (And the clock ticks.) A toast to them, to bring them closer. Last night ... last night these same bottles moved upon the shelf in a slow dance, between the ants and the beetles. Never been so calm as when the world fractures. Watch as if privileged. What would we say it meant if we all saw it? None but the brave do though. I mean none but the damned – remarkable though I've sometimes felt the damned to be. (They don't butter you up; don't kid themselves.)

The bed or the nettles? Dressed as I am or in pyjamas? Does it matter? Always thought it foolish, such theatrical fussing about appearances. Won't be around to see myself dragged from the nettles or lifted from the bed. The bathroom floor or the bath then? The living to be considered, I think; to be spared, though not entirely. Ridiculous this need to be discovered! Memorial corpses: Whoever finds me will understand nothing. The sea, then, the salt breakers of childhood? Cradled in the Gulf Stream? No; fear of water as deep as the need to be found.

The first pill. The second. The third. Perhaps they are duds. The fourth. The fifth. A drink again. And again. The sixth. A high valley with graveyards. The seventh. A drink. Graveyards again. Dull thoughts. Imps behind the gravestones. Why expect visions? God after such despair? The eighth. The ninth. Nothing. (A letter to Boots ...?) A hint of swooning to come though. A face ... not a face, no, a presence. Whose? Some grace in it. A formal dance. The tenth. What a tedious method. A revolver or a knife? The eleventh, or was that (counting never my strong point)... the twelfth. Why count for God's sake? Dying not to be measured. Sweep them into a pile and gobble ... Might be sick. Might be ... Twenty now? Thirty? All of a sudden past the foothills. Graveyards again. How monotonous, but to the point, I suppose. Certainly a dullness now. Another handful. That presence again. Grace in it, yes, much grace. When did I last see mother? Months? Years? Unremarkable she should appear to me now who was never shocked by weakness or perversity. Peeing out of the window that summer and father raging! "At least it's the back window, Charles, and not into the wind." My mother the wit. Dead calm as often as not. A lovely evenness. A grace ... (What do I name by that word? Wrong question.) To her a letter maybe. Too late! Too late! A darkening dullness. The yards, the feet going. Inches merely. Glass over. Done.

"Oh what have you done, Mr Templeton?" The salesman lodger bends over me, a girl beside him, bending too. A nightdress. Half darkness. "Call the ambulance, Barbara! The phone's in the hall."

Neither in my bed nor in the nettles but on the floor by the door apparently. I had been on my way somewhere it seems when dying. Wherever I move my hand I feel vomit. Here and here and here and here.

"Not much," I mumble. "Not enough. Sorry!"

CHAPTER FOURTEEN

The Church Commission met at Glasgow Airport in mid-February. Most of its members were ministers, and most of these greeted each other loudly. William waited until the excitement had died down, then introduced himself as the Reverend Alan Walsh's representative, smiling at his willingness to use a description which at first had struck him as ridiculous. But what else was he so far as these people were concerned?

Overnight bags and suitcases had been boldly labelled. The occasion, it seemed to William, had something of the air of an annual excursion, a welcome break in the monotony of day-to-day pastoral work. He sat quietly with his coffee in its plastic cup, noting that the group already had its joker, and that this joker already had a particular fan. A minister from Edinburgh, he walked and talked at the same time, and, as his punchlines approached, bore down on his fan, who laughed in extravagant appreciation. The fan, also from Edinburgh, was pale and young, and might have been pretty had she been able to relax. But her concern to please made her lips tight and her eyes move restlessly. (A horizon without people, William thought, would have thrown her into a panic.) The group also had its gruff member, who participated by appearing to find his companions unworthy of any kind of attention. He too was a minister, who stooped even as he sat, the heel of his right shoe cocked nervously on his left knee. A few times, whistling under his breath, he glanced at William as if here at last was the individual he had most dreaded to meet – the individual who, by moving effortlessly to the centre of the group, would require everyone to ask himself what he was doing there.

"This is the Commission for North Africa?" William asked, not caring if his question should seem like a criticism.

"It is indeed," the gruff minister replied. "As you will see."

The aircraft tilted against the sun. The pressure of William's feet on the floor was not that of apprehension but of acceptance, resolve. He was going where he was going. Had he been asked, he might have chosen to go later, but he couldn't easily have said why later would have been preferable. Who knew where he stood until demands were made? He took it as a good sign that he had chosen to sit beside the gruff minister, and that he was quite at ease with his decision, taken before departure, not to speak much. It didn't even seem to be an impertinence to read now and then over the minister's shoulder. "Can The Church look inwards and outwards at the same time? How can two such different but necessary functions be combined without confusion?" Nor did it seem an impertinence to try to gauge the minister's smell. Aftershave, yes, but what else? What was this desolate dryness underneath? Questions formed themselves in William's head which, had he been sure that he was flying to his death, he might have asked. "Are you as dry as this because you have forgotten your sins? Never confessed to fear? Never rejoiced?"

The course of the aircraft was settled. The gruff minister dozed above *The Church Times*. His hands, tense even in sleep, had thrust the paper into his crotch. William read that it might become necessary for two or three ministers to share a parish. The young lady from Edinburgh three times turned in her seat and smiled at him. He nodded back, soberly, anxious not to make her a fan. Everyone else, composed by the drone of the engines, appeared to be sleeping.

After his assurances to Sophie (she had been sullen and

irritated) that he would return – that he was not embarking on a new career – and his letter to Margo (it was as if the decision to go abroad had emboldened him, made him feel that he had the right to address her) telling her what had been happening to him, William was glad to sit still.

At the other airport the light was brighter, harsher, and outside it was very still. Through the airport windows the palm trees appeared black, not green. Someone who was to have met the Commission had not turned up. The joker was silent and so was his fan. Now, though, the leader of the Commission emerged, or was thrown up by the setback. He had a sort of smiling meditativeness, as though he too had been a joker once but, denied fans, had decided on the more complicated business of amusing himself. His face was grey, grey and broad, his lips alert even in repose, the folds of flesh about his mouth alert too. The animation didn't quite reach his eyes, however. His eyes were weary. William found himself admiring the weight of his weariness, his refusal to try and reassure the party that the absent man was even now approaching, pushing through the high glass doors of the airport lounge, looking around as though he knew exactly who he was looking for. No. His example in waiting was such that William was glad to wait with him, near him – though with the young lady from Edinburgh on his left, her hands working unhappily in the pockets of her dress, it wasn't as easy as it might have been.

"I'm a nurse, you know," she said.

"What precautions should I take against sunstroke?" William's lack of interest in his own question was startling, however, and prevented the nurse from doing more than open her mouth.

The ten members of the Commission sat on a padded circular seat of black leather, in the middle of which and higher than their heads were plants of a kind William had never seen before. Huge heart-shaped leaves and a smell that was dense, cold and scouring.

"What plants are these?" William asked.

"I don't know," the nurse said.

One of the ministers could have sworn that they had had the same bus driver two years ago. He tried to reintroduce himself, but he wasn't remembered. He sat down again, his affability, unwanted, appearing in the swaying bus as foolishness. Another said that he recognised the bazaars and even some of the bazaar owners. The joker, breaking a long silence, said that he recognised some of the street girls. But his fan had deserted him and his remark came over as the height of tastelessness. William glanced at the nurse, for she was sitting beside him, as far back from the window as she could, squinting into the glare. She didn't seem to have heard the joke. Nothing was familiar to her apparently, and in the absence of familiarity she had lost herself. Sensing her condition, the fear within it, William knew that he should speak. Nothing outside the bus and little inside it was familiar to him either, but he hadn't lost himself. Indeed he realised, preparing to speak, that the time for such foundering – the self at its centre guttered and out – had passed for him. His hand, he noticed, was on the nurse's forearm: the decent companion.

"I expect we can relax when we get to our quarters. Even have a little walk. I'd like to convince myself that the palm trees are real. Look how still they are."

If, when she turned to him, the nurse responded at all, it was to some agreeable memory his manner evoked. He was sure she couldn't have repeated his words. Patting her forearm, he smiled, as though, had there been any point, he might have apologised for what was happening.

The bus was on the open road now – a bad road, made

worse by the dead bodies of crows and dogs and by broken sacks. Also on it were jeeps and lorries, some of the lorries empty, others carrying sacks of grain. And weaving in and out, as if wrapped in playfulness, was a white sports car. The bus driver, amused perhaps that this familiar stretch of road was only the first of many unfamiliar stretches to his passengers, was laughing and singing.

Beyond, the start of the desert was marked by a dull haziness. Where sky and sand met, an obscurity.

In the evening, unbelievably, toasts were drunk by some of the company to absent friends. One of these was the Reverend Alan Walsh. A Church character, apparently. Without him the Commission might not have got started, it seemed. What a tragedy that a man with such vision should have ended up ill and in a backwater! So said the gruff minister, and there were murmurs of approval. William was asked to say a word or two.

"I don't think it's right to regard homes for the elderly as backwaters," he said, remembering the minister's pride and closeness, his nose for weaknesses, the sound of his footsteps in the corridors of the Montgomery. "Don't worry, though: I'll give him a full account of the Commission's findings. If you like, you can think of me as Walsh's eye."

"It is William, isn't it?" the little nurse whispered, still too timid to risk more than the simplest exchange.

"It is," William said.

"I'm Helen."

They were not the only Commission in the area. When William got off the bus the next morning he saw other groups like theirs. Briefly and awkwardly they eyed each other. The expectation seemed to be that there would be someone to show them around; but there wasn't. The minister who had emerged as the leader at the airport walked off on his own. Thinking that it was manifestly a setting in which to stick with the group would be wrong, William walked off alone too.

He walked down a little street or lane, on either side of which were tents, huts, trestle tables, piles of sacks, buckets. Everything seemed to have been bleached, and he had the impression that this was why those he passed appeared to be finding it difficult to make decisions: they were in an element which frustrated their need for colour. Another impression he had was that almost anyone would have been welcomed as a helper. One could have entered any of these tents and registered oneself as willing.

Willing? Was it a co-ordinated operation that was taking place in the colony, or a series of operations – rival ones at that? So many different languages were being spoken that William didn't know. In the second street that he entered he heard English, American, French, German, Italian, Swedish, Dutch, Spanish, and many languages he couldn't identify. There was a great amount of shouting, but the reasons for this – beyond the fact that the colony or encampment meant crisis, disaster – weren't clear. But the shouting was in street after street, as though, continually throughout the day, bad news and worse news and better news and no news was passed from one to the other, right through the colony. It struck William as self-indulgence – a kind of international melodrama – the more so because he felt like shouting too. He walked with his left hand pressed to his chest. At least, if he did start to shout (what would he shout?), it wouldn't be noticed. He would be just another member of the vast confused chorus. He struggled to restrain himself, however. And, struggling, became exhausted.

The line of starving children was long. William wondered why they had to stand. The terrible docility he thought he could grasp, but not the standing. They were naked also, which made the uniforms and badges and footwear of the helpers seem like vain credentials. Stopped before the line, he felt his toes in their sandals curl against grains of sand. All he was able to notice were the joints and the eyes. The knees in particular.

Knees and eyes. Towards and past the enormous container (soup? porridge?), knees and eyes. Knees and eyes. But wasn't he just looking? He moved abjectly on, looking, not looking. Starvation, he thought, had made the children look alike. Beings he could hardly tell apart, their features as if drawn upwards into their eyes. Eyes. Knees. The white hands and white sleeves of the women giving out the food.

He went back to the bus at noon. Lunchtime. The plan was that, having eaten and shared their impressions, they would continue their work in the afternoon. What work though? Were they to wander about watchfully for three or four weeks, now in one part of the colony, now in another? Making report when they got back home, recommending? William asked the gruff minister and Helen and another young woman, called Grace, what they thought. Grace was crying bitterly, so he looked to the other two. (He didn't feel that tears, under the circumstances, deserved any respect.)

"Well look," the gruff minister said angrily, raising his voice against the shouting which could still be heard in the background, "we're the only ones to have come back for lunch. What do you think Geoffrey and Paul and Andrew and the others are doing – just watching? Ecclesiastical voyeurs? Anyway, I'm eating because I'm diabetic. What's your excuse?"

"But why shouldn't we eat?" Helen asked. "What good will it do anyone if we don't?"

Nonetheless, William flung away his sandwich, a lettuce

sandwich, the lettuce and the bread coming apart in mid-air. On his way back to the colony he dug them both into the sand with his foot.

Walking back into the dust and the shouting of the colony, William had the odd sense that the shouting would never die. That even after the colony had been disbanded and starvation driven from the earth, it would be there, an echo of death, of death and frenzy.

In the following days, each member of the Commission found something to do. But, as if these activities were perversions of a kind, they weren't spoken about. Each returned in the evenings as if sworn to secrecy about his day. It had to be imagined what had distressed the distressed; fatigued the fatigued; excited the excited.

Only the airport leader wasn't ashamed to admit what he did. He had attached himself to some Swedes, he said, because he had always admired Swedes, their cool practicality, and because he spoke a little Swedish. He did anything they told him to do, however menial. The lack of shame and embarrassment with which he described how he had been affected (moving among the ill and dying, he had vomited, apparently, fainted, even fouled himself) seemed to William almost masochistic. The reserve of the others then seemed to be the result either of fear – they weren't doing enough – or of pride – at last they had found themselves.

Once or twice – if only to get her to say what she had been up to, William thought of telling Helen what he did. Did they have the same perversion? If not, were they complementary? He didn't ask; and she didn't say. He simply wondered if all the commissions were like this, their members, nursing such virtues as they found in themselves and struggling to keep down their vices, falling strangely silent as the days passed. Did others, like William, find that they could do little unless close to the inspired, to those who, among the afflicted, were light, imperturbable, humorous even? And did they, like him, find that they cursed themselves for this dependence, hoping earnestly that, with time, they would learn self-reliance?

Sometimes, though, the fact that the visit was only for a few weeks sobered him. Mightn't it be more modest not to think of improving himself? He thought that it might be, and then he would be calm, abiding with the knowledge of his weaknesses and sleeping tolerably.

But some nights he slept intolerably. Waking, he wondered if he had shouted out. It was the same dream each time. In his parents' garden were four figures, dressed in white. White masks and long loose white sleeves. The light was odd – a sort of pale amber twilight – and the garden had been recently dug, readied for strange seeds. One of the figures was to sow these, the others supervising, but he could never get his arm out of its sleeve. It wouldn't lift. The others, frustrated and angry, turned away. At which point William – a neat, eager teenager – stepped forwards and tried to release the arm that wouldn't move. But it proved not to be an arm at all, only a stump. A stump with boils and sores and something that looked like a mouth. There was laughter then, at William's terror and amazement, making him flee across the freshly dug garden, leaping the hollows that awaited the strange seeds, fearful that unless he was careful he would wake up one morning to find that he too had blasted limbs.

At a place on the edge of the colony some jeeps were parked. They had long, open backs and in these were stretchers, mattresses, cushions, blankets. There was a strong smell of disinfectant, but there was also a smell of sickness, and if you looked at the air above the backs of the jeeps, William believed, you could see a shimmering, as of disembodied fevers. A hot wind blew in from the desert, and in the mid-sky, above this wind apparently, some heavy black birds hung.

The woman who fed the starving here did so with the minimum of display and feeling. And she did not seem to look at those she fed. That was William's first impression. But as he watched her give out the porridge and touch the head of each child that passed he felt otherwise. The movements which made up the small ritual seemed to be the result of a patience greater than any he had seen before and made possible, moment by moment, a greater patience still. The head touched; the porridge scooped from its container; the bowl filled; a smile, nonetheless intense for being quick; the head touched again. William didn't think that the children looked any better for the meeting, though. But why should they? Why shouldn't they pass on as if this was to be their last meal ever? (And to whom did they pass on? A group of men, presumably their fathers, who might have been a hundred but who were probably only twenty-five and who walked as if stilts, very thin stilts, had been grafted on to their ruined limbs.)

When the last child had been fed, the woman rose and slowly – it seemed an expression of regret – straightened her headscarf. William went up to her. She was a little tense now, a little tired, but she smiled warmly when William asked her what he could do. She sat down again on the low stool from which she had been feeding the children, and, bowing her head and massaging her neck, carefully considered his question. When she looked up it was as if to praise him for appearing at that particular moment. Appalled by the size of their task yet reverent towards anyone who was prepared to try and reduce it, she encouraged William.

"You could go out with the boys," she said, her accent

American. "They're done in. And one's sick today. Over there."

Between his enquiry and her answer a vitality had come to him, at which – as though he might be tempted to use it licentiously – he blushed.

"The boys" went out several times a day. Sometimes they saw no one and came back empty. Other times they found more than they could carry in one journey, having to make several trips in quick succession. Some of the starving, one of the drivers explained to William, wouldn't accept lifts. They had to be pointed in the direction of the colony and watched until they reached it. William's task was to help them onto the back of the jeep and sit with them during the journey, which could be ten miles or twenty miles. Deaths occurred quite often on the backs of the jeeps. It was hard for newcomers to spot the actual moment: between starvation and death from it there didn't seem to be a definite line. William felt insensitive beside the others who could spot the moment even before it came. And he wouldn't have much time to learn.

One day William and the driver came upon just one person. It was evening. Several times William had had the feeling that the desert created disaster in order to be respected, and he had it again now. One moment there was no one, the next the figure was there, born from the dunes, famished, flung forth. The driver, fatigued, stayed in the jeep while William helped the man aboard. These skeletal frames were hard to handle: the bones were elusive, William found, shockingly so, and the skin either too tight or too loose. His judgement of their terminal needs was poor. Sometimes his clumsiness had made his charges wince, wriggle away.

The man lay back in rags on a mattress. Slowly the jeep circled the hollow in which he had been found, heading then for the colony. It was the first time William had only one to watch. He had to concentrate himself: he couldn't count heads, compare conditions, go from one to the other. To only this one in rags could he give succour.

Suddenly from the rags the man produced a small pistol. Supine, he raised his right arm and pointed the pistol directly above him, as at a spectre many miles high and rapidly escaping. There was an impression of extraordinary strain, as though, this time, the aim had to be perfect. The pistol went off and the arm that held it fell instantly, the pistol striking the wooden floor in the back of the jeep. The jeep stopped and the driver jumped out. He and William then found that the gesture – as of climactic repayment or vengeance – had been the man's last.

Another day William and the driver found ten refugees. William's touch finer now, born of better patience, they helped them into the back of the jeep. One of them was agitated, though, and wouldn't lie down. He kept pointing and – palms together, head leaning on them – making gestures which suggested sleep. The driver tried to get him to lie down, pointing at a mattress, himself making the gesture of sleep. But the man, standing up in the back of the jeep, pointed repeatedly towards the desert, making the gesture of sleep so often that William and the driver might have believed that millions slept out there. Millions. At last the driver thought that he saw a mound. Sticking a red flag in the sand beside it, he indicated that they would return after they had taken the ten to the colony. The man seemed to understand.

The light must have changed, defining the desert differently, giving a clearer impression of space and recession, because when they returned they saw the red flag immediately.

Kneeling together, William and the driver began to burrow at the mound. Several times a wind whipped sand into their faces. His goggles making the light orange, William burrowed on, more and more tentatively. It was he who was the first to touch a limb, but instead of recoiling – as he had thought he would – he held fast to the limb, his other hand raised, as though to still the wind and register his discovery. Pushing the sand carefully aside – such a terrible absorption in his task! – he uncovered the body of a child. A child of bones. Then another. Then an old woman of bones – or was it a young woman appearing old? For some reason he led the driver in the task. The driver laid the bodies side by side – William still digging – in readiness for the jeep. There were seven in all. When he had uncovered the last one, William felt the area around the mound – a mad repetitive thoroughness in his movements – in case some lay in shallower graves still. But there were no more. On all fours on the sand, then, William let his head hang. A good position for weeping. (But there would be no weeping.) The thought he had was oddly simple: those in shallow graves had been victims of some kind – murder, rape, pestilence, starvation. They lifted the corpses into the back of the jeep then, William remembering Sophie's remark about the difference between dead and living bodies.

And then, abruptly, the Commission's time was up. The bus stood ready to take them to the airport. A wind had been blowing for several days, getting stronger, it seemed, by the hour. William had heard it said that the colony should be fortified. In the old days, apparently, encampments had been protected against the weather. Ignorant of the history of this part of the world, however, he couldn't imagine what these protections would have been like.

At Glasgow Airport, he exchanged addresses with Helen, but with no one else. He didn't think he would see her again – he didn't think he would even write to her – but their last wave could have been mistaken for that of lovers. Others too waved goodbye in this way. It was as if, in spite of themselves, their isolation from one another, their sense of shame and insignificance, they had become a kind of brotherhood.

March 4th, 1985

Some would call Sandra Mclehose a good sort, but I'm not so sure. Here I am anyway. Like me, she was once married, and like me, it's a long time since she last saw her children. We treat the fact that (to put it mildly) we are in disgrace as a joke. What else can we do? It seems we are powerless to make amends. Powerless. Amends. What do I mean by these words? All they do is sound vaguely in an expanding space that has lost reference points. At this rate my vocabulary will be shrinking. It is shrinking. Sandra's cannot afford to shrink, I'd say; it's small enough as it is. Can you tell a bore by the number of words he uses? Maybe. We're bores together then. Surely we are.

But we have our diversions. Today, for example, it's been decided that I cannot wear my clothes any more. They smell so horribly that when I am in my own presence, so to speak, I cannot smell Sandra, and that's saying something. She has kept her husband's clothes in a wardrobe, for she had hoped to get round to selling them. Now we discover they fit me perfectly. I won't say that they too don't smell, but it is the smell of a man on his way up or at least holding his own. A most respectable smell. I should be honoured. No wonder he left Sandra. After a week or two in his clothes mightn't I be inspired (inspired!?) to try and leave her too?

She lies on the bed laughing (not quite the right word, I think: cackling is better) while, unsteadily, I try on shirt after shirt, jersey after jersey, trousers and shoes, ties even. All fit perfectly. The shoes are worn as I like shoes to be worn, and the jackets hang comfortably. Remarkable. But when I begin to act the part Sandra gets angry. I am to remain myself even although the clothes constrain me to make an effort. She shouts that I'm to mind my manners, though I'd have thought that, in my new clothes and with the wardrobe open beside me, my manners have improved. I strut and she curses; hold out my arm as if we are going for a civilized walk and she curses; smooth my lapels and adjust my trousers when I sit and she curses. She shouts that she'll rip the clothes off me if I don't watch out. "Remember who you are!" she bellows. Remember who I am when I've forgotten who I was! "Was", "is", "will be" – all buggered. I may have to drop "I" from my vocabulary altogether. In these, clothes, though, I am changed a little, yes definitely changed a little. It has to be said. It's hard to be gross and disgraceful in such clothes. I tell her I'll have to break the clothes in; make them my own. I say to her ... I say to her that she doesn't understand.

Should I have tried the stage? I mean isn't this stubborn pleasure in these clothes and what they suggest to be applauded? She shouts at me and struggles to get off the bed. I continue to appear better than I am, more possessed, more purposeful. A flicker of remembered decency in a malodorous house and an even more malodorous relationship. Between three and four drinks Sandra may be a good sort but after that she's not. After that – and she's seven or eight after that, I think – she's an ignorant, dirty, nasty bitch. It is three in the afternoon.

She gets to her feet and comes at me. It's not the first time I've been attacked, and not the last, I imagine. We struggle and fall to the floor. My shirt – his shirt – is ripped off me and my trousers taken down. Sandra is horribly strong. A real thug. I stop struggling. Everything is ripped off me. Too late she tries to turn it into a sexual game. Straddling me, she lifts up her skirt and cackles. Too late! I lie naked, drunk, exhausted, wondering where my old clothes are, thinking that in their repossession is my only hope.

I look for them, staggering, find them, put them on. Sandra is sorry now and holds out her husband's jacket. I charge it like a bull. Holding me by the knees, she moans "Willy!" Now nobody calls me Willy and gets away with it. She calls me it again. "Willy!" (Has she confused me with my cock?) I hit her, hit her cursing face, get hit back. "Couldn't you just have put the clothes on!" she screams. Apparently not. Apparently clothes change you, give you ideas, airs.

Back in my own clothes, I cry bitterly. Downstairs Sandra is banging doors. It is Saturday afternoon or Sunday afternoon. Time for a drink, I'd say. A quarter past three.

CHAPTER FIFTEEN

William had been away from the Montgomery for almost four weeks, but it seemed longer. He couldn't get used to it again; he couldn't take it seriously. The news that Mr. Clow had died of a heart attack at breakfast one day (pitching forwards into his porridge with a little cry) and Miss Adams (asking for William repeatedly, it seemed) of pneumonia barely affected him. And the sight of a new arrival, a Colonel Galston, walking up and down the corridors asking for his aide-de-camp and slapping his left wrist with three fingers of his right hand – a movement at once effete and imperious – barely amused him. Not even the news that the minister had had a slight stroke and was being looked after by matron in her cottage in the grounds made much impression.

And Sophie: to her he could respond least of all, so concerned was she to get him to put his trip to Africa behind him, to involve him once again in the life of the Montgomery. She had viewed his decision to go abroad unfavourably, a piece of bravado at best, a sign that he was at the mercy of the minister at worst, and he hadn't been able to persuade her otherwise. Now, if she referred to the trip at all, she did so as if it had been an ill-considered holiday. She would remark on his suntan, his cracked lips, his fatigue and what she called his "faraway look" or his "tragic look". But she wouldn't ask any questions. She acted, too, as if – with the minister ill and matron frequently away, tending to him – the Montgomery was on the verge of happier times. Her theory seemed to be that if the minister had a second stroke and died matron would take early retirement. William told her that she shouldn't hope for another's death, death being willing enough, as he had recently seen. And he would annoy her further by calling her Queen of the Montgomery and by singing, under his breath and wearily, "When I shall be King and you shall be Queen."

His dislike of her absorption in the Montgomery (the very absorption he had once admired); her dislike of his detachment from it: after a few days they were barely speaking. "Why dream of things to do over there," she would ask impatiently, "when there are plenty of things to do here?"

"That's not really how it is," he would reply, equally impatiently. "You don't seem to understand."

The only thing that touched him was a letter from Margo, written in reply to the letter he had sent her before going abroad.

"Dear William,

I can't describe how good it was to hear from you after all these years. I'd heard from Lesley that you were alive and well and working as a nurse (she liked your white jacket!). But to have it confirmed by you was important. I won't say I ever gave you up for dead, but there were times when it was close. When you feel ready for it, recovered even further, you must meet us all again. What a strange thing to say! But I mean it. Even after your final outings with the children – over which I think we should all agree to draw a veil – they asked after you, asked when they could see you again.

I have my own life now, more or less, and it'll stay that way. I do hope you'll understand. How much there is to say! At this stage, though, and on paper, it seems hard to say it. But it'll come, I'm sure.

Please write again soon, and continue to take care of yourself.

Love,
Margo

William replied almost immediately, surprised to find that after a few sentences something of his old manner with his wife – the manner of their best years – returned.

"Dear Margo,
I was delighted to get your letter. It was waiting for me on my return.

I'd love to see you all again, and it shouldn't be too long before I can manage it. Don't worry, though, I do appreciate that you have your own life now. (Come to think of it, so have I!) It would be best if we didn't conceal anything from each other, I think. Certainly I don't expect you to feel that you have to conceal anything from me. Not even at my most irrational did I imagine that you would wait for me, look forward to the time when I would return to heal your wounds. Another's hands were bound to do that. Good luck!

After this month away I feel terribly unsettled. How to get going again after such an experience! Here, they live longer than they want to and frequently refuse their food; there, they die before their time because they have no food. I feel quite displaced. It is a common reaction, I suppose, but I have no one to talk to about it, so excuse me for going on. The minister who set up the opportunity for me is ill, so I can't talk to him. Not that I'd have been inclined to anyway, for his motives are suspect. Very suspect. I think, you see, that my ruin was his objective: by sending me to a "refugee colony" he hoped to terrify me into drinking again. (I've even thought that there may be something suspect about his interest in the starving – not to mention the old. God help me, but are there people who like others because they – the others – are about to become corpses?) But I'm as sober as I've ever been – all senses. The only other person I might have spoken to is a nurse I'm friendly with (her name is Sophie) but she thinks my going abroad was an ego trip. I expect time will return me to myself and show me my place again, but at the moment it doesn't seem like it.

Actually, I do remember my last "outing" with the children. It's one of the few things I do remember from that time. Terrible!

I'll write again soon.

Love,

William

William hadn't been to matron's cottage before (few of the staff had). It was hidden from the Montgomery by trees, and through these trees, a cold March wind blowing, William now walked. His collar was turned up, his hands were deep in his pockets. It was evening. Clouds scudded across the face of a full moon; a cloud-bank obscured it entirely; then it sailed free again. The effect of such intermittent moonlight, William felt, was to make the trees, the path through them, the swaying branches, the high wall and even matron's cottage seem provisional (as if there by grace of the moonlight, not otherwise). He paused before knocking at the cottage door, and was then obliged – such was the noise of the wind – to knock three times.

It was the minister who had asked to see him, though since matron insisted that the patient wasn't to be troubled with difficult news, William didn't see what his visit could achieve. She had asked him to be light and general about his time abroad, to avoid details – in short, to hold back from the worst. He had offered to wait until the minister was better, but matron, ruffling her hair, had said it had to be now.

The minister, bent slightly, was sitting in an armchair at a coal fire. His chair – as if to warm the side that had been affected by the stroke – had been turned sideways. Seeing William, he lifted his right hand in greeting and pointed to a chair opposite. William said that he was glad to see the minister well, at least recovering, and sat down. For a moment matron stood in the doorway – William had the impression that she was holding her breath – before withdrawing to make some tea.

"A nuisance, this," the minister said, shifting in his chair, grimacing.

"It's just a matter of rest."

"So Alice tells me. But rest is time out."

"Time out of what?"

"Of life. And to wait for life to begin again is to realise, at least at my age, that it may have other plans." There seemed to be more saliva than usual in the minister's mouth: his words were heavier, a little slurred.

"You'll be all right," William said, more casually than he had intended, reaching over to adjust a yellow tartan rug that was slipping from the minister's waist.

"You think so?" It wasn't asked uneasily, but aggressively, as if it was the minister's hope to discredit William's opinions one by one.

"Matron is sure of it."

William, still adjusting the rug, was discovering the extent of the minister's portliness. The flab was packed above and below the waistline, and between two rolls of this (whether by accident or not he couldn't easily have said) William poked a finger.

"Oh leave it!" the minister said, grasping William's wrist and lifting it away. "Don't fuss; it doesn't matter. Tell me now …"

Then he broke off, looked away, William remembering how something similar had happened during their interview on Christmas night. Uncertain cerebral activity, he supposed, giving an impression of preoccupation, enigmatic hesitation.

His eyes when they recollected themselves had forgotten their purpose. But they had found another one. William was to be observed: posture noted, complexion checked, steadiness under scrutiny considered. It was as if in his uneasy convalescence the minister had got it into his head that his chief business was to reassess what was normally taken for granted. And just as the word "protectress" had once occurred to William in relation to matron, so now the word "reassessor" occurred to him in relation to the minister. He sat very still, so still, in fact, that he seemed to have consented to join with the minister in this scrutiny of himself. But at last he smiled, as though, so far as he was concerned, he had passed the test easily, had come over as fit, ready, resourceful, dignified. But the minister wasn't so pleased.

"I suppose when I'm stronger," he said, looking into the fire, "you can tell me how you managed it. For it is remarkable ..."

"How I managed what?"

"How you've been able to return from your trip so sanguine, so collected. I never could."

"But I haven't, Reverend," William said. "I'm fatigued and unsettled."

"How odd," the minister went on, as if he hadn't been listening, "that it should have been I who remained behind who was struck down."

"I wouldn't say that you've been struck down. That's putting it too strongly."

"As you wish," the minister muttered.

There came another blankness then, another void, and when he returned from it – returned to the room with its flickering firelight and matron entering prettily with the tea-tray – the minister had lost interest. He was bored now, indifferent. And so, William felt, it would probably continue, the blankness alternating with the petulance, the rages with the inertia, until the minister either recovered or, rising up from his chair with a great shout (William could imagine this very easily), died.

Matron asked William about the garden. With spring approaching, what were his plans for it? She asked it rather pointedly, he thought, as if his plans for the garden were well known to be bound up with his plans for himself. He had no plans for it, he believed, none at all, but in order to pass the time before he could politely leave he spoke in a quiet voice, now and then raising it slightly against the wind, of the need for more borders and for vegetables. He realised after a moment or two, however, that matron wasn't listening, more interested in the minister's unhealthy silence than in anyone's plans for the garden. He spoke on, nonetheless, even suggesting that garden tables and chairs wouldn't be a bad idea.

Just before lunch the next day, William left the Montgomery by a back entrance. Carrying his suitcase (still covered with labels from his recent trip), he walked, not down the main drive, but through the grounds – carefully in and out of trees, bushes – rejoining the drive at the front gate. At one o'clock a bus passed here, stopping for anyone from the Montgomery who wanted it.

Making sure that he couldn't be seen from the Montgomery, William took up his position by the gate, waiting uneasily, tensely (as tensely, he fancied, as his letters to them were waiting to be discovered by matron and Sophie).

It was a grey day, very still, the landscape, flat at the best of times, appearing even flatter because of the greyness. It was not how he had imagined himself waiting. He had imagined that the day of his departure would be the first day of spring, with warm sunshine and birdsong. He had imagined that there would be abundant signs that he had taken the right decision. But all he could hear in the grey stillness were the questions he didn't want to hear. The old questions. Who are you? Where are you from? Where are you going?

What will you do? Who will receive you? The belief that had inspired his flight – that he had more to give than service to the privileged elderly – was still with him. But as he waited, the suspicion grew that it was vain of him to suppose that he would find a worthier occupation, a grander commitment. And why the idea that service to the elderly – privileged or not – was negligible?

The bus was late, but it was often late on its journeys round this corner of Lanarkshire. He pictured its arrival, the automatic doors opening, the familiar driver with the high forehead and the red hair smiling down at him. But beyond that he could imagine nothing. The bus was always stopped and waiting, and he – as if it represented just one of several possibilities – was always looking up at it.

It began to drizzle. Still William stood where he was, his back to the Montgomery, his ears straining for the sound of the bus. And still he looked in the direction the bus would take after he had boarded it. But then, as he put on his over-coat, he felt the action of doing so induce an experience which, a year before, he would probably have put down to his liver (disordered bodies imagining disordered worlds). Behind him, it felt that the Montgomery was breaking up. At first the tremor was gentle, running the length of the ground floor and then ceasing. Then it was more pronounced, caus-ing a few bricks and slates to fall and dust to rise. And then it was violent and sustained, causing the building, with horri-ble slowness, to collapse inwards. There were clouds of black and purple dust and there were screams. Then – as if there had never been a place called the Montgomery – silence and calm daylight.

The bus – it was all that could be heard in the stillness – came into sight at last. But by now William had picked up his suitcase and was walking up the drive. Soon he heard the bus pass and go on – heard it as if it had been only his intention to board it – as if he were returning after a long absence. It had been an essential absence, apparently, as essential as rest after exhaustion, bereavement after death. The balance might not last, he knew, but it had been struck for the moment. He was returning neither cowed nor in triumph, neither an underling nor an upstart.

To get to the front door, he had to pass the dining-room window. Lunch was still in progress. None of the elderly saw him though as, awkwardly but purposefully swinging his suitcase, he walked by. Sophie did however. And looked at him, he feared, as if she had known for days that he was going to try – and fail – to leave the Montgomery by a back entrance. He recalled the first time he had seen her, the time when, in the middle of helping an old man along one of the Montgomery's lovely autumn paths, she had looked up and seemed to ask him who he was. Her look was more knowing now, he had to admit, less curious, less patient even; but he liked to believe there was appreciation in it still. More appreciation than censure. Why not? Wasn't there more to himself, William Templeton – proudly he permitted himself the thought – than there was to this crusading young woman of twenty-four or twenty-five?

To acknowledge, though, that her doubts about his loyalty had been justified, he gave her a sober wave and nodded, passing on then into the entrance hall, where he came upon matron setting out fresh copies of *For All Seasons*.

"Oh, William," she said, barely looking up. "Could you clean the zimmers sometime? They've got sticky again."

"Right, matron," he said, passing through without stopping.

Later that afternoon, he suggested to Mrs Walker that they take a turn in the garden. The drizzle had stopped and the clouds were high. Mrs Walker remarked that spring was in the air.

"And soon it'll be summer," she added, appearing to savour each syllable.

"Yes," William said, regretting that when summer did come it would be apparent that the garden had been neglected again.

"Do you know what?" he said, pacing slowly with Mrs Walker down an avenue of rhododendron bushes.

"What?"

"If I made more of the garden, we could spend more time in it. I think we spend too much time inside. Too much damn time inside."

"I agree," Mrs Walker said. "But don't delay; none of us here has terribly much time left."